GETTING OLD IS CRIMINAL

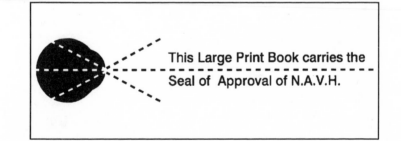

This Large Print Book carries the
Seal of Approval of N.A.V.H.

GETTING OLD IS CRIMINAL

RITA LAKIN

THORNDIKE PRESS

An imprint of Thomson Gale, a part of The Thomson Corporation

Detroit • New York • San Francisco • New Haven, Conn. • Waterville, Maine • London

Copyright © 2007 by Rita Lakin.
A Gladdy Gold Mystery.
Map and ornament illustrations by Laura Hartman Maestro.
Thorndike Press, an imprint of The Gale Group.
Thomson and Star Logo and Thorndike are trademarks and Gale is a registered trademark used herein under license.

LIBRARY OF CONGRESS CATALOGING-IN-PUBLICATION DATA

Lakin, Rita.
    Getting old is criminal / by Rita Lakin.
      p. cm. — (Thorndike Press large print mystery)
    "A Gladdy Gold mystery"—T.p. verso.
    ISBN-13: 978-0-7862-9752-8 (alk. paper)
    ISBN-10: 0-7862-9752-2 (alk. paper)
    1. Gold, Gladdy (Fictitious character) — Fiction. 2. Older women —
Fiction. 3. Retirees — Fiction. 4. Fort Lauderdale (Fla.) — Fiction. 5. Large
type books. I. Title.
PS3612.A5424G476 2007
813'.6—dc22   2007027199

Published in 2007 by arrangement with The Bantam Dell Publishing Group, a division of Random House, Inc.

Printed in the United States of America on permanent paper
10 9 8 7 6 5 4 3 2 1

This book is
for Alison with Love
from her Grandma

You don't stop laughing when you grow
old.
You grow old when you stop laughing.
— *Anonymous*

Happy 101st Birthday!
Harold W. (Rudy) Truesdale
Eureka, California
Born 1906, twelve days before the San
Francisco earthquake hit.
One of the first commercial pilots ever.
Now the oldest living one.
Hired by TWA.
First airline captain to ever marry a
stewardess.
Surveyed the road and pool at Hearst
Castle for friend Howard Hughes.

Advice for longevity: a glass of red wine every night.
— *Submitted by Burrille Catamach*

"Life is not measured by the number of breaths we take, but by the moments that take our breath away."

— *George Carlin, 70, comic*

INTRODUCTION TO OUR CHARACTERS

Gladdy & Her Gladiators

Gladys (Gladdy) Gold, 75 Our heroine and her funny, adorable, and sometimes impossible partners:

Evelyn (Evvie) Markowitz, 73 Gladdy's sister. Logical, a regular Sherlock Holmes

Ida Franz, 71 Stubborn, mean, great for in-your-face confrontation

Bella Fox, 83 The "shadow." She's so forgettable, she's perfect for surveillance, but smarter than you think

Sophie Meyerbeer, 80 Master of disguises, she lives for color-coordination

Yentas, Kibitzers, Sufferers: The Inhabitants of Phase Two

Hy Binder, 88 A man of a thousand jokes, all of them tasteless

Lola Binder, 78 Hy's wife, who hasn't a thought in her head that he hasn't put there

Denny Ryan, 42 The handyman. Sweet,

kind, mentally slow

Enya Slovak, 84 Survivor of "the camps" but never really survived

Tessie Hoffman, 56 Chubby, with a big fat crush on Sol

Millie Weiss, 85 Suffering with Alzheimer's

Irving Weiss, 86 Suffering because Millie is suffering

Mary Mueller, 60 Neighbor and nurse, whose husband left her

Oddballs and Fruitcakes

The Canadians, 30–40-ish Young, tan, and clueless

Sol Spankowitz, 79 A lech after the ladies

Dora Dooley, 81 Jack's neighbor, loves soap operas

The Cop and The Cop's Pop

Morgan (Morrie) Langford, 35 Tall, lanky, sweet, and smart

Jack Langford, 75 Handsome and romantic

The Library Mavens

Conchetta Aguilar, 38 Her Cuban coffee could grow hair on your chest

Barney Schwartz, 27 Loves a good puzzle

New Tenants

Barbi Stevens, 20-ish, and Casey Wright, 20-ish Cousins who moved from California

and:

Yolanda Diaz, 22 Her English is bad, but her heart is good

Building P - Petunia
Lanai Gardens

IRY & MILIE 114
HY & LOLA 216
MARY 314
DENNY 119
EVVIE 217
BELLA 216
ENYA 219

mailboxes & elevator

Sol Spankowitz lives in Phase Three.
Jack Langford lives in Phase Six.

GLADDY'S GLOSSARY

Yiddish (meaning Jewish) came into being between the ninth and twelfth centuries in Germany as an adaptation of German dialect to the special uses of Jewish religious life.

In the early twentieth century, Yiddish was spoken by eleven million Jews in Eastern Europe and the United States. Its use declined radically. However, lately there has been a renewed interest in embracing Yiddish once again as a connection to Jewish culture.

alter kockers lecherous old men
bubbala (bubeleh) endearing term
bubkes trifling, worth nothing
chupeh bridal canopy
dumkupf dunce
fahputzed overly done
feh! phooey!
gornisht nothing
haimish friendly

kibitz giving unwanted advice

kvetch whine & complain

lantsman countryman, someone from your home area

maven someone who knows everything

matzo unleavened bread for Passover

mensch a dignified person

mishmash a mess

mamzer trickster, untrustworthy person

nosh small meal

pupik belly button

putz penis (insult)

rugallah pastry

schlep dragging a load

schmear to spread like butter

tsimmes fuss

tush a baby's bottom

yenta busybody

■ ■ ■ ■

SIGH NO MORE, LADY

■ ■ ■ ■

The Jacuzzi bubbles tickled. Even the champagne tickled as the silvery liquid glided down her eager throat. She looked up at the mirrored ceiling. Then at each mirrored wall. Happily, the bubbles were up to her chin so she didn't have to look at her ninety-five-year-old turkey-wattled neck. Her eyesight was failing, so in the haze of her cataracts, her white hair once again seemed as blond as it had been in her salad days. In her tipsy state, she remembered when she'd been compared to Carole Lombard — or so the boys had said in those courting days when they were trying to get into her bloomers.

What was management thinking? Esther Ferguson wondered. Everyone here was close to pushing up the daisies. Why would they have installed so many mirrors? The first three years she lived here, she had draped all but the mirror over the sink. It was Romeo who'd made her take the fabric down, the better to admire her.

Esther loved Grecian Villas. Close to the heart of Fort Lauderdale, conveniently located near the beach and the chic Las Olas Street shopping area — what more could anyone want? Everything in the deluxe retirement community was first-rate. A fabulous dining room that outdid Las Vegas. Food from a class-act chef. Lush lawns. Indoor and outdoor pools. Views of the ocean. First-run movies any night of the week. Bridge players with their brains still intact. Granted, she paid through the *pupik,* but she could afford it. Her dead husband, Harry, had left her very, very, very rich. And she had no family except for her rigid son, Alvin, and his annoying wife. They were waiting for her to croak. They'd get the money, all right; they could have whatever was left. But she intended to spend as much as she wanted on herself as long as she lasted.

She giggled. This place alone took five thousand a month. Oops, she thought, and hiccupped, as she spilled a bit of her champagne into the Jacuzzi.

She looked toward the half-open mirrored door. "Romeo, where art thou, snookums?"

A velvety voice replied from the living room bar, where she could hear him tinkling with the glasses, "Coming, my Juliet."

Her lover put on a CD. Tchaikovsky's Romeo and Juliet Overture wafted toward her. How perfect. Who would have thunk it? Mad, passionate love at ninety-five with a gorgeous guy twenty years her junior. Well, not so mad and not all that passionate, either. The body parts didn't move much, no matter how much oiling, but, oh, the romance.

He knocked. "May I enter, m'lady?"

"Need you ask, m'lord?"

"Of course. A gentleman always knocks before he enters his loved one's private chambers."

"Knock away, oh dear one, and bring your gorgeous self right in."

Romeo entered, the diamond stickpin gleaming against his silken white cravat, his red damask robe in dramatic counterpoint. His unshod feet glided toward Esther as all his mirror images reflected and re-reflected. Removing Esther's empty champagne flute, he handed her another and spoke softly to her. " 'Eyes, look your last! Arms, take your last embrace.' " He leaned over and kissed her forehead.

For a moment she was confused. What did he say? But then she smiled and raised her glass heavenward. "Thank you, God. Take me anytime you want and I will die happy."

Esther was surprised when Romeo pushed her head gently, but firmly, down into the bubbles. He held her under the water as he whispered into her disappearing ear, " 'Good night, good night! Parting is such sweet sorrow.' "

ONE:
ALONE AT LAST

Here I am, Gladdy Gold, happily up to my neck in warm bubbles, soaking in this wooden barrel hot-tub-for-two, drinking piña coladas in front of our *fale,* which is the Polynesian word for our picturesque private thatched hut. Remarkably, the hut has cement floors, yet is air-conditioned. Our bathroom is in the open air and our shower is a waterfall, surrounded by an exotic jungle full of vines with leaves the size of elephant ears. Wow! What bliss. What happiness.

Just a few days ago, the girls — even though we are in our seventies and eighties, my sister Evvie and our friends, Sophie, Bella, and Ida, will always be "the girls" — and I had been on a bingo cruise where, much to my amazement, we not only caught a killer, but won at bingo, too. That was all well and good, but I missed my new boyfriend, Jack. Lo and behold, he turned up at the port where we docked. So Jack and I left the girls to fend for themselves on the good ship *Heavenly,* and now we are on this heavenly island of our own. It took sixteen grueling hours to get here, snatching moments of sleep as we leaned against each other in bumpy planes. Well worth it, now that we're here. Alone at last.

I sip the last of my piña colada, then lean my head back against the edge of the hot tub and sigh contentedly. The sky is beginning to darken. Dramatic slashes of red illuminate the patchy clouds. Red sky at night, I think, sailor's delight.

I had no idea how much I would like being away from everyone. What's not to like? I look around me.

On the picnic table next to the hot tub, Jack has placed the portable CD player and CD he bought at the Samoa airport when we landed very early this morning. Corny music, but what with the lack of choices in an airport in the middle of nowhere, the well-worn theme from *Titanic* will have to do. When we landed this morning, there was a crowd of natives greeting the plane. I guess the twice-a-week flights are a big event here.

I have the luggage I took with me on the cruise. Jack has nothing but the suit he was wearing when he showed up at the port. And proud of it. So, he's impulsive; I like that about him. You should see him now, wearing the wraparound skirt called a lavalava, the male version of a sarong, which he bought in the airport gift shop along with a shaving kit and a toothbrush. Winking and leering at me, he told me he wouldn't need anything else. I couldn't resist buying the matching lady's muumuu.

All day today has been prelude to right now. Dressed in our new native attire (and me with an exotic frangipani flower in my hair) Jack and I had an early lunch of island fruits — papayas, pineapple, and bananas — served to us on the porch of our quaint little thatched hut. Then a long, barefoot walk on a beach with the whitest sand I've ever seen, gathering shells and drinking those addictive piña coladas from actual coconuts. Whispering sweet nothings in each other's ears. Mmm, wonderful. Topped off with fresh ahi tuna for dinner, caught by a local fisherman and fixed for us in the intimate candlelit dining room of our charming island hotel.

Jack's waited a long time for us to finally get away from the girls and consummate our love for each other, and he is doing his best to make it memorable.

So the scene is set. A perfect day continuing on into a magical night. Music, drinks, the smell of jasmine all around us — romance everywhere. I can hear Jack whistling Céline Dion as he comes out of the hut with another round of drinks.

But am I ready? I think so. Finally. I hope I've finally put my late husband to rest. I still have little tremors, little qualms about how this will change my life. This is no one-night stand. This is a prelude to moving in together, marriage, and total commitment. I admit it: Even at my age I fear change. I am comfortable with my cozy, circumscribed life. My simple daily routine, answering to no one but myself. Who ever said falling in love was as easy as falling off a log? For that matter, what's so easy about getting on a log, let alone falling off one, and what's a log got to do with love, anyway?

At the sight of Jack coming toward me, wearing that silly, adorable lavalava, I feel my heart go pitter-patter. I instantly shut my mind off. He is so handsome and so sexy. And he wants me.

He bends to me. "Madame, a refill?"

"But of course."

He pours and then gives me a gentle kiss. "Shall I join you?"

I splash as I move to make room for him.

I can't take my eyes off him, nor can he stop gazing adoringly at me.

Just as he drops his lavalava and sets one foot into the tub, we hear the muffled, tinny sound of a bugle — three short, shocking blasts. Jack, startled, falls into the tub on top of me. I go under, my mouth filling with bubbles. We scramble up and out of the tub as best we can, reaching for towels to cover ourselves.

"May I approach?" The voice of a native bellboy calls from behind a palm tree. He waits for an answer: The hotel's idea of a subtle way to warn lovers in case they are — well, as we were — in a state of indelicacy.

Jack and I exchange despairing looks. What timing! I shrug. Jack calls out, "Permission granted."

I giggle at his formal pronouncement and squeeze his hand. Our messenger comes forward, eyes suitably lowered at the sight of two wet, embarrassed, towel-clad guests.

The bellboy hands Jack a fax. Naturally, he's the man, so he gets it. The boy doesn't wait for a tip. There are no pockets in towels.

Jack reads it, with me looking over his shoulder.

"What!" we both shout at the same time.

The message is short and to the point:

Come home. Sophie is dying.

We scramble into our clothes; Jack into his one and only suit while I quickly and unhappily choose a traveling outfit. At the reception desk we learn that the fax came from the ship *Heavenly*. Jack's cell phone is useless, so we have to use the hotel's phone. Jack shrugs at the irony. He found us the most out-of-the-way place to go so we wouldn't be disturbed and now, in an emergency, we can hardly reach anyone on the outside.

After endless tries, with many excuses from the obsequious manager about old equipment, time differences, and that being the charm of getting away from the wearisome world, we do manage to reach Captain Standish on the *Heavenly*. He informs us that Sophie was airlifted from the ship and was sent back to Fort Lauderdale with her three companions.

"What happened?" I ask him.

"Something about her heart," he informs me.

"Do you know where they took her?"

"I assume she was brought to your local hospital. So sorry."

Now the wires are crackling, or whatever

24

it is that makes any more conversation difficult.

We disconnect from Captain Standish, then try calling the two hospitals nearest to where we live. No Sophie Meyerbeer listed at either of them. No answer in Sophie's apartment. Or Evvie's. Or Ida's. Where the hell can they be?

I say the words, but they're choking me. "We have to go home."

Jack nods. "But there isn't a plane until next Monday."

The manager, who has never left our side, says cheerfully, "You're in luck. The last flight out today leaves in two hours. If you wish to leave, I can book you on it. Of course you'll have to pay for your one night."

"Of course," says Jack bitterly. I know it's the night we won't have that rankles.

If Evvie were here watching us gloomily huddle together on the airstrip in the steamy night air, waiting to board the little puddle jumper, she'd remind me of the movie *Casablanca.*

She'd utter that famous line, *We'll always have Paris.* But we can't even say we'll always have Pago Pago.

Two:
Finding Sophie

Another sixteen or so hours of miserable plane travel. Jack and I make small talk to avoid what we both would rather not discuss. When we get home should we call from the airport or just grab a cab and go? Hopefully it won't take too long to get my luggage. Once again we sleep fitfully. And I worry. What could have brought on the attack? Sophie's never had that happen before. How bad is it? Why can't we locate any of the girls? I am in turmoil and agony.

I try to console myself that she is with Evvie, Ida, and Bella. Bella won't be of much use, but Ida and my sister are level-headed. They can handle things. Or if Sophie's recuperating at home in Lanai Gardens by now, everyone in the entire Phase Two will attend to her. I bemoan the fact that I take my girls for granted. None of us think of our age and what lies ahead. Especially Sophie. She has such a love for life. She never complains. She's always smiling and good-natured.

Please, God, let her be all right.

Somebody once told me a story about a friend who kept buying airline tickets and making hotel reservations. "How can I die," she asked, "when I'm booked for France? Or Israel? Or wherever." For Sophie, it's going downtown to buy yet another colorful, coordinated outfit.

Jack holds my hand most of the trip, bless him.

When we arrive at the Fort Lauderdale airport, the baggage is slow in coming out, as usual, which adds to our anxiety. The heat is suffocating hot — typical for late August. I already miss the coolness of our island getaway. Finally we're on our way home.

We hurry out of the cab as soon as it pulls up in front of my building. And there's Tessie, her frizzy black hair bouncing as she throws her newspapers in the trash barrel. My luck, she's wearing one of her typical muumuus to hide her large size. The irony of a muumuu here is not lost on Jack.

"Tessie. Where's Sophie?"

Tessie looks at us curiously. "Where do you think she is? She's in her apartment with the rest of your gang."

27

"Thanks." I run past her. I can't wait for the elevator. I rush up the three flights with Jack right behind me.

Tessie yells after me, "Hey, Gladdy. Where's the fire?"

We hear raucous laughter coming from inside Sophie's apartment. And at the same time it dawns on me that Tessie didn't look worried.

No one hears us knock. The screen door is unlocked so we walk in, Jack and I still schlepping my suitcase. Silence falls as we step into the bedroom and they see us. Astonishment flashes across every face.

There roly-poly Sophie is, propped up in bed, dressed all in lavender: nightie, bed jacket, and ribbons in her matching lavender hair. Looking very healthy. Holding court. Eating chocolate. The girls surround her, seated on kitchen chairs and munching on goodies. Her bed is a riot of fashion magazines and candy boxes.

"What are you two doing here?" Evvie asks, amazed.

"I thought you were ill," I say to Sophie, with ice in my voice.

"False alarm," answers Sophie gaily. "Pacemaker needed adjustments."

"But how did you know?" Evvie asks, frowning at me, sensing something is not

28

right or we wouldn't be back this soon.

"You missed all the excitement," Bella says in her usual whisper. "We all got to ride in a helicopter."

"I thought I would faint," Ida adds, patting her tight bun. "You know how easy I get motion sickness. I closed my eyes the entire trip."

Sophie admonishes, "And you missed all the good scenery."

"And unfortunately *we* missed the last bingo session of the trip," Evvie says, aiming her annoyance at Sophie.

"But we're covered," Bella adds gleefully. "The Bingo Dolls are playing for us. We left them money."

Sophie playfully throws a candy bar at Evvie. "I said I was sorry. I can't help it if I got sick. I needed to get back to my darling Dr. Friendly."

I can feel Jack behind me, stiffening. I don't dare turn to look at him.

Sophie continues, "And he was right there waiting at the hospital for me, bless his heart."

With a cash register clicking away in his head, I think unkindly. Special run to the hospital. Click. Overtime. Click. Quick exam. Click. I'm surprised Dr. Friendly didn't make her stay overnight, like all the other times, and take yet another angiogram and who knows what other expensive tests and procedures. I think he is one step above being a quack, but Sophie worships him so no one is allowed to say a bad word about him.

Bella giggles behind her hands. "Just like dialing nine-one-one. Only more exciting." She reaches for another jujube.

"One-two-three, he checked me out, gave me a new prescription, and sent me on home. Now I take Dijoxin."

Bella adds, "Now she takes ten pills a day."

"I don't mind," Sophie coos. "If my darling Dr. Friendly —"

But I'm not about to let her off the hook. "I tried calling and never got an answer."

Sophie looks puzzled for a moment, then brightens. "I turned off the ringer so I could sleep."

Jack's voice cuts through the levity. I was wondering when he'd reach the point where he'd had enough. "Who sent the fax?"

Everyone looks up at him, bewildered.

"What fax?" Evvie asks.

Jack searches every face, but sees only surprise. Except for Bella, who suddenly drops her candy box onto Sophie's lavish pink bedspread.

Oh, no. I see where this is going.

Bella raises a shaky hand. All eyes are on her. "I did."

"Why?" Jack snaps at her.

Her thin, reedy voice gets even softer. "Because Gladdy always worries if someone doesn't tell her if someone was sick and someone . . ." Bella stops. She's run out of clarity.

Evvie is amazed. "When did you do that?"

"When everyone was packing. I went up to the captain . . ."

Quick-witted, quick-moving Ida is also astonished at such unusual action from our timid friend. "You went all by yourself to the top deck and found your way back to the cabin by yourself?"

Tiny Bella grins with pride, holding her five-foot-tall frame erect in her chair. "The captain said he'd send a fax for me. I told him what to say and then he picked a cute sailor to take me back." She blushes. Bella always blushes when she's the center of attention.

Sophie is all excited. "How sweet. What did you say in the fax?"

Bella stutters. "I . . . I don't remember."

Ida snarls, "She never does."

Jack pulls a crumpled piece of paper from his jacket pocket and waves it at Bella. "Let me refresh your memory. 'Come home.

Sophie is dying.' "

By now I want to crawl away and hide.

The girls respond true to form. I can see it in their faces: Evvie realizing that the fax ruined my romantic getaway. I think she feels bad about that. Or does she? She's on the fence about my relationship with Jack. Ida is visibly pleased by this new happening — Ms. Man-hater sees Jack complicating our lives. Sophie is delighted at having so much attention. And Bella, well, Bella is a shambles.

Me? I just want to get out of there. "Jack, let's go," I say timorously.

"Not yet," he says icily.

And here comes the dreaded question. He asks, "Bella, how did you know where to send the fax?"

Considering that Jack and I had both agreed not to tell anyone where we were going, there were only two people who could have broken that vow, and Jack knew it hadn't been him.

Bella, stunned into silence, can't even look at me.

Evvie sees the trouble I'm in. She makes a pathetic attempt to save me. "Maybe Bella has ESP?"

"I told her," I confess, needing to let poor Bella off the hook. "I knew she'd worry about me, so I left her a note and warned her not to ever tell anyone."

I don't think I'll ever forget the look on Jack's face at that moment.

Now I realize how foolish I'd been. I'd thought that someone should know our whereabouts in case of emergencies. But a lawyer perhaps. Not sweet Bella who now feels awful. I shouldn't have put that responsibility on her.

Without another word, Jack walks out. I rush after him. I can already hear the girls mumbling behind me. I catch up to him at the staircase.

"Wait," I say.

"What for?" he says angrily.

"What can I say? It was just one of those crazy things that happen."

"While we're on this subject of Sophie and her maladies, what was the nine-one-one reference?"

I'd rather not tell him. But I do. "Sometimes Sophie panics and she just picks up the phone and dials emergency. Or maybe she wakes up in the middle of the night and feels frightened or lonely and she doesn't want to wake us. And she needs someone who cares. It happens with many of the women here."

"And that made Bella giggle? Why? The

hospital is across the street. You could walk to it from here! Why nine-one-one?"

"It's their way to beat the system," I say. "Over the years one woman tells another, and now they all do it."

"What?"

"They know if they go to the emergency room, they'll wait hours until they get attention. This way, dial nine-one-one, the ambulance arrives in minutes; they get a team of three fussing over them, getting their history, giving them oxygen. Then they are rushed over and get immediate further attention."

"Which the taxpayer pays for," he says with disgust.

"I didn't say I condone it, but they are very good at saving their own lives when the system really doesn't care."

"This is no time for a political discussion. I'm exhausted. I'm going home."

"Jack, wait. What if something happened to you? How would anyone know?"

"Believe me, they'd find a way."

"You're walking away because I made a mistake by telling Bella? I'm sorry our trip got ruined, but we'll have another chance . . ."

"Do I really need to tell you?" His voice is soft. He turns and starts down the stairs.

I know what he is thinking. I know how long he waited for us to be alone and how hard he worked to make it special. "I'm sorry."

He doesn't respond.

I call down after him, not caring whether anyone might be listening. "Please, Jack, stay. Stay with me here."

He pauses on the bottom step.

"Overnight." I say it breathlessly, hopefully. I want so desperately to make it up to him.

He looks up at me, sadly. "I don't think so. Go take care of your 'girls.' "

With that he continues walking. I watch him from the balcony until he turns the corner. He doesn't look back to see me break into tears.

The last thing I remember is the sound of the lawn sprinklers turning on as I drift off to sleep.

"What if something happened to you?"

"Jack, I'm talking to you. Answer me."

But all I see is dimness. I can't find him.

"Jack, where are you?"

The dimness evaporates as if it were fog, and suddenly I can see him. There he is, lying in the alley, bleeding to death. I scream. "Jack, don't leave me. Jack!"

I wake abruptly. It's the middle of the night. I've been dreaming of the first Jack, my husband, who was shot forty years ago. But it's Jack Langford I'm thinking about now. I couldn't bear it if I lost him, too.

THREE:
OLD ROUTINES

I wake to a pounding noise coming from outside my apartment. I drag myself out of bed and make my way to the door. Through the screen I see Evvie in a bathing suit, one of her collection of wild Hawaiian designs. Her red hair, now sprinkled with gray, is curly as always from the humidity. She looks so much like our mother with her softer, round body. Unlike tall, angular me, who resembles our father. She carries a matching towel on her arm.

"Good morning, sleepyhead," she says cheerfully.

I force my bleary eyes to focus. "What time is it?"

"Time to get moving. You missed morning exercises. I figured jet lag, so we let you sleep. Rise and shine. Get your swimsuit on."

"Coffee," I mumble. "Shower."

"Okay. A quick cup and a quick wash and

get on down. See you at the pool."

I want to go back to bed and not get up again. Ever. I don't want to go to the pool. I don't want to face my girls. Or anyone else. I just want to hide my head in my pillows and sleep. All I can think about is the way Jack looked at me last night as he walked away from me.

As I turn away from Evvie, she calls out to me. "If you're not down in fifteen minutes I'm coming to get you. Everyone's waiting to see you."

In the kitchen, I grope for my coffeepot. Evvie's moved down the walkway and is now peering at me through my window. "Glad? It's a shame your vacation was spoiled. Is Jack all right about coming back early?"

I choke on the lie, but I say, "Yeah, just fine."

"There's something I want to talk about with you later today. Seeing how happy you are with Jack has given me an idea."

Yeah, right. Happy. I manage to nod. "Later."

But all I'm thinking is, Go away. Leave me to my misery.

As I make my way across the brick path to the pool, I try to compose myself. Of course, when they got home those yentas told everyone I'd left the cruise ship and gone off with Jack. I mean, I wasn't with them, so where would I be? The rest of the neighbors will be dying to hear about what Jack and I were up to, but I will go to my death before I tell any of them. How am I going to look my neighbors in the eye? Will they be able to read the failure in my face?

Walking past Denny Ryan's garden, I hear voices. Our handyman spends as much time as he can in his beloved garden. Today he is talking to his new girlfriend, Yolanda Diaz, called Yolie by all. Since she came to work for Irving Weiss as caretaker to his wife (and our dear friend) Millie, who has Alzheimer's, we've all come to adore her. As our Denny does. But, what's this? She's crying, and Denny in his gentle way is trying to comfort her. Seems like something is bothering her, but she won't tell him why. A lover's quarrel so soon? I think sadly, What? Another spat in the Garden of Eden?

I arrive at the pool area quietly to find everyone at their usual pastimes. Tessie is doing laps. My gang are walking back and forth in the shallow end of the water, chatting. Mary is sitting by the side of the pool, crocheting. She seems to have made peace with her husband, John, leaving her. Is that what I have to look forward to? Finding some hobby to take Jack's place if he doesn't come back to me?

Meanwhile, the snowbird Canadians who fly down every winter to flee their icy weather are sunbathing and reading their hometown newspapers. Enya, our concentration camp survivor, engrossed in a book, as always, sits off to one side alone. Hy and Lola are holding hands across their adjoining chaises — he, Mr. Pain-in-the-you-know-where, and she, clueless as ever.

The young, secretly gay "cousins," Barbi and Casey, dressed more casually than when they are at their computer research office, are playing cards, content in the knowledge they are accepted here and the girls and I won't betray their secret.

As usual, dear Irving is sitting in the shade, whispering gently to immobile Millie. There's no way to tell whether her Alzheimer's is any worse, but between Irving and Yolie, she is well cared for.

As for me, I hope not to attract anyone's attention.

But no such luck! At the sight of me, Hy leaps to his feet and starts a round of applause. Everyone hops to attention and joins in. "Get the goodies," he orders Lola. In moments there's a box of assorted *rugallah* opened on one of the round white plastic tables. One of the Canadians opens an ice chest and takes out cold drinks and places them alongside the baked goods. Tessie's out of the pool and rounding up the napkins, which are instantly made useless by her wet hands.

Just about everyone is surrounding me. Oh, God, I think. Save me. Then they sing out, " 'Hail the conquering hero . . .' "

Evvie leads me to the food table during the rousing cheer. Our neighbors wait breathlessly until I pick a *rugallah.*

"Good choice. Raspberry," says Mary, and then everyone else dives in.

They're all talking at once. I'm sure the girls filled them in on our exploits during the bingo cruise. I guess they want to hear it again now that I'm back.

"You captured a killer?" Tessie.

"Single-handed?" Irving.

"No, we already told you, we all got him." Ida.

"We got him during a hurricane." Sophie.

"No, it was a tsunami." Evvie.

"A what?" Tessie.

"Didja get a reward?" Hy.

Bella starts to speak, but Ida stops her by slapping a hand over her mouth. Ida faces Hy. "None of your business."

"Congratulations," Barbi and Casey say in unison.

"So where's Jack?" Mary asks.

My head is spinning. Evvie seats me in a chair and shifts the nearby umbrella to shade my face. "Have mercy, she's jet-lagged," warns my sister, always protective of me.

I'm feeling nothing but anger. Anger at all of their nonsense. And most of all anger at myself. I could be in Jack's arms on our island paradise instead of here. Coulda, woulda, shoulda.

Tessie pulls a chair close. "Lots of news here. The Peeper struck again."

Mary adds, "And again and again."

"Dumkupfs," Hy says with disgust. "I told these ladies to pull down their shades. They're just asking for it."

I know I should show some interest. This man, whoever he is, has been frightening many of the women who live on the first floors of buildings throughout the condo. But my heart isn't in it.

Tessie leans over and swats Hy.

"Ouch," he says. Then to me, "You missed my joke. Wanna hear it?"

A chorus of "No" blasts out at him. He ignores it. He circles round me, hands on hips, gyrating his tush as he always does.

He begins, "At eight you take her to bed and tell her a story."

Even though I try not to listen, he goes on and on. The group gives up, knowing they can't stop him, and they disperse, ambling back to their other pursuits.

"At eighteen, you tell her a story and take her to bed. At twenty-eight, you don't need to tell her a story to take her to bed."

Irving makes the universal gesture of repulsion, waving his hand. *"Feh."*

Hy gestures back, meaning *who cares what you think.* "At thirty-eight, she tells you a story and takes you to bed."

Ida reaches out and smacks him with her wet towel. He ducks, not missing a beat. "At forty-eight, you tell her a story to avoid going to bed." Hearing rumblings of impatience, he talks faster. "At fifty-eight you stay in bed to avoid her story. At sixty-eight if you take her to bed, that'll be a story —"

Almost as if rehearsed, the entire poolside gang (except Enya and Irving) shouts the punch line loudly, cutting him off. "At seventy-eight, what story? What bed? Who *are* you?"

Hy walks away in disgust. "I waste my talents on you ingrates."

In spite of my misery, I find myself laughing out loud. Some things never change. I am beginning to feel a little better. I'm here. Whether I want to be or not. So be here, I tell myself. I'm with people who care about me. I'm with my *lantsmen*, my neighbors, my family.

FOUR:
CATCHING UP

Since the weather is so pleasant, the girls opt to work outdoors. Evvie called the meeting of Gladdy Gold and Associates Detective Agency, insisting it was time to catch up with our mail and calls since we've been away. But as nice as it is to see my neighbors and friends, I just can't get with it. I want to care but I don't. Jack is the only thing on my mind. How serious is this fight? Is it something he'll get over quickly? I wish I knew.

We are gathered around a picnic table on the grass in the shade. Behind us ducks quack as they swim past under the little wooden bridges that dot one of the many ponds around Lanai Gardens. Lucky for me, the girls are all so self-absorbed that they haven't mentioned Jack's reaction to our coming home so early, though I would have expected more response from Evvie. Sophie is applying new nail polish. Something lavender to go with her latest hair rinse. Her ten vials of pills are stretched out in a row. She intends to take them after her nails dry. Bella, our recording secretary, is eagerly waiting to take notes on the meeting. Evvie is catching me up on all the new calls that came in to our answering machine while we were away.

"This one sounds promising," she says. "His wife's become addicted to the shopping channel and she just keeps ordering stuff. But what makes it worse, with her bad memory she orders the same things over and over again. He doesn't know how to stop her."

"Pass," I say listlessly.

"Tell him to cut up her credit cards," Ida suggests in her toughest voice. She is busy reading the directions on our brand-new cell phones.

After our harrowing experience on the cliffs of Puerto Rico, when I would have sold my soul for a phone, I promised we'd now have cell phones. To my surprise, they've already bought them.

"This is complicated," Ida says. "What's text messages?"

"Who cares," Evvie tells her. "Just learn how to talk on it and get voice messages."

"But this manual is thirty pages long."

"Ignore it. Learn everything on a need-to-know basis."

"What about programming numbers?"

"No," insists Evvie, "we don't need that. We're only going to use it for emergencies."

I pretend to read through my mail, but all I want is to go back to my apartment and cry.

"What about this one?" Evvie asks. "Here's a woman who thinks someone is stalking her."

"Tell her to call the police," I say sharply.

The girls look at me, surprised at my prickly answer, so unlike me. I sigh. I'd better be careful and not take my frustration out on them. I don't want to answer any questions about what happened between me and Jack.

"Yeah, I guess you're right," Evvie says, throwing the girls an anxious look, which I pretend not to notice.

"So tell Gladdy what we were talking about for you," Bella says to Evvie. Always the peacemaker, she knows it's time to change the subject.

Evvie sits up taller and gives me a perky grin. "I decided I am finally ready to start dating again. I simply must get out of my rut." She runs her fingers through her fading red curls. "Time to wash that gray right out of my hair."

Sophie, who changes her hair color with her moods, applauds. "Bravo."

"I mean, look how happy you are with Jack. I've just been stubborn. Now I'm ready to spread my wings and fly." Evvie leans back in her deck chair and spreads her arms wide. "Adventure, here I come."

Oh, my dear sister, if you only knew.

Sophie adds, "We've been making lists of what things she should try. Like maybe she puts an ad in the personals in the *Sun-Sentinel*."

"Or join a matchmaking service." Bella grins at the thought. "Then you can lie about your age like everyone else does."

Evvie adds, "I'm even toying with the idea of getting a computer and doing that on-line dating, like with Match.com."

Sourpuss Ida gives her opinion: "Waste of time and money."

"I don't care. I'm ready and Glad will help." She turns to me. "Won't you? You're the expert."

Luckily, before I can sputter some kind of inane comment, I am saved by a familiar voice.

"Good afternoon, ladies." Sol Spankowitz bears down on us, full set of false teeth gleaming. He carries the inevitable racing form, so he must be on his way to meet his racetrack buddy, Irving. "Welcome home. I only just heard you were back, and I couldn't wait to welcome you personally." All of this is directed at Evvie, who makes a face showing her displeasure.

"You look so tanned and healthy," he says, looking down at her chest as usual. She pulls up her halter top to hide any cleavage showing, then reaches over and pushes Sol's chin up, so he's forced to look at her face.

The lack of any positive response doesn't stop him. "I was thinking maybe I could tempt you into a little breakfast date tomorrow?"

"Date. He said the magic word," says Bella excitedly.

"I'll call you this evening and we'll make plans." With that he waves his farewell and jauntily strolls away.

"And my phone will be off the hook," Evvie says under her breath. She shoots Bella a dirty look. "He's not what I had in mind."

Bella is practically jumping up and down. "I can't believe it. You said the date word and a minute later, you're asked."

"So, Miss Popularity," Ida says caustically, "what Prince Charming *do* you expect to show up on your welcome mat?"

Evvie thinks for a few moments, trying to find the right words. "I want someone . . . someone debonair. Worldly. A man who'll sweep me off my feet. Maybe even handsome. Someone who'll understand me. Not like that pathetic schlepper, Sol."

Bella says, "So give him a broom and he'll sweep."

Sophie looks up from swallowing her pills as she mixes yet another metaphor. "Look at him like a practice trial."

"Look at him like the loser he is," adds Ida, negative as usual.

Evvie scowls. "I'd rather have the heartbreak of psoriasis."

I can't sit another minute. I stand up. This date talk is driving me crazy. "I think it's time we dealt with the problem of our Peeping Tom. Let's go to the office and find Greta Kronk's file."

"Right." Evvie jumps up. "We have to find the drawing labeled 'sneaky peeky.' It may identify the guy who's been peeping in all those apartments."

Greta Kronk had been a longtime resident of Phase Two. After she died, on a hunch I suggested we keep all her sketches. I sigh. I still bemoan the fact that the police refused to do an autopsy on her. We later proved she was murdered. If we'd found out earlier, we might have been able to save the next victim.

Bella is confused. "What?"

Ida says, "Remember when poor crazy Greta was smearing paint on our doors and cars, she always left a nasty little poem? And then when we went to her apartment, we found out she did sketches to match the poems?"

Bella smiles. "Now I remember, when you remind me."

Sophie says, "I can't go. Mah-jongg. And Bella, you're playing, too."

Ida tells us she has to write letters to her grandchildren. We all avoid commenting since we know what little good that will do — they never answer any of her mail.

Evvie puts her arm through mine. Meeting is over. Thank God.

The condo office, where all the Lanai Gardens records are kept, is really not much more than a large broom closet. Actually, board members converted part of one of our many storerooms for this purpose. An old wooden desk, an unmatched chair, a two-drawer file cabinet, a bulletin board, and that's about it. Evvie looks up at me from where she is searching the lower file drawer. "It's not here."

"How can that be? It has to be there."

She wipes the dust off her hands. This place is only cleaned when someone thinks about it, and that isn't often. Evvie looks through the mess of papers on the desk as well. "Nope. The Greta Kronk file is gone, along with the poems and sketches she did of almost everyone in Lanai Gardens. You think the Peeper took it?"

"Who else?"

"But the office is always locked."

"And the key is always under the mat. Probably fifty people know that, and just about that many knew all about Greta's pictures, too. Try and keep any secrets around this place."

We secure the door when we leave, and yes, we put the key under the mat.

I glance up toward the third-floor catwalk, where my apartment is, and catch a glimpse of a couple standing there.

They see us at the same time. "Mrs. Gold?" the man calls down.

"Are you waiting for me?"

"Yes," he says, "We might have a job for you."

Evvie pinches my arm excitedly. "I hope this is a good one."

As Evvie and I hurry up the stairs, only about a dozen or so doors open, allowing their residents to get a look at what's going on. I find it amazing that, what with the huge yenta population around here, no one has seen the Peeper yet. Anyone could have snuck into the condo office — any resident, that is. But a stranger on the property would have attracted immediate attention. That's why I'm sure it's one of our men, an insider, who is the Peeper.

But who? If I've learned anything as a PI or from my lifelong love of reading mystery novels, it's that the guilty party will have to make a mistake sometime!

FIVE:
BACK IN BUSINESS

As they sip the tea I offered them, I examine my visitors. Mr. Alvin Ferguson, mid-sixties, I think, wears a dark wool suit and tie. Prissy. Nervous. Keeps patting what few strands of grayish brown hair he has across his rather bald pate. His wife, Shirley, who looks about the same age, wears a bright, large-patterned heavy rayon dress with matching closed-toe shoes. Her hair is a multicolored mishmash of gray, brown, and a bit of dirty blond. Either it's time to get to the beauty parlor or she likes the way that looks. If Sophie were here, she'd have plenty to say about Shirley Ferguson's style, or lack of it. And yet, their clothes appear expensive. The heavy fabrics must be stifling in our Florida heat.

"This is your office?" Alvin asks. He looks around my living room with concern. Family photos everywhere. No business equipment in sight. I could point out our answering machine in the kitchen, plugged into the same wall socket as my toaster, or our new cell phones, but I doubt if he'd be impressed. His expression reads, *This is how you run a business?* He should see our business files, stored in a seltzer carton behind my shoes at the bottom of my bedroom closet.

"For now," I tell him. "We're thinking of renting a regular office, but we've been so busy, we haven't had time to look."

Evvie grins at me as if to say, *Nice move!*

"I like it," says Shirley. "Very *haimish.* Instead of boring stuffy office stuff, a person can feel cozy here." She stretches her arms out to illustrate her comfort.

I'm making a guess here — after all, I've only just met this couple — but I'll bet that whatever Alvin says, Shirley will reply in the negative.

He looks at the wall sampler Bella stitched for us last Hanukkah. " 'Don't trust anyone under seventy-five'?" he reads disdainfully. "This is your motto?"

"It's just our company joke," Evvie explains.

"Cute," Shirley says. See what I mean?

"How may we help you?" I say, to move things along.

Alvin clears his throat. "My mother, Esther Ferguson, died on July 27th — nearly one month ago."

Evvie says, "Sorry to hear it."

"Well, she was ninety-five."

"That's a good, ripe old age," says Evvie encouragingly.

Shirley jumps in. "She died in her bathtub in her apartment in the Grecian Villas retirement complex."

That's informative. Grecian Villas is probably one of the most expensive and elegant retirement hotels in all of Fort Lauderdale. Evvie's glance tells me she made the same connection. She is smiling, which means she is sure that this couple can afford to pay. That's one of the advantages about sisters knowing each other so well. We can often read each other's minds.

Alvin pushes his teacup away. "I need to tell you up front that I'm interviewing a number of private detectives."

There goes Evvie's smile. We don't have the job yet.

"Alvin," his wife warns, "enough already."

"Well, I need to make sure, don't I? I can't turn this sensitive matter over to just about anybody. This is a serious situation." He turns back to me and Evvie. "I think my dear mother was murdered."

Shirley butts in quickly. "Just so you know

which side I'm on, I don't. The woman was nearly one hundred, for God's sakes." She glares at her husband.

"I know it was that man."

"She was living with her lover," Shirley reports.

"Don't call him that. It's disgusting."

"Well, he was! They weren't just playing Parcheesi." Shirley grins at me. "She called him Romeo and he called her Juliet. Isn't that sweet? I should be so lucky to have such a romance at that age." She gives Alvin a look that threatens it might not be him.

"Philip Smythe was taking advantage of her," Alvin insists. "He knew she was loaded."

"We met him once," Shirley says to me and Evvie. "Don't you just love British accents? I could tell he made her happy. He really loved her. He was a saint."

"He was stealing her blind." Alvin's face is getting purple with anger.

"Alvin. We went through her bank accounts. All her money was there. She didn't marry him or leave him anything in her will. You're crazy, carrying on like this. We were her sole heirs."

"I know he did it! I can't let it alone. I want justice!" Now he is standing; his collar seems to be choking him.

57

Shirley stands up, too. "So what's his motive?" She turns away from her husband and addresses us. "I'm really sorry we've wasted your time. We don't need a detective. What we need to do is go back home to Seattle."

That explains the wardrobe. Only out-of-towners wear rayon and wool.

Evvie frowns. There goes our job.

Alvin clenches his fists, defying her. "I say we do need a detective."

Shirley says, "So all right, waste our money and hire these girls already. They seem nice enough. All I can say is I'm not schlepping to one more PI. I'll wait for you outside."

Alvin turns to us and announces, "So be it. I am formally hiring you to prove that my mother, Esther Ferguson, was murdered by Philip Smythe!"

"No fool like an old fool," Shirley mutters as she heads for the door.

Evvie says mildly, "You'll die of the heat out there."

Shirley walks out, then walks back in. "You're right." She stands under the air-conditioning vents, arms folded. "I'll wait right here."

I go to my mahogany credenza; lying there in the top drawer, amid the dessert and cocktail forks, is a small stack of copies of

58

our boilerplate contract.

Alvin takes one when I hold it out to him. "Just tell me where I put my John Hancock."

"Are you sure, Mr. Ferguson?" I ask him. "Don't rush into signing with us if you need to interview others."

"No, this is it," he says. He signs the contract and starts to write us a check. "How much is your retainer and who do I make it out to?"

Evvie jumps right in. "Five hundred will be fine. To Gladdy Gold and Associates."

I'm about to comment about that amount and the fact that he didn't even read the contract, but Evvie kicks me in my ankle.

Alvin manages a tight little smile. "I'm a man who makes decisions and I've decided."

"Thank you," I say. "Now how about another cup of tea? Please sit down again and you can fill us in on some details."

With that, Shirley sits back down as well. She's not about to miss anything.

As Evvie refills their cups she asks, "Have you been to the police?"

Alvin shoots Shirley a dirty look. "My *wife* wouldn't let me."

"And make a fool of yourself? They'd laugh us out of the station."

I ask, "Was there an autopsy?"

Again Shirley answers for him. "What for? She fell asleep in a tub and died of old age."

Alvin's expression is sad, thinking of his dear, departed mother, I suppose. "They didn't bother."

"You could have requested it," I tell him.

Angry looks are exchanged between husband and wife.

Evvie needs to change the subject. "So your name is Ferguson. I assumed you were Jewish."

Alvin tells her they are. "Our family was one of those at Ellis Island who got their names changed because of poor communication."

I smile. I've heard that story before. When the frightened immigrants faced the authorities asking for their names, they were so flustered, they said in Yiddish, *Ich hab fargesen."* Meaning, I forgot. And that's why there is a huge branch of Jews living in America named Ferguson, who are thought to be Scottish.

Evvie's curiosity is on a roll. "What about this Philip Smythe? What a la-de-da name."

"Who knows?" Alvin says. "Maybe Immigration changed his name, too."

Practical Shirley chimes in, "Now you're on the payroll, find out for yourselves. Me,

I prefer to think of him as Romeo."

From the open screen door I watch them leave down the walkway, still arguing.

Evvie looks at me expectantly. "So when do we start?"

"When the check clears, that's when."

SIX:
THE PEEPER

Dora Dooley, eighty-one, resident of Phase Six, apartment 114, was doing what she usually did late at night. She was sitting in her sunroom, watching today's tape of her favorite soap opera, *World of Our Dreams.* That VCR was the best Christmas gift she'd ever received in her whole life, and it was from her darling neighbor, Jack Langford, after he'd learned she hardly slept nights. It had taken Dora a while to catch on to rewind, fast forward, and play, but she still had all her marbles and she learned. So every morning she watched her soap, recording it all the while, and looked forward to watching it again that night. And every night before she let her eyes close, she always rewound the tape, readying it for the following day.

Dora was very thin, and so tiny that her bird-like legs barely reached the edge of her worn recliner. She wore a heavy flannel gown, wool socks, and her favorite purple chenille robe she'd had for over fifty years — it was still as good as new. Her warm comforter was at the ready for when it grew really cool.

Tonight, Dora had started playing her tape before eleven o'clock, early for her. But today's show was so exciting she couldn't wait another moment to watch it again. Evangeline and Errol were meeting for the first time in three years. Dora shivered with excitement. She'd known Errol would hunt for Evangeline until he found her again. He was possessed by her. But Dora also knew from reading her fan magazines that Errol, played by Leroy Johnson, had left the show three years ago because the producers wouldn't pay him the money he wanted. But Errol was back, so they must have settled. And that's what Dora did now. She settled back and pressed play.

At first she thought she was imagining things. Dora suddenly felt weird, as if someone was staring at her. Something made her turn to the window and her skin began to crawl. There was a shadow out there, peering in. She squinted and realized the shadow was dressed all in black, and wore a superman mask! She pulled her blanket over her head, hoping she'd imagined it and it would go away. But when she snuck a look out of the corner of her blanket, the shadow was still there! Oh, no! What was it doing? She saw a hand moving . . . She closed her eyes, horrified.

Instinctively Dora reached over and grabbed the weapon she always kept beside her recliner — her kitchen broom. She raised it high and banged on her ceiling as hard as she could.

"Jack!" she screamed. "Jack Langford, get down here at once! And bring your gun!"

When she looked back at the window, the disgusting figure was gone.

Dora climbed out of her recliner, so she could meet Jack at the door. She shivered in disgust as she thought about what that Peeper had been doing outside her window. None of her soap friends would ever behave in such a disgraceful manner.

As soon as Dora opened her front door, Jack hurried in. "I just got home. What is it? What's happened? Are you all right?"

Dora smiled, imagining that she was one of the characters on *World of Our Dreams.* It was nice having a cop living in her building, especially such a handsome and attentive one.

SEVEN:
MAYBE MEN ARE
FROM MARS

Night two. Is this going to be my way of keeping track of my loneliness?

Luckily I was so jet-lagged last night that, except for my nightmares, I didn't have time to record my first night without Jack. Not that I ever had a night *with* him. I fell asleep after a dinner I couldn't eat and woke up in the morning with a headache. Or was it an ache in my heart?

Night two is not off to a good start. My usual routine is to watch the ten o'clock news and then read until my eyes close, but I have no desire to watch TV or open my book. I have to pull myself out of this. I'm driving myself crazy. I'm acting like a teenager.

I look at the phone. Staring at it doesn't make it ring. Ring, I demand silently.

You make the call.

Great. The phone is talking to me.

No, I can't.

Do it. You know you want to.

Mind your own business.

Just reach out.

It's after eleven o'clock.

Ooh, he's a big boy. I bet he stays up 'til at least eleven thirty, maybe even midnight.

I need sarcasm from a phone?

Call him up!

All right. Stop nagging.

I can't believe I'm having a conversation with myself as a phone. I reach out tentatively for the receiver. I dial Jack's number, then quickly hang up before I reach the last digit.

Coward.

Shut up.

I pace. I sit down on the edge of the bed. I get up again. I dial again. It rings. And rings. And rings. Then his answering machine picks up. I hang up, fast. He's not home. Where is he after eleven o'clock at night? Where would he have gone? None of us seniors ever venture out past nine p.m. I'm about to dial again, but what's the point. What if he's in the shower and didn't hear the phone? A memory flashes into my head of Jack dropping his lavalava as he was about to get into the Jacuzzi with me. For a brief moment I see his body and feel faint with longing. And then to miss it all. Because of my stupidity. I had to put the girls first, didn't I? Oh, this is torture. I wait ten minutes; the hands on the clock are moving much too slowly. He's got to be out of the shower now. I dial. Get the same result. No shower. Face it. He's not home. Or even worse he's there and doesn't want to talk to me. I hang up on the answering machine. I will not leave a message.

Now I'm wide awake. Angry. Frustrated. Annoyed. First at him and then at myself. I head to the fridge for something to eat. Anything. Luckily nothing appeals to me. Carrot sticks won't do it.

Jack, where are you? Call me, damn it!

"Now, you sit on this bench," Evvie tells me the next morning. "You'll be able to see and hear everything."

I sit down. "This is your idea of a date?"

"No, it's his, and I didn't want this date in the first place. I need you to help me out."

"So why didn't you say no?"

"Because I'm stupid. So stay here and drink your coffee and do your crossword puzzle. Look inconspicuous."

I can hardly be inconspicuous since I'm six inches away from the picnic table at which Evvie is supposed to wait for Sol Spankowitz. We are seated in a grassy area near the duck pond — which places us directly in the path of everyone walking to the pool, meaning they can't miss us. Sol's idea, I'll bet, to show off having a date with Evvie.

Evvie pinches me. "Tell me to run now while I still have the chance."

"Why isn't he taking you out to a restaurant?"

"Probably because he's cheap. The man is an idiot. Uh-oh, speaking of idiots, here he comes."

"Well, at least he's on time. That's a good trait in a boyfriend."

"Don't say anything nice about him; do me that favor."

"I promise." But I can hardly keep my face straight.

Sol is practically bouncing along the path, he's that happy. He carries a yellow wicker picnic basket with pink ribbons, something I'm sure his late wife, Clara, bought. He wears one of his inevitable bad-taste outfits, lime green checkered pants, a striped orange shirt, and unmatched socks. I'm beginning to suspect he's color-blind.

"Good morning, good morning, O princess of the Dawn." He tries to kiss Evvie's hand, but she snaps it away before he can touch her.

Sol is oblivious to my presence, which is good, because this is a scene I wouldn't want to miss: my usually unflappable sister, dealing with a man who's gaga about her, a man she despises. I pretend to look at my puzzle while I hide my grin.

Romance at our age is fraught with pitfalls. Boy, am I ever aware of that with Mr. On-again-off-again Jack Langford. But while my blissful life with Jack Gold was cut tragically short, Evvie survived an unhappy marriage and a bitter divorce that left her never wanting to go down that path of hurt again. She's been skittish ever since. She's dated on and off through the years, but no guy has ever really touched her heart. This is the first time in many years that my sister has been willing to take another tenuous shot at dating. Albeit, one forced on her. Sol is not a good starting choice, I fear.

"How come we aren't going to a deli or something?" I hear Evvie ask. She looks at the wicker basket with fear and loathing.

"Because the deli has come to you. It's a beautiful day, why should we be indoors?" Never mind that almost all the delis we know have seating outside. And besides, everyone prefers eating indoors in the air-conditioning. With that, Sol opens the basket and removes two lumpy paper napkins and two bananas. And two bottles of water.

Evvie looks disgusted. "This is it?"

He unwraps the napkins to reveal two bagels sloppily filled with cream cheese.

"Bagels with a schmear," he says proudly. "I made them myself." He hands her one.

"This bagel is ice cold." Evvie immediately drops it on the table and pushes it back to him.

"Fresh out of the freezer. And I filled up two bottles I had in the house with water from the sink. Who needs that fancy overpriced water they sell in Publix?"

Evvie moves slightly away from him. "The bananas are black."

"Ain't you never heard of blackened bananas? That's like blackened chicken. A delicacy."

"Yeah, I heard of them," she mimics. "They're the ones I always throw out."

Sol begins eating with gusto. Evvie shakes her head over and over again. She is mumbling something under her breath. It sounds like, "Please let this be over with already."

Mary Mueller passes us, carrying her crocheting, on the way to the pool. She stares in amazement. "You and Sol, an item?" she asks Evvie.

"Pretend you don't see us. It's an optical

illusion."

I can't help it. I giggle. Evvie throws me a dirty look.

Sol is finished eating. He wipes his hands on the soiled napkin that originally held his bagel. "That was spectacular. I love breakfast en brochette."

"En brochette? What are you talking about?"

"It's French for being outdoors." Sol gets up. "Let's go."

"I haven't eaten yet," Evvie says spitefully. Not that she'd ever touch that mess.

Sol quickly grabs her portion and tosses it into his picnic basket. "You can have it after."

Evvie stands up, too. "After what?"

Sol winks at her. "You know."

"I know what?"

"We'll go to my apartment, and . . ." More winking. His eye looks like it's in spasm.

Evvie gapes at him, astonished.

I give up pretending to look at my puzzle. I can't believe what I'm hearing.

"We had breakfast; now it's time to you-know-what."

Evvie's face has turned as red as her hair. With a voice as icy as the bagel, she says, "Tell me exactly what 'you-know-what' is at

71

nine a.m. in the morning."

Sol is getting a little testy. "Hey, I brung you a bagel and a schmear. What more do you want? You owe me."

Evvie crosses her arms. Her eyes have narrowed to slits. "Just exactly what do I owe you?"

Sol is getting uncomfortable. "You know."

She is yelling now. "I don't *effing know,* so tell me!"

He beams. "The F word. I, personally, wouldn't say such a thing but it's so cute coming out of your adorable mouth." He moves crabwise around the picnic table, arms outstretched to embrace her.

Evvie's had it. She smacks him across the face. "Cheapskate!"

At that moment more of the swimming group walks by. Hy and Lola, Tessie, the Canadians. They all stop and stare.

Tessie breaks rank and runs over to Sol, her love gleaming in her eyes. "*Bubbala,* what did she do to you?" All two hundred fifty pounds of her towers over him as she strokes his few strands of hair.

Sol, now befuddled, sees the crowd forming and makes a run for it. His shoelaces are untied, forcing him to hop and skip down the sidewalk, a rather odd sight.

When he's gone, everyone turns back to Evvie.

Evvie walks over and pulls at my arm. "Get up, Glad. We're leaving." She faces the crowd, her look menacing. "Not one word out of anyone."

The would-be swimmers attempt to swallow their grins, not easy to do. Tessie continues to look back in the direction where Sol disappeared.

"Hey, lady PI, what about last night?" Hy asks me.

"What about last night?" I ask.

"Didn't Jack tell you? I thought you'd be the first to know."

Jack? No, Jack tells me nothing anymore. I sigh.

Evvie says, "Spit it out already. I need to go home and get some Extra Strength Tylenol."

Tessie shoots her a dirty look for her poor treatment of the man for whom she carries a torch.

Hy reports. "Late last night in Phase Six, Dora Dooley spotted the Peeper just about the time Jack got home. If he'd only been a couple of minutes earlier, he might have caught him."

What was Jack doing out so late? I wonder suspiciously. But then another thought occurs to me — Jack must have gone to Dora's apartment when she yelled for help. This makes me feel a tiny bit better. That's why he didn't answer his phone.

Lola adds, "He's her hero. He's so good to Dora, always there when she needs him."

I wish I could say the same thing, I think enviously.

"Jack promised he'd get Morrie to write up a report. I was sure he'd tell you since you're the big, important PI around here," says Hy. "You know . . . maybe in pillow talk?"

Now it's my turn to want to smack someone, but I restrain myself. "I'll check it out with him," I say stiffly.

By now Tessie is grubbing around in the wicker basket that Sol abandoned when he fled. "Hey, Evvie," she asks, "mind if I finish off your breakfast?"

"Be my guest," Evvie says, head high, walking off like a queen departing her loyal subjects.

I follow her. All I can think of is that now I have a real excuse to call Jack. On business.

EIGHT:
THE FERGUSONS
INVESTIGATE US

Alvin Ferguson stares probingly at my girls. They stare back with varied expressions. Apparently, when he thought about the fact that Evvie and I had associates, Mr. Picky decided he wanted to meet with them as well. So do we have that job yet? Now I'm not sure. Will he take back the retainer? We've already banked the check. Does he have a legal right to? This guy is going to be a pain in the neck.

Shirley sips a cup of tea at the dining room table, next to me, where we can easily watch the action taking place in the living room. Alvin has been interrogating the girls for twenty minutes. His wife has been smirking the whole time. I think she secretly enjoys how easily he irritates people.

Alvin began by asking Ida questions about her family, which got her back up. She wasn't about to tell him she doesn't ever hear from them.

He wanted to know if Evvie had ever been to college, which she felt was none of his business. She said, "Yes, to the college of Life." She dared him with her eyes to question this, so he moved on.

He asked Sophie about her marital status. She didn't want to tell him she'd been married. Twice.

Now he is tackling Bella.

"But, Mrs. Fox, you can't see very well and you cannot hear very well — what *can* you do?"

"I can . . . I can . . ." Bella is flustered. She looks to me for help.

"Mr. Ferguson, Bella is an excellent operative," I pipe up. "You'll have to take my word on that. All my associates make up a great working team."

Bella is relieved to be off the hot seat.

Alvin doesn't look convinced.

Shirley smiles at my taking her bossy husband down a peg.

Alvin tries to save face. "Money is no object, as I've said before."

Shirley winces. It's obvious she would like to slap him, but he still holds the purse strings. "It won't bring your mother back, Alvin."

"I need to know the truth!"

The girls are practically panting — it looks

like the job is in the bag.

I break in. "We'll get on the case right away."

"Done," he says. "You'll call when you need more money?"

Shirley closes her eyes. Giving away their money is too painful to watch.

Sophie and Bella pinch each other gleefully.

"What can you hope to accomplish?" Shirley says to me, after taking a few long, cleansing breaths to calm down. "Romeo certainly isn't going to confess to you, that's for sure."

"I honestly don't know. But our first goal is to find out everything we can about Philip Smythe."

"How long do you think this is gonna take?" She demands a closing date. They can't support this investigation forever.

Ida jumps in. "There's no way of knowing."

Evvie says smartly, "We have other clients, you know."

I say, "We're on your side, Mrs. Ferguson. We want answers quickly."

Shirley Ferguson stands. She's had enough.

"Wait," I say. "Is there anything else either of you can tell me that might shed some light on what could have happened between the two of them? Was Esther's behavior in any way unusual? Either before or after she met Philip Smythe?"

"Not that I can think of," Alvin says quickly.

"I can think of something," says Shirley, after a brief pause.

We all turn to look at her.

Shirley takes a cigarette out of her purse and slips it between her lips. She knows she can't smoke in here, but I guess it helps her feel a semblance of calm. "She changed her address."

When she has all our attention, she goes on. "After she met Philip, she wrote and told us that from that date on we were to write her at a P.O. Box number."

Alvin gives her one of his what-do-*you*-know looks. "And that means something to you?"

"Yes," she says quietly, which she does to irritate him. "It meant that she no longer received her mail at Grecian Villas. Now, why do you think she would have done that?"

"Big deal," says Alvin.

"I would certainly think so. In Grecian Villas, all she had to do was walk downstairs from her apartment to her box in the lobby and lift out her mail. The new address meant she would have to get someone to drive her to the nearest post office and get her mail there. Why bother?"

This gives Alvin pause. "I never thought about that."

"She didn't want Philip to see her mail?" Ida asks.

"I wonder," I say. "She didn't want Philip to know she had a family?"

"My feeling exactly," says Shirley.

"But why?" asks Sophie.

"I don't really know." Shirley puts the cigarette back in its pack. Then she smiles wickedly. "Maybe she was ashamed of us."

"But you mentioned last time that you met him," I remind her.

"Yes, we did. Once. Only two weeks before she died."

Alvin adds, "I had business on the East Coast and I thought I'd surprise her."

"And let me tell you," Shirley says, "she was surprised all right. And not very happy to see us. But Philip, he was thrilled. He chastised her ever so sweetly for keeping her lovely children from him. I thought he was wonderful."

"I thought he was smarmy," says Alvin. "I immediately knew my mother was in danger."

■ ■ ■ ■

When the Fergusons leave, a few minutes after admonishing us to get on the case quickly, there is a collective sigh of relief in my living room. Everyone stretches out to get more comfortable.

"What a nosy guy. Like he needed to know my private business?" Sophie is still insulted.

"Poor Shirley," Bella whispers. "He must be awful to live with."

"She ain't no walk in the park, either," Ida adds.

"Okay, so they deserve each other." Bella feels better about it now that that's settled.

"Okay," comments Ida, "the first check cleared, now we're official. Where do we go from here?"

I get up and start to clear the tea things. "Directly to Grecian Villas, where the alleged crime took place."

But while the girls head back to their own apartments to get ready for the drive, I quickly dial Jack's number. As it rings, I plan what to say. *I hear you almost caught the Peeper . . .* Then the answering machine picks up. Suddenly Jack is never at home. Where does he go? Does he have any idea he's driving me mad? Life is too short

to spend it being miserable, so I leave a message this time. I tell him I *have* to see him.

NINE:
GRECIAN VILLAS

We pull up to the front door of the retirement hotel where the ill-fated Esther Ferguson and Philip Smythe (a.k.a. Romeo) lived. We've taken the case. Alvin has instructed us to go full steam ahead and not worry about expenses. Music to our ears. Even though Shirley told us otherwise.

The girls have dressed up for their foray into the land of the obscenely wealthy. No flip-flops today. They *ooh* and *ahhh* at the sparkling white archways and pillars that grace the front of Grecian Villas' main building.

Inside, the theme continues. Marble gray-white floors and whitewashed walls hung with paintings of ancient and modern Greece. Furniture in muted tones. Floor-to-ceiling windows everywhere. Well-dressed residents lounging about a huge lobby reading or quietly chatting. Soft music piped in through hidden speakers.

"Elegant," whispers Evvie.

"Too quiet," retorts Ida.

"Works for me," says Sophie to Ida. "I could live in a place like this. It fits my standards of living."

Bella just stares — up, down, everywhere, her mouth hanging open.

A resident directs us to the office of the general manager, Rosalie Gordon. The room is soothing, the manager elegant. She is tall, in her forties, dressed simply but stylishly. Her assistant, a slightly chubby woman in her twenties, works across the room. She is introduced to us as Myra. Like her boss, she wears muted colors. They blend in with the wall décor, as if even management should be inconspicuous to the residents of this luxury community.

After a few pleasantries about the weather, Mrs. Gordon starts her spiel about the facility. Do we want to know about the amenities first? The health and wellness plan? Which of us is interested in joining the happy Grecian Villas family? She is busily pulling out brochures for us as she speaks.

I stop her quickly by taking out our card and handing it to her. For a moment she studies it, confused. "You're all private investigators?"

I say, "Yes," and the gang nods eagerly.

"We're investigating the death of Esther Ferguson."

She looks even more perplexed, as does her assistant.

"At the behest of her son, Alvin."

"I see," says Mrs. Gordon. "It's not about the missing Oriental rug? I already told him it must have been lost by the movers."

"It's not that. It's about how she died."

"This surprises me. We'd already spoken to him, and I had hoped I'd allayed his fears about how his mother died." She pauses. "Obviously not. But I'm afraid there is nothing to investigate, Mrs. Gold. It was a sad occurrence, but not unexpected after a long and comfortable life. Apparently, Mrs. Ferguson was drinking champagne in her bath and fell asleep. She died very peacefully, I should think."

Myra jumps in. "She was found hours later by that dear Mr. Smythe, her beloved companion."

My ears perk up at "dear."

"What is your opinion of Mr. Smythe?" I ask.

Myra gushes, "Wonderful, wonderful. The man is a saint."

"I would have to concur with that," adds Mrs. Gordon, managing a small smile.

Evvie glances at me. That word *saint*

again. Interesting.

"How long were they together?" Evvie asks.

"Three wonderful months." Myra lays one hand over her heart. "They met the first week Philip arrived, and it was love at first sight."

"Where was he when Mrs. Ferguson passed away?" Ida jumps in. I can see that Sophie and Bella are intimidated in this posh environment. They stand stiffly and silently.

"Playing his usual bridge game with the Feig sisters and Alice Brown. You might speak to them. They'll tell you how enchanting he is." Myra can hardly hold back her enthusiasm.

Mrs. Gordon is a bit more sedate. "All the ladies here adored him. The man was so generous with himself. On dance night, he took turns dancing with all the ladies. He was a regular Fred Astaire. On shopping days, he escorted a group of them and helped carry their bags. After all, the ratio of women to men here is ten to one, and Mr. Smythe is a very robust seventy-five years of age. Very friendly. Very healthy."

"Wasn't Mrs. Ferguson jealous?" Sophie finally gets the courage to speak. "Didn't it make her mad?"

"Au contraire," says Mrs. Gordon. "Esther got a kick out of all the other ladies vying for his attention. Everyone knew she was the love of his life."

"We're all going to miss him. He was a shining light among us," contributes Myra.

"Miss him?" I ask quickly.

"Yes," Myra says mournfully, "he left soon after the funeral. He said he could no longer bear to be in a place where every little thing reminded him of his precious Esther." With that, Myra's eyes tear up.

At my request, Mrs. Gordon reluctantly takes us all up to the Smythe-Ferguson apartment. She explains, "I don't usually do this. So please hurry. Of course, new tenants live here now. All of Esther's things were taken out by her son."

I'm not going to find any clues here, but it's good to get a picture of how they lived.

"Did Mr. Smythe have his own apartment?" I ask.

"Oh, yes, briefly, but soon after they fell in love, Esther insisted they move in together."

"Who paid the rent?" I ask.

"At first they shared it, but then Esther insisted on taking it over." Myra giggles. "She practically twisted his arm. He was such an old-fashioned gentleman."

We look around, suitably awed. Large, spacious, elegant. The girls are obviously shocked by the mirrored bathroom.

"The guests seem to like it." Now Mrs. Gordon hurries us out. "My tenants are due home shortly. I think we've been here long enough."

Back in her office, I ask Mrs. Gordon if she happens to remember where Mr. Smythe lived before he came to Grecian Villas.

"Of course I do. We who have the upper echelon of retirement resorts know all about one another. He lived at Seaside Cliffs on the other side of the state, in Sarasota, before he came to us."

"And now? Do you have a forwarding address?"

Indeed she does. "He's moving the first week in September to one our competitors, Wilmington House in Palm Beach. Lucky them."

She writes down the address on the back of her card and gives it to me. "When you see him, tell him everyone at Grecian Villas misses him."

When we are outside, we take a last lingering glance at the spacious Grecian Villas. Bella and Sophie sigh.

"Only five thousand a month," says Evvie.

"A mere pittance."

"Who cares," says Ida as she walks quickly toward our car. "I like where we live better."

"I can't wait to meet this guy," says Sophie.

"Me, too," says Evvie.

"Me, three," says Bella.

"I can wait. Believe me," says Ida, our lady of petulance, "no man can be that good."

Yes, some can. I think of Jack, hoping he'll have returned my call by the time we get home. I'm anxious to put this fight behind us.

But I admit I'm intrigued about "Romeo" as well. Lover or killer? I wonder. Hopefully we'll find out soon.

TEN:
CASE REVIEW

Ida pours us another round of coffee, all decaffeinated except for mine. We are in her apartment this time around. Shoes off, exhausted from our meeting this morning and lunch on the way home. I need my nap and am dying to check my answering machine, but the girls want to rehash what we know so far.

Ida's place is sparsely and simply furnished, spotlessly clean. She isn't into any specific type of décor. Her living room walls are covered with photos of her grandchildren, who live in California. They are very old photos, since she has not heard from her family in years, even though she continues to write to them. It's obviously heartbreaking for her, but she has yet to tell any of us what caused this terrible rift. Nor are there any photos of her ex-husband — she never talks about him, either.

Her "Florida room" — as enclosed sunrooms are called down here — is for her many crafts. She sews, embroiders, quilts, and knits. Most of which she gives away. She makes stuffed toys for poor children at Christmas. So many things to keep her busy through the lonely nights?

Sophie warms up some macaroons in Ida's toaster oven. To make them softer, she claims.

Once the food and drinks are ready, the meeting of Gladdy Gold and Associates is off and running.

First we discuss the latest Peeper incident with Dora Dooley.

"We should do another follow-up, anyway," Evvie says, "before we call Morrie again." The girls all adore Jack's son, Detective Morrie Langford. Not only because they think he's cute, but because he's always willing to help us — after I do a little convincing. Frankly, right now I'm not in any hurry to face Jack's son with our relationship so up in the air.

"Maybe Dora remembers some details by now. Maybe she did get a look at the Peeper," adds Ida.

"I'll do it," I say quickly. Any excuse to stop by Phase Six and maybe run into Jack. Or casually drop in on him. He has to be home sometime.

Now Ida is ready to give her report as everyone noshes contentedly.

"I got the manager of the Seaside Cliffs Retirement Resort in Sarasota on the phone a few minutes ago, and it was as if I was talking to that Mrs. Gordon at Grecian Villas. Same story. Everybody loved Philip. He was the belle of the ball, so to speak."

"You mean, beau of the ball." Evvie can't resist.

Ida ignores her. "The really interesting part is that he had a special lady he lived with who died of heart failure. A Mrs. Elsie Rogers. Same response. He moved out because he couldn't bear living where everything would remind him of his beloved. Boo-hoo. Everybody cried at the funeral and they cried when Philip Smythe left. Sound familiar?"

We exchange glances. This is a surprise.

"Sure sounds like a pattern to me," Evvie says as she helps herself from a bowl of strawberries.

Sophie asks, "So what kind of pattern?"

Ida, not surprisingly, spouts a caustic opinion about men. "My guess is he picks out a woman in a retirement place. Gets all the sex he wants 'til she drops dead. You know how men are. That's all they ever think about. Maybe he wears them out, that's why they die. Then he leaves."

Bella sighs. "What a way to go."

Evvie laughs, shaking her head. "Ida, there must be one nice guy in the world."

Ida stiffens and raises her chin high. "Maybe Mahatma Gandhi . . . and he's dead."

"Nicely put," I say mockingly to Ida, but she is immune to my sarcasm. Her husband must have been some piece of work to inspire her bleak attitude about men.

"But why leave?" Evvie asks. "He can probably choose his next lady friend from a hundred panting others, since he's such a great catch."

"Good question," Bella says. She suddenly grins. "You know who he reminds me of? Our Peeper. He goes from window to window looking for love."

"Cheaper than going from retirement home to retirement home," says Sophie. Everyone laughs.

"Love ain't what he's looking for," says Ida snidely.

"Maybe this Romeo guy would be embarrassed to have another hot chickie in the same place," Sophie says, back on track.

"That must be it. Well, what do you expect him to do?" Evvie adds. "Tell all the women to get in line and pick a number. Like at the meat counter?"

"Next!" says Bella playfully, raising her hand and pretending to jump up.

"It also would look peculiar if every one of those same chickies died," says Sophie.

"But they're old. Of course they'll die." This from always-practical Ida.

"You're old, too," Sophie points out. "You'll die, too."

"So will you, so shut up. Who asked you? I'm making a point here."

"Girls, girls . . ." I say, to no effect.

"Girls, stop fighting," Evvie says loudly, rapping her spoon on the table.

"Stupid, where's your logic?" Ida says, glowering at Sophie. "How can he know *he* won't die before his lover?"

Bella looks confused. "But isn't that sweet? He makes one woman happy, then goes off to the next. Like the Pied Piper."

Sophie pretends to shiver. "Don't talk about rats. They scare me."

Evvie sums it up. "So what are we saying here? Philip Smythe is a healthy, active man in his seventies still looking for love?" She grins. "Over and over and over again."

"Sex!" Ida interrupts.

"Okay, he finds someone to love *and* have sex." This she says pointedly at Ida. "She dies eventually of natural causes. He truly feels sad and leaves."

My turn. "But Esther's son is sure Philip Smythe killed her."

Evvie says, "He also admitted that Philip didn't take any money from her, other than let her pay the rent."

"Yeah," agrees Bella. "No motive. *Gornisht.* Nothing. Nada."

Evvie gets up and does stretches. We missed our usual exercise today. "You want to know my opinion? I think Ferguson is all wet. His mother died. He's grieving. Philip Smythe sounds harmless to me."

Bella says, "Maybe we should tell Mr. Ferguson and give him back his money?"

"Are you crazy?" Sophie asks. "I can't wait to start spending it."

Ida has a one-track mind. "I agree with Evvie. Doesn't sound like much of a case to me, either. This guy, Philip, has nothing better to do in his old age than get laid. For him it beats playing bingo."

"I resent that remark," says the bingo maven, Sophie, still simmering.

"Me, too," echoes Bella. "Besides, we made big bucks on that bingo cruise."

"Nevertheless," I say, "we have to find out the truth. We have to find a way to take a closer look at this man."

I get up and start clearing the remains of

the food off Ida's table, a signal that our meeting is near an end.

"How will we do that?" Bella gathers up the silverware.

"I think we have to follow him to Wilmington House in Palm Beach."

"But that's about an hour drive, and an hour back." Sophie brushes crumbs into the napkin in her hand. "It's not like it's around the corner."

"And it won't be so easy to get in." Evvie is in charge of the cups and saucers. "All those retirement places are enclosed and have very tight security. I can't see us just waltzing in and out. I agree we need a different approach."

"I will just have to move into Wilmington House," I boldly declare.

My statement is met by silence.

Sophie recovers quickly. "Just you?"

Ida picks up on that. "You'll need help."

Bella next. "Four eyes are better than two."

For a moment they are quiet again, absorbing this. Then Bella's, Sophie's, and Ida's hands shoot up. And in unison they say, "Me, pick me."

Evvie simply stares at them, eyes narrowing.

"First things first," I say, realizing I am now about to get into deep water. I ignore the raised hands and keep going. "I need to make an appointment with the manager at Wilmington House. I'll have to make a strong pitch for letting me move in temporarily."

"Oh, no," Evvie says with consternation, thinking back to the relatively polished attire we wore for our first visit to Grecian Villas, "my clothes aren't fancy enough for Palm Beach. I'll have to go shopping."

"Wait just one minute," Ida says. "Who voted you in?"

"Yeah," says Bella, folding her arms across her chest. "I could go. I have no pressing engagements."

"What are we, chopped liver?" Sophie finishes the round. The chorus has spoken.

Evvie turns to me. "Of course I'm going with you, Glad, isn't that so?"

Oh, boy, this is some pickle. I feel my sister Evvie is the right choice for me. We've had a lifetime of thinking alike and working so well together, but I look at those three pairs of sad eyes accusing me, correctly, of favoritism. This is a no-win situation. "Let me think about it," says the coward.

Ida stomps toward the door. "Don't bother. We know who you'll choose, so just do it and get done with it."

The others follow her.

There is a decided chill in the air. But Evvie is grinning.

And I feel rotten.

Eleven:
Where Is Jack?

Dora Dooley is where she usually is, planted in front of her TV, which is so close to her she can almost touch it. She got up to let me in, then hurried back to her recliner, where she now sits watching her show avidly and ignoring me.

It is very hot and stuffy in here. Dora is wearing lime green pedal pushers and a matching sweater with a long-sleeved cardigan over it. She's already informed me she doesn't like air conditioning and she won't open windows for fear of a draft. I fan myself as best I can in this stifling room. I intend to get out quickly. Not only because of the heat, but because I'm dying to see Jack.

"So can you tell me a little more about the Peeping Tom the other night?" I say as loudly as I can.

"Shah," Dora says. "Wait for the commercial." I assume she's hard of hearing since the sound is turned up very high.

I sit and stew, fanning hard, as she watches a torrid love scene. The way I'm feeling, that's the last kind of thing I need to be looking at — all I'm aware of is that Jack lives right above this apartment. From what I can gather, the characters on her soap opera are both married to other people and feeling terribly guilty. However, it doesn't seem to interfere with their lust.

Finally the commercials arrive, and the volume rises even higher. One of my pet peeves is that the advertisers do that on purpose.

Dora cackles. "Won't take long until Penelope finds out her husband, Percy, is boffing her best friend, Elizabeth."

I nod obediently.

She cups her left ear at me and shouts, "Who are you? What do you want?"

"I'm Gladdy Gold, Phase Two. We're trying to find the man who is peeking in women's windows. You were his latest victim."

"I didn't see much. All I saw was a mask and his hand wagging his little *peepee* at me."

That's that. "Someone told me you might have gotten a good look at him."

"With my eyesight?" She indicates the

closeness of the TV set.

"Your neighbor, Jack Langford, didn't see him either, I suppose."

She waves her hand at me. "Shhh, *World of Our Dreams* is on again. They sure got sexy actors on this show."

"Well, thank you anyway." I move to leave.

She grasps my sleeve as I pass her chair. "Ask me anything. I'm an expert. This is my favorite show. I've been watching it since it came on in 1951. They started in kinescope and went to tape in 1964. Ask me who broke Victoria Ainsworth's heart in 1972. Errol Forsyth, that's who. He slept with her sister, Evangeline, and she tried to commit suicide."

"Very sad," I comment.

"And in 1987, Eugenia Huffington got the first face-lift on live TV." She cackles again. "That was something else. The producers on this show sure likes stuffy character names, though. Evangeline, Eugenia, Moira . . ."

Loneliness, I think. Let me count the ways people keep themselves going. Whatever gets you through the night. I should talk. I don't have anything to help me. My eyes look upward again. How did I let myself care this much? Is the pain worth it?

I can no longer breathe. I carefully extradite myself. "Gotta go, Dora. Need to check some facts with Jack upstairs."

I head down her hallway. "I'll let myself out."

She calls after me, "Don't waste your energy climbing the steps. Jack ain't home."

I turn back. "He's gone out for the day?"

"No, he's just plain gone. Took his suitcase this morning and left. Didn't say a word to nobody."

My stomach starts churning. No, it's not possible.

"But he did come and say good-bye to me and that he hoped I was okay after my close call with the pervert."

Gone. I can't believe it.

I walk outside, head down, lost in my troubled thoughts. Where did Jack go? Maybe to finish an unfinished romantic vacation on some other beautiful island with someone else? What was my crime? That I ruined our vacation? Wasn't I just as frustrated as he was? So I worried about my girls. Thanks a lot, Jack, for being so understanding! I'm so mad I want to spit.

"Gladdy?"

Startled, I look up and Jack is standing there. Right in front of me. Dressed for traveling. With a suitcase. For a second I think I'm hallucinating.

But, no, it is him.

I try to cover my astonishment. "Coming or going?" I say sarcastically.

His eyebrows rise and he stares at me for a moment. "I'm going away for a few days. I came back home to pick up a couple of things first."

He doesn't offer to tell me where he's going and I'll be damned if I'll ask. "I was interviewing Dora. About her Peeper." God forbid he should think I was there looking for him.

Even though I really was.

"Come on up," he tells me. "Let me drop my suitcase and I'll make us a cup of coffee."

I am torn. What should I do? Play hard to get? Indifferent? Show him how upset I am? Or just see what happens?

He doesn't wait for my answer. He assumes I'm following him, that egotist! What am I having debates with myself for? I came here to see him and here he is. Huffing and puffing, I hurry after him up the stairs.

The few times I've been in Jack's apartment, I've never felt at ease. I'm still not comfortable even though it's a pleasant place, tastefully done, definitely with a woman's touch. His late wife, Faye's. And I know he's uneasy for the same reason. As he makes coffee, I glance yet again at the family pictures of earlier times. Jack and Faye smiling up at each other with Morrie and his sister, Lisa, looking like the happy kids they were. Jack and Faye's wedding photo. How young and lovely they looked. How adoringly they gaze at each other.

Jack serves me the coffee just as I like it, one sugar and very little milk.

I thank him and he says, "You're welcome."

And here we are. I'm balanced on the very edge of the peach floral couch. He's perched on the rim of the matching armchair that faces it.

"So . . ." I'm the first to break the silence.

"So, what?"

Oy, enough already. "Sew buttons."

"Huh?"

"That's what my mother used to say when we kept saying 'so.'" At Jack's puzzled look I bat my hand at him. "Don't bother trying to get it. It's a non sequitur."

"Oh. So. Sew buttons. I get it."

I'm running out of repartee. "Jack. Where are we?"

"In my apartment."

"Funny."

He finally smiles. I do, too.

"I've missed you," I admit.

He doesn't comment. I want to reach out and touch his hands, which are folded on his lap. They are only inches away. If I touch them, he'll touch me and we'll be all right again. I can't do it and he won't. His hands might as well be back in Pago Pago. The chasm between us is too deep.

As if reading my mind, he moves his hands to the arm of the chair. "I've been doing a lot of thinking . . ."

I don't like the way that sounds. Come on, let's kiss and make up. I want to say it, but first I need to know how he feels about me.

"And . . . ?"

"I think we need to separate for a while."

Separate? I feel my body stiffen and my eyes widen in shock. "Why?" I blurt.

"Because you're not ready for me."

I stand and pace around the room. "Just because I told Bella where we'd be? I was committed to you. Didn't I fly for sixteen uncomfortable hours to run away with you? I was as upset as you were that we were . . . interrupted."

He stands, too, looking eager. "All right. I already have a packed suitcase. I'll just grab my passport. Let's go back to your apartment and you pack a quick bag and leave a note. We'll go to the airport and hop onto the first flight going anywhere."

I automatically take a step away from him. "Wait. What's the hurry? We don't have to rush off."

"Why not? What if I say, we'll find the first judge, or a rabbi, if you insist, and get married."

"I don't understand. Why can't we tell our families and friends first?"

"We can inform them afterward, when we get back, and then we'll have a big party."

I don't know how to respond. My mind is running in a dozen directions.

"Glad. Do you see what you're doing? You keep stepping backward. Not forward. Not to me."

I stop in my tracks. I suddenly realize that I've moved halfway across the living room away from him. "You're confusing me. First you're angry and you are ready to leave without telling me where you're going. You don't call. I worry myself sick wondering where you are. Or if you'll ever talk to me again. Now I accidentally run into you, and you're racing me out the door to the nearest altar."

"And what's so bad about that?"

"I need to think."

"About what?"

"I don't know. This is too fast."

"What are you waiting for? When we get to be ninety?"

I find myself shouting. "I don't know!"

He's shouting, too. "Gladdy. What will it take for you to be ready? What will it take to make you sure? What do I have to do?"

I keep shaking my head as if to clear the cobwebs. Why can't he understand?

Now his voice gets lower. And he is shaking his head, too. "I'm sorry. I can't make us work. To paraphrase the poet, 'she who hesitates is lost.' "

He strides out the door and leaves me standing there.

A moment later, he sheepishly walks back in. "I forgot. I live here."

With that I race past him and slam the door behind me.

Twelve:
Rain and Pain

I hurry back to Phase Two. I walk fast and I talk out loud to myself. I feel crazed. What did I do? I've lost Jack again. What's wrong with me? What's wrong with him? What was so terrible if I didn't want to run away with him and elope that very second? Wet, sloppy tears run down my face. Huge wet tears. Then I realize it's raining. That's rain pouring down my face. Big sloppy tears of rain. The rain is crying with me. It's a typical Florida instant downpour. It feels like tons of water drowning me. Drowning me and my sorrow. Why did I think I could ever find love again? It's too hard. It's too much . . . what? Pressure? Is that what I feel? Why can't Jack understand how much my girls mean to me? How much we've all needed one another and helped one another through the years? I just can't abandon them. He acts as if it's so simple. Let's just run off. But life is more complex than that.

A few people run past me hurrying for shelter. I don't want shelter. I want to drown standing up. I want to keep running in this downpour forever.

"That's it!" I scream to the skies. "I've had it! How dare he tell me I'm not ready? How dare he make me move to his time clock? And what about all those beautiful words he said to me that first night in the Greek restaurant? It doesn't matter how much time we have left. A year. A month. As long as we're together. What happened to those sentiments? He's dumped me again!"

Someone passes me, looks at this crazy, drenched woman screaming to the skies. She pauses. Thinks maybe I need help, and then another cloud bursts and she runs to the nearest sheltered area.

"That's it, Jack Langford. Forget it. I'm done. Not one more tear will I shed for you. Not one more thought will I give this stupid relationship. I'm through! I'm going to get on with my life. I was fine before I met you, Jack Langford, and I'll do very well without you, again!"

The first thing I hear when I reach our club room is Tessie saying, "Let's kill all the doctors."

Ida says, "That's supposed to be lawyers."

"Them, too." Tessie sees me before the others do. "Look what the cat dragged in!"

I am totally soaked and my teeth are chattering.

The room is filled with women now staring at me. They are seated in a huge circle, sewing. Then I realize, it's the monthly Hadassah meeting.

Lola jumps right on me. "You're too dumb to come in out of the rain?" She takes after her husband, Hy, quick with the unkind cuts.

I see my girls and instantly realize that Bella, Ida, and Sophie are sitting next to one another as usual, and Evvie is seated as far away from them as possible. I guess the feud is still going strong.

Evvie jumps up and runs over to me. She takes her sweater and wraps it around me.

"Florence Nightingale, she thinks she is," says Sophie snidely. Evvie shoots her a dirty look. The girls won't be quick to forgive Evvie for grabbing the plum role of being my partner when and if we go to Wilmington House. More aggravation. Just what I need.

Ida yells, "Someone turn the air down or she'll get pneumonia." Nobody moves quickly enough, so she turns the thermostat up herself.

I am still shaking. But I don't know if it's from the rain or shock or just plain rage. I try to calm myself. Sophie hurries over and offers me some hot tea. She avoids looking at Evvie.

"We got caught in the rain, too," Irving says. He's with Millie in her wheelchair, seated near the door. Of course, Yolie is there with them, holding Millie's hand. All three look bedraggled. Irving waves to me.

"Come see how we're doing," Mary suggests, holding up the square she's working on. Their Hadassah chapter's good works project is making quilts for underprivileged children. The colors are bright and the patterns cheerful. This was Ida's idea.

Someone pulls a chair over for me, and one of the members who had come in to the meeting directly from swimming offers me her towels to dry myself.

Sophie informs me that they were in the middle of an important discussion. Doctors. "Of course, I was bragging about my darling Dr. Friendly."

Ida shoots me a look of resignation. "As if we could shut her up."

I think dismally to myself, it was Sophie's "condition" that brought me to my current misery. But I can't blame sweet Sophie; I can only blame myself for causing it to happen. If only I could have . . . I stop myself. Woulda coulda shoulda . . . Sophie has a real problem and my feeling sorry for myself won't help her. I think about Sophie and her pills and wonder if Esther Ferguson took pills, too. Maybe too many? Or maybe Romeo fed her pills along with romance. But I can't think now. My brain feels too fuzzy.

"We were also sharing war stories. Of some of the terrible experiences people have had with doctors and hospitals," Mary informs me as she offers me a cookie. Mary used to be a nurse and she ought to know. "My poor cousin went to Mexico for a cure for her MS. I warned her not to go. They injected her with bee venom and charged her twenty thousand dollars. They almost killed her down there."

Tessie says, "I was telling them about my niece who went into the hospital for a knee replacement and they replaced the wrong one."

The women continue sewing while they talk. From what I can tell, they are already at the piecing process where they sew all their small cotton fabric patches together to create the pattern of the top half of the quilt.

I should take part in this discussion, but I

don't want to. I let myself lean back against the wall and close my eyes and allow the pleasant hum of words to wash over me.

"Well," Chris Willems, from Phase One, comments, "I hear hospitals now write on the leg in ink saying 'cut this one.' "

"It's about time," adds Jean Davis from Phase Four.

"I had a doctor tell me I had something called fibro myalgia. Which I didn't have. And later on I found out he told all his patients the same thing. Maybe he owned stock in Celebrex." This from Tessie.

"Maybe he was just lazy," comments Bella.

"Well, things like that wouldn't happen with my GP, Dr. Friendly. In fact, I think he's found a cure for Alzheimer's." Sophie announces this with great pride.

Ida reaches over and pokes her. "Don't talk stupid. No one has such a cure."

Sophie pokes Ida back, barely missing her with her embroidery scissors. "And how do you know he doesn't?"

Evvie glances over toward Irving, who's sitting with Millie, listening to this. She whispers to Sophie. "Miss Insensitive, be quiet."

"What are we supposed to do? We're old and helpless." Ellie Fisher, in her nineties, from Phase Three, says this in a small, frightened voice. "Our lives are in their hands." She puts down her sewing to dab at the tears in her weak eyes.

"Yeah, those mamzers come down here to bleed us seniors dry," Tessie adds.

"Not all doctors are here to cheat us. There are some fine ones, too." Mary is the voice of reason.

"You have to learn how to protect yourself," Ida comments.

"I'll drink to that." With that, Tessie downs the rest of her bottle of Dr. Brown's Cel-Ray tonic.

"How?" Ellie squints as she tries to thread her needle. "What about that couple I read about? His wife died because she accidentally took his pills and the dosage was too high for her. They were both taking the same pills for the same illness. It could happen to any of us. Our pills change so often and the dosages change, too. Half the time I don't know what I'm doing."

They look to Mary for some advice from a professional. She thinks for a moment. "I've got an idea. We form a group and take care of one another. For example, how many of you can still see pretty good?"

A smattering of hands go up. "Okay. I do, too. So we now are the medications group. Especially call me and I'll help anyone who has trouble figuring out their pills."

"Good idea," adds Evvie, one of the well-sighted ones. "We can make charts in very big letters and with black felt pens so you know when to take what, and also write the names of each prescription in very large black letters on the bottles so you know which is which."

There is applause at that.

"You can call yourself the Pill Poppers," suggests Sophie, who always has to name everything.

I find myself thinking about Philip Smythe and Esther Ferguson again. Were they taking any pills? Is it really possible she was overdosed? I remind myself to look into this later.

"Where do we sign up?" asks Jean Davis. "I can barely see the writing on those little bottles. Every morning I pray that I take the right ones."

"I'm always scared I took them already, so sometimes I don't take them at all. I need help," Chris Willems adds.

"We can work out a system where you keep all the bottles in one basket or on one shelf and after you take one, you move the bottle into another basket or shelf and that way you can keep them straight," Mary suggests.

Ida instructs them, "Call me. I'll keep a list of who's available. And send someone up to help."

"And what about picking doctors? How do we know we're not getting a quack?" Chris asks.

Evvie answers excitedly. "We ask Barbi and Casey. They know how to find out anything on their computers. They can do a search for us and get recommendations. And also find out the doctors who get sued a lot."

"Who's Barbi and Casey?" asks Flo. "I never met them."

"They're the young ones who live in our building," Bella answers shyly.

I hold my breath waiting to hear one of my girls say more. But they don't. My eyelids are beginning to close. I am so tired. As they continue their plans I find myself dozing off. The stress has exhausted me.

I feel a hand shaking me. It's Evvie. "Wake up, Sleeping Beauty. The sewing bee has ended. All medical problems have been solved and the rain has stopped. Care to go home?"

THIRTEEN:
WILMINGTON HOUSE

As usual, Evvie is my copilot. Her lap is filled with maps and whatever else she thought necessary to bring with us on the hour drive up north to Palm Beach, home of the posh Wilmington House. We've dressed up as best we could this morning with our limited "better" wardrobe. Torn between pantsuits and skirts, we ended up wearing dresses. The ones we usually save for weddings. Though we hated to have to wear stockings.

I've even had my old Chevy wagon washed for the occasion.

Evvie reads to me. " 'Palm Beach is twelve miles long and three quarters of a mile wide, home to some of the richest families in America and their biggest dirty secrets. The famous Rush Limbaugh drug arrest. William Kennedy Smith's rape case . . .' "

"What are you reading?"

"An old gossip magazine I found in the

laundry room." She flips through the pictures. "Juicy stuff. Everybody who's anybody's been here. Even John Lennon once was, and the Trumps still go there."

"You know, sister? Maybe this isn't going to be as easy as I expect. The rich are not so easy to deal with."

"Nonsense. When we explain why we're here, *no problema.*"

As we drive down the area's main artery, the lavish Worth Avenue, Evvie continues her travelogue. "Wow, look at the stores: Tiffany and Cartier, Armani. Look at the cars — Ferraris, Bentleys, Rolls-Royces. Look at those wardrobes, double wow! And look at those old guys with young girls."

"Maybe they're nurses."

"I doubt it. I can see the diamonds sparkling from here."

Finally we arrive at Wilmington House and it's as imposing as the town around it. I recognize the style of the architecture as Art Deco. The cars in the parking area are equally impressive. I search for a spot that's far from the entrance, hoping to hide my pathetic old wreck among those of the working staff.

A young man hurries out to take our car. He looks puzzled. As we march past him, Evvie murmurs, "Taxi."

Once inside, we are meant to be awed by the luxury around us. The Art Deco colors, olives and grays, are muted and restful. A tall, thin, forty-ish brunette stands before us quivering with officiousness. She introduces herself as the manager, Hope Watson. She wears a navy blue suit with a tailored white blouse and is as stiff as the starch in her shirt. Ms. Watson is disappointed. We weren't what she expected when she gave us this appointment a couple of days ago.

"May we speak to you privately?" I say in my best modulated voice. Evvie immediately straightens her shoulders and holds her head higher.

I can tell by the look in Ms. Watson's eyes as we are ushered into her office that she knows we shop at Target and not at Saks. And she knows exactly what we paid for our outfits.

"May I ask your business here?" Hope Watson takes a stance, arms folded, behind her desk in her simple but lavish office. "I hope you haven't come to sell something. We have a purchasing department that handles that."

"No, we're not sales reps," I begin.

"Where do you come from?" she asks.

"Fort Lauderdale," Evvie informs her.

"Where in Fort Lauderdale?"

I know what she's fishing for and I am tempted to lie, but that would be a mistake with the likes of her.

I answer. "In Lauderdale Lakes, actually. West Oakland Park Boulevard." Might as well give her what she's already guessed. "In the fifties." Which tells her we're nowhere near the beach, or anything else expensive.

"We have a gigantic Publix supermarket," Evvie offers as a possible honor. "And we're not too far from the Inverarry golf course."

"I see," she says icily.

I'm sure she does.

I try to bring her back to the point of our visit. "We have been hired by a Mr. Alvin Ferguson —"

Rudeness comes with the snobby attitude. She interrupts me. "I've never heard of him."

I jump back in. "He comes from Seattle. His mother, Esther, was living in Grecian Villas in Fort Lauderdale until she died at the end of July."

Hope glances down at her appointment book, trying either to annoy me or ignore me.

I keep on. "She died there, but Mr. Ferguson thinks his mother was murdered."

I was hoping to lead up to this subject in

a more subtle manner, but subtlety would be lost on this tough bird. I decide shock is more likely to get Ms. Watson's attention back.

It does. She looks up. "Whatever in the world has any of this to do with Wilmington House?"

Evvie jumps in, always less patient and even less subtle than I. "The man they think murdered his mother is coming here to live as of September first, in three days. Philip Smythe is his name. We really must move quickly." I'm sure Evvie would have liked to add "so, there!" but resisted the temptation.

"What!" Ms. Watson blanches, then hurries to her door, opening it wide, as if she's suddenly discovered lepers in her office.

Evvie finishes her sentence as fast as she can. "And we were hired to investigate him. That would mean moving in here for a while. We're private eyes."

Ms. Watson's eyebrows shoot up. Now she finally bothers to really look at us, and what she sees infuriates her. She stalks back to her desk and picks up the phone. "Security. In my office immediately."

She slams the receiver down and screams at us, her face blotchy with rage. "Do you know where you are? You are in Palm Beach, for God's sakes! Palm Beach! Go back to where you belong. To that . . . that . . . slum."

In my car, with the air turned up high, Evvie and I, still panting from having scurried out of Wilmington House, stare at each other incredulously.

"That went well," she says, then bursts into laughter.

And so do I.

We laugh until we are almost in tears.

"That phony bitch," Evvie rants. "The nerve of her. She can't hide that Brooklyn accent from me. And what's she got to be so snobby about? It's not her money. She probably makes *bubkes.*"

I'm starting to hiccup. My side hurts from laughing so hard.

"Boy, did she steamroll us." Evvie tickles me and I tickle her back. A childhood thing we used to do when we were having a good time. "We shoulda worn our tiaras. La-di-da!"

"All she was missing was a bouncer at the door. She should hang a sign up — no hoi polloi allowed." I lift the sun screens off the windshield, getting ready to leave.

"She hates us, she really hates us." Evvie parodies Sally Field's famous Oscar speech.

I start the motor. "Well, since we're out

already and have time to spare, anyplace you want to stop on our way home?"

"Wait a minute." Evvie puts her hand on my hand holding the keys. "Hold on just one minute."

"What?"

"Are we going to let her get away with that?"

"What are we supposed to do? She threw us out."

"What are we, wusses or gladiators? Are we going to give up without a fight?"

"I'll call Alvin Ferguson and let him get in touch with their board. Let him handle her."

"Then Shirley will want their money back for our not doing the job. No way."

"You want to go back?"

"Yeah. I'm not afraid of her."

"We'll only get thrown out again."

"Hey, we're PI's, right?"

"Yes, PI's without credentials. So far none of our clients have ever asked to see them. One of these days we're going to have to do something about that."

"You should ask Jack's advice."

Yes, I think bitterly. Next time I run into him. It suddenly occurs to me — will he move out of Lanai Gardens just so he won't have to ever run into me again? I look at my sister. I need to tell her about Jack leaving

122

me. Then I glance at her eager face and I can't bring myself to spoil her day.

"Well, I want another shot at her."

I grin. "You sound so hard-boiled. Just like a Mickey Spillane."

She gets out of the car and jabs, boxer-like, with her fists, her short legs pumping. "It's our turn to do a little steamrolling."

I shrug. "We've come this far. Why not?"

We find Ms. Watson in the large lobby near the entrance, chatting with guests. I note that they are in pantsuits, so I guess frilly dresses were the wrong choice. And their hair: Fresh out of the beauty salons, all of them. Oops, didn't think about our washed-out, non-coiffed colors. No wonder Hope Watson wasn't fooled. When she sees us now, she excuses herself and comes directly at us at a fast clip, teeth bared.

Evvie takes the offensive and she intends to keep it this time. "Calm down, not in front of the guests. We need to talk to you again. Believe me; you won't want us to cause a scene."

Teeth clenched, Ms. Watson forces herself to take a deep breath. She strides back down the hall to her office with us following close behind.

Of course her first act is to dial the phone.

Evvie reaches over and disconnects her. Ms. Watson is stunned.

"You call Security again and we call the local paper and give their gossip columnist an item about what alleged murderer is moving into what formerly first-class retirement hotel."

The woman is stymied and actually speechless. I'm pretty speechless, myself, at this new Evvie. If I were Ms. Watson I'd start screaming at the top of my lungs for help. Luckily she just plops down on her desk chair and stares at us.

Evvie is on a roll. "Here's the scoop. Just listen and ask questions later. We want to use a spare apartment here, hopefully for a short while. We need to find out as much as we can about Philip Smythe. We want to do this quietly and without a fuss. When we've learned all we can, we will leave just as quietly as we came in."

Of course, Ms. Watson can't wait. "Are you telling me you know Philip Smythe is a murderer?"

Now that she's paying attention, I speak. "We don't know that he is. My client may be wrong. We would like more than anything to clear him if we can. But a woman died. There is a bereft son. He needs to know the truth about his mother's death."

"Why doesn't he go to the police?" she asks, finally pulling herself together.

"Because he has no proof. He wants a private investigation before he can seek out help from the police."

"This is your problem, not mine. Give me one good reason I should put up with this nonsense."

"Because I think you believe in right and wrong and integrity and honesty. Because if this man killed a helpless woman, he deserves to be brought to justice. Because if we don't clear him, you will never be sure whether your elegant residence is harboring a murderer. You will never have a comfortable day."

Evvie nails it home. "Imagine what that will do to your reputation."

Evvie has her fingers crossed. I know she's thinking, will we pull it off? I pinch her arm to make sure she doesn't say anything right now. Let it sink in.

Hope Watson hesitates. We wait.

"If one word leaks out —"

"It won't," insists Evvie. "No one will ever know why we're here."

"You promise there will be no upsetting of our routine? There is no way I will allow you to wreak havoc in my well-run facility."

Evvie jumps in. "You'll hardly even know

we're here." She makes a zipping motion with her finger across her lips. "We'll be as quiet as little mice."

Hope Watson sighs. "I shall have to bring this up before the board. I cannot make such a decision on my own."

"We understand, and we'd be glad to go before the board to explain if you wish. As would Mr. Ferguson."

"That won't be necessary. I am quite capable of explaining your mission."

She walks us quickly to the outer lobby. "Should you be given permission," which she says in a doubtful tone, "I would suggest you look around and see how we live here at Wilmington House. It is a place of peace and decorum. You will mind your manners."

"Yes, we will," I say dutifully.

"But don't think you shall have the run of the place. You will be watched constantly. By me."

"Agreed."

As she opens the door for us, Hope Watson has the final word. "And do something about your abominable taste in clothing!"

And we're thrown out again.

Driving home after our victory, Evvie is elated. "There's so much we need to do.

Somebody's got to pick up our mail. We gotta make sure we leave the air on low. What'll we do with all the food in our fridges? Wait til Hy hears we get to live with the rich folks!"

"You're so sure we're getting in?"

"Positive."

"You know there's a gossip columnist on the Palm Beach paper?"

She shrugs, grinning. "How should I know? I made it up. Besides, we could never reveal anything that Philip Smythe might read about."

"Whatever got into you? Talk about bossy!"

Evvie is delighted with herself. "Who knows? PMS? The frustrated actress in me? Maybe it's just sexual frustration. It is definitely time for me to meet a guy again. And be happy like you."

Evvie leans back in her seat. "Now, aren't you glad you picked me as your partner?"

Fourteen:
More Peeper
Problems

As Evvie and I drive back through Lanai
Gardens, I find myself looking at our condos
through Hope Watson's eyes. Low-rent area?
Yes, I guess you could call it that. Our pretty
lawns can hardly compare to the extravagant
grounds at Wilmington House. The stucco
paint on our buildings is getting shabby. We
need a lot of repair work to fix last year's
hurricane damage. No comparison to the
perfection that the rich can afford. Never
mind, though; it's home.

"Hey, look over there." Evvie pokes me.
We are about to pass Phase Five, when I
see the police car. I pull over. To my surprise, there's Morrie Langford in conversation with some of the residents. I recognize
Dora Dooley, Jack's neighbor, among them.
I park and Evvie and I join them.

For a moment I am startled. Morrie
reminds me so much of his dad. Same tall
height, same posture. Full head of lustrous

brown hair, now salt-and-pepper on his father's head. What Jack must have looked like in his thirties. Another jolt for me and I feel my pain once again. Morrie and I have become good friends since we met professionally. Now I feel at a loss as to how to behave with him. Does he know Jack and I have broken up?

"There's Gladdy," says Sylvia Green, a tall, usually cheerful woman I know only slightly. "Just the person we want to see."

And in minutes, we get the story. Our Peeper struck again. The woman who saw him got so frightened that they had to take her to her doctor this morning.

Dora is practically jumping up and down, pointing an accusing finger at Morrie. "You promised your father you'd catch him."

He smiles at the tiny woman. "I promised I'd try."

Morrie addresses us. "I want to help but there's not much I can do. I can't spare any cars to cruise your premises all night. Unfortunately, it's not our top priority."

"Then what are we going to do?" Alice Potts is wringing her hands.

Morrie makes a suggestion. "Perhaps putting up motion-sensor lights on every building will make a difference. He won't be able to avoid the bright lights. That might deter him."

I notice Jack's son won't look me in the eye. I guess he's already heard the news. "I'll call an emergency meeting of our phase. You do the same with yours," I say to the Phase Five women. "But installing lights will be very costly."

"This has gone on long enough," Alice insists.

"Yeah, you said that right," Dora echoes her. "Are you done now? I have to get back to my show."

Sylvia has a solution. "Maybe if all the phases chip in we can afford those lights. I'll pass the word along to all the phase presidents."

I promise to get in touch with my group right away.

Morrie gives me a cursory nod and leaves.

Evvie, watching him leave, looks surprised. "What's with the cold shoulder? What's eating him?"

Guilt, I hope. Like father, like son? Leave when the going gets tough?

As I turn into my parking spot I see Denny's old car pulled out so that Irving and Yolie can help Millie into the backseat.

Evvie heads upstairs to my apartment, but

I amble over. "Hi. How is everyone?"

Everyone seems nervous, that's how everyone is.

"Is something wrong?"

"No, nothing," Irving answers quickly. "We're taking her for a checkup. And some tests. Just a checkup."

"Oh, okay," I say. "Hope everything goes well."

Denny mumbles something incoherent and Yolie doesn't look at me and I swear Irving is sweating.

Millie giggles one of her inappropriate laughs. "They're such liars." Then, as it is with her, it's as if a light goes off and she's comatose once again.

Denny rolls out of the parking area, burning rubber.

Strange.

I know one day we're going to have to convince Irving to put Millie in an Alzheimer's hospital. He looks exhausted. I know he can't take much more.

"Yes, Mr. Ferguson, I'm pretty sure Evvie and I will be getting into Wilmington House. The board might call you to confirm what we're doing."

I nod at Evvie, who is leaning so far over my shoulder in order to listen that she is practically on my lap. I'll bet Shirley's doing the same on the other side of the phone. I listen a few moments and then Evvie pokes me, covering her mouth in order to hide her laughing openly.

"That's a very good idea, Alvin. In both our names. And very generous of you." Now I can hear Shirley yelling, "Are you crazy?" in the background. "Thank you. We'll keep you informed."

I hang up. Evvie hugs me. "Wow! A charge account at Wilmington House!"

"Down, girl. That's to pay the rental on the apartment and for the few sundries we might need."

"Yeah, yeah." Evvie dances around the room. "I heard him. Toothpaste and hairspray, stuff like that."

"We have a fiscal responsibility to keep our charges low."

Evvie heads out the door. "I heard you. Yum yum! I just can't wait to move into our fancy retirement hotel. Maybe I'll nab some old rich guy and never have to leave again!"

Lying in bed that night, I can't stop thinking about Jack and wondering where he is. I remember how the two of us showered in our outdoor waterfall in Pago Pago. How cool the water was. The first time we saw each other naked. How his body fit so well against mine. How we teased, saying we'd wait until later, but later never came. I play the scene over and over again, each time demanding of myself that I stop. But I can't.

Maybe I'm kidding myself. Maybe I don't need the aggravation of having a man in my life. Everything was much simpler before. And yet — that incredible feeling of pleasure. At what price?

Now I can hardly wait to get to Wilmington House where I can worry about Esther Ferguson's Romeo and not my own. And what price did she pay for her pleasure? Oh, such dark and dreary thoughts.

I turn on the TV and catch a comedy show.

I will not let Jack get me down.

Fifteen:
No Escape for the Wicked

Like fugitives, we tiptoe our way to my car, looking every which way to make sure we aren't seen by the girls. Evvie and I are going to prepare for the big move into Wilmington House. First stop: shopping for ritzy clothes. We only have a couple of days — I hope we can find something.

Frankly, I didn't think the Wilmington board would vote us in. But I guess the convincing argument was that they desperately needed to know if they had inadvertently allowed a killer into their midst. I'm sure they tried to look for an out in Philip Smythe's rental agreement, but the first and last month's rent must have been already paid. And I'm sure his former records and bank statements reaffirmed he was more than able to afford to live there.

Evvie is merrily singing Gilbert and Sullivan under her breath. " 'With catlike tread upon our prey we steal . . . tarantara,

tarantara! . . .' " She stops. "Oh, oh." She points toward my car, where three determined figures stand with crossed arms and grim faces. Evvie mutters under her breath, "Guess the yenta grapevine told them we were heading out." Then she waves with phony cheerfulness. "Hi, girls, what's up?"

"Going somewhere?" Ida asks. "I thought you had mah-jongg this afternoon."

"Just not in a mah-jongg kind of mood today."

"More like in a spending-a-rich-guy's-money mood?"

"Lay off, Ida."

I feel terrible. Ever since Evvie abruptly announced she was going with me before I could tactfully pave the way, I have felt so guilty. "I'm so sorry. I wish I could take you all with us, but it's just not possible."

"We know that," Bella says, her arm around Sophie. "It would be silly to have a mob hanging around."

"But you could use us as accessories around the fact," says Sophie, in her inimitable way of expressing herself.

"You're not mad anymore?" I feel so relieved.

"Of course not," says Bella. "You need to leave some of the troops back at the home office. The Peeper case is still hot on the

135

griddle."

"In fact," says Ida huffily, "we've already arranged the multi-condo meeting, so there. We are very capable of running the shop without you."

I have a feeling they've already had one prideful meeting without Evvie and me. To come up with these fancy words to throw at me. Good for them. They've got spunk.

But Bella is hurt. "Why didn't you invite us along today? You know Soph and me are good with fashions."

Sophie nods vigorously. "Versace. Dior. Pucci and Gucci. Hey, we saw *The Devil Wears Prada* last year with that wonderful Meryl Streep. I'm a regular fashionista."

"We can't afford them," I say. "We can't spend that kind of money. It's not fair to Mr. Ferguson."

Ida imitates him. " 'Money is no object.' I say spend."

"I know that," says Sophie, "but I know how to recognize a knockoff, and I know where to find them."

"Yeah," Bella adds, "you need us. The two of you dress like it's still 1945."

"Thanks for nothing," says Evvie hotly. "Besides, the styles always come back. Now it's called retro."

Ida laughs. "You are going to make great

big fools of yourself. Those rich ladies will smell Wal-Mart and run for the hills."

Bella and Sophie pull me toward the car door. "Not if we can help it."

This is not just a thrift shop — it is an upscale thrift shop, clothing donated by women with do-re-mi who have tired of their casually worn attire. The girls are having a ball. Sophie and Bella are pulling things off the rack faster than Evvie and I can try them on. Trying to match us to our new personas. Even Ida has caught the excitement. I see her hiding behind a mirror, holding a last-season Donna Karan up to her body and daydreaming.

I've decided to go for sleek and sophisticated. A quietly rich woman who keeps to herself a lot. One who watches things from the sidelines. Evvie is going for raffish abandonment. Her chance to act on a stage at last. She chooses to play the role of a former socialite who landed a rich husband. Maybe many rich husbands. And she outlived them all.

"Get a load of this," Evvie says gleefully, holding up a three-strand "diamond" necklace.

Sophie, the jewelry maven with the son in Brooklyn Heights who taught her everything about gems, examines it closely. "A really good imitation. You can pull it off, Ev. If you pretend to believe it's real, they'll believe you," says the expert. "It will go beautifully with this Givenchy scarlet red cocktail dress and matching boa. And the Jimmy Choo knockoff shoes."

By now the checkout counter is piled with clothes. I wait with bated breath for the total. I worried needlessly. As it turns out, two hundred dollars and change for two wardrobes. I'm impressed. Sophie and Bella high-five each other.

While they shopped and tried on and giggled and chatted, they planned.

"Have we got a surprise for you this afternoon," announces Sophie to Evvie. "The perfect opportunity to try out your new personas. Are we all gonna have fun!"

The staff of the senior recreation center in Margate has tried to make the ordinary gym look festive. Balloons float above the small tables and rickety chairs set up for this four p.m. event. Two facing chairs at each table. Photos from magazines of young, happy-looking couples are taped onto the walls. There is much giggling among the waiting women, ranging in ages from sixty-ish to ninety-ish, who line up against the wall.

They have clearly dressed up for the occasion.

The men of similar age hover in a cluster across the room, pretending not to scope out the action, except for the gregarious few who mingle among us to get a much closer view. Could the mingling be because these men have thick glasses and hearing aids?

The girls and I stand in line to pay our admission at the door. When it's my turn, Evvie pipes up that I'm just a *looky loo*, since I already have a boyfriend. And therefore maybe I only need to pay half price.

Yeah, Evvie, and how come you haven't noticed that said boyfriend is never around these days?

"Full price to all," says the tough ticket taker with frizzy orange hair. "This is a fund-raiser, honey, not a nonprofit, so cough it up."

My girls put on their name and number tags and stay close to one another. Ida is ready to bolt, but Sophie reins her in tight. Bella is all giggles. Evvie, wearing one of her new outfits, is attentive. There is an air of anticipation as the women size up the men and vice versa.

"What a bunch of *alter kockers*," Ida decides.

"And you old broads ain't that great,

either," says a burly, fat-gut guy standing behind her.

Bella laughs. "Ignore him." She puts her arm around Ida.

Ida groans. "This is a waste of time, coming here."

Evvie, raring to have a good time, says, "I like to think of it as practice. When we get to Wilmington House, Gladdy and I will need all the flirting experience we can get."

I look at her doubtfully. "Flirting?"

She gives me one of her pretend innocent looks. "Why, we might have to — to get information out of Romeo. You know, like Juliet?"

A pretty young woman wearing a pink, fluffy cocktail dress and a lot of makeup walks to the podium and taps a pencil on the wood for quiet. All eyes are on her. The men on the women's side scurry back across the room. Brimming over with enthusiasm, she calls out, "Hello, my name is Cindi, and welcome to Senior Match Dance!" She waits for the applause. "How many of you have been here before?"

A smattering of hands go up.

"The rejects," whispers Ida, making sure fat-gut is no longer standing nearby.

"How many here for the first time?" A much larger group now.

"Helloooo, suckers." Ida again.

Sophie smacks Ida on the back with her purse. "Shut up already; let's have some positive thinking. We're here for Evvie. She might meet the man of her dreams tonight."

"More like her nightmare." Ida ducks before Sophie can hit her again.

Cindi is revving up to play cheerleader. "Are you too old to date?"

A chorus of *yes*ses shout up at her. Not the right answer. That stops her for a moment. "Of course not. You're never too old."

"A lot you know," shouts an eighty-five-year-old up front.

"How many of you are sick of staying home nights?"

No one responds. Is she kidding? Who goes out at night? Nobody.

Cindi will not be discouraged. "Tired of blind dates?"

A white cane is seen waving from the back. Followed by a reedy voice. "What's wrong with blind dates? Try me; I'm a bundle of laughs."

"I'll try you, honey," shouts a homely woman to the left, "if you promise not to ask anybody what I look like."

More laughs at that.

Cindi is losing a bit of her rah-rah, but is game to go on. "Tired of waiting for the

141

phone to ring?"

A voice down center shouts, "It hasn't rung in forty years. Think I should give up?"

Lots of agreement there.

Cindi keeps bulldozing. "Aren't you sick of wasting time going from one bad date to another, going through long boring dinners that will lead to nothing but frustration?"

I hear a voice near us call out, "Dinner? Who gets that lucky? Lucky is lunch, where you get a greasy hamburger on a stale roll, in a fast-food place with a lot of screaming kids."

"Or an ice-cold bagel with a schmear, sitting on a free bench," shouts another. I can't believe it. It's Evvie reliving her breakfast with Sol.

"Hey, whatever happened to Dutch treat?" calls a male voice across the room. "Why do we guys always have to be the ones to pay?" A chorus of male *yeahs* goes with that.

There's a lot of back-and-forth jeering.

The pencil is tap-tap-tapping. Cindi is shouting now, hoping to prevent an uprising. "And that's why you've come here! Equal opportunities for everyone! A chance for thirty men and women to date in one night. The shortcut to love at first sight. You'll look at him, and he'll look at you, you'll ask each other questions. You'll know

142

if there's a spark." She holds up her left hand; something glistens on her ring finger. "That's how I met my husband and that's why I'm a believer. It's never too late to fall in love!"

The room erupts in applause. And catcalls. Mostly catcalls.

Sure. Never too late to get hurt again. I think it, but I'm not about to shout it out. Frankly, I wish I were home reading a good mystery.

"Easy for her to say. She's twenty and skinny and gorgeous." I look back. This time it's Bella making her little comment, feeling self-righteous.

Cindi is closing fast. "Okay, let's party! Women, each of you take a seat at one of the tables. Men, line up in a straight line. When the music starts, you start dancing your way around the room, but stay in line. When the music stops, sit down next to your nearest lady. Try to be relaxed, ask questions, look one another in the eyes, and say something that describes who you are. When the music starts again, the gentleman will say thank you as he gets up," she says pointedly, "as will the woman, and he moves on, dancing to the right. The next round, the women dance, the men sit, and the women get to choose their men."

Huge applause at that.

"At the end of the dance portion, we'll match up the requested numbers and the social hour will begin. If you don't get a partner, well, there's always next week."

"If I live that long," shouts a ninety-year-old in the far corner, leaning on the wall for support.

"Ladies and gentlemen, the ball is in your court. Have fun!" Cindy nods to her assistant at the sound system.

There is much tentative moving about. The girls grab seats next to one another. I don't want to participate, so I just stand around. I can't think of anyone except Jack. The girls grin nervously, except for Ida, who has already lost all interest.

"Break a leg," says Bella, unclear on the concept.

With much pushing and shoving, the men manage to get in a line. The music starts. It's "Hava Nagila" — of course everyone knows that one. The women energetically sing along and tap their feet as the men, obviously self-conscious, stomp their clumsy way around the room in a parody of dancing. The blind man has his dog with him. The dog has better rhythm than most of the men. There are two men with walkers, one with crutches, and one old geezer attached to an oxygen cart, walking with the aid of his nurse. God bless them all, for never giving up trying. But, I better keep out of their way.

The music stops, mid-note. The men freeze. They look around frantically, sizing up the goods. A redhead with big hair and a lot of makeup catches several eyes. Three men run for the seat next to her. One gets it, sneers. One sulks away to a different seat. The other one trips and falls. Two medical assistants in white coats hurry to his aid.

The talking starts, the room is filled with rapid conversation.

I wander from table to table and pick up snippets of conversation.

I pass table number one: A short, tubby guy with a bad toupee, panting from that slight exercise, leans toward his woman, informing her intimately, "Right away, I have to confess, I got psoriasis."

"How nice for you." The woman in the purple pantsuit and Mickey Mouse T-shirt quickly moves as far back in her chair as she can.

Another table. A very thin, intense man wearing a badly fitting forest green leisure suit, and a green tie with goldfish on it, leans over to a short woman with too much perfume and three pairs of glasses hanging around her neck. He whispers, "I've just joined Jews for Jesus. Would you like to hear about it?"

"God, no."

And another: Oh, oh, here's Ida.

Her guy is hot to trot. He's got his opening gambit prepared. Big smile with a mouth that is missing most of its teeth. "I'm a Gemini. What's your sign?"

"My sign tells me you should get up right now."

He stutters. "But there's no music."

"Let me hum a few bars for you." She sings. Badly, on purpose. " 'I'm gonna wash that man right outta my hair . . .' "

Her date sits there, paralyzed with fear. He closes his mouth.

She shuts her eyes as if napping.

And here's Bella: "I wasn't always like this. I was born a princess." She sees me and waves. I walk away, leaving her in fairy-tale land.

Evvie at her table: "I should have been a movie star. I should have been Doris Day."

A rather unattractive man replies in kind: "And I should have been Rock Hudson."

"In your dreams."

They both look toward the sound system, waiting for escape.

There's Sophie, already holding the hand

of the nondescript man at her table. He looks dubious. She says, reading his palm, "You are going to meet a wonderful woman today. She is wearing a midnight blue, crushed-velvet dress, V neckline, with a matching fake flower in her hair."

Need I tell you what Sophie is wearing?

The music starts again. I sit down on a bench and stare up at the basketball hoops and watch the balloons float around. What else have I got to do? I can think about Sophie's medical troubles. Not solved. Irving and poor Millie. Where will that end? Not happily. The Peeper, still getting away with it. Not solved. And this difficult case of Romeo and Juliet. Either there's no case at all, or — I suddenly shudder. Why do I have this strange feeling that we might be treading on very dangerous ground?

Oy.

Sixteen: Movin' Out

Why am I not surprised that there is a small crowd surrounding the mint green Cadillac parked in my usual spot? In fact, I'd be amazed if there weren't. Never mind that it is early in the morning and Evvie and I want to get started for Palm Beach. The word got out, and hail, hail, the gang's all here.

Alvin Ferguson is a man of his word. He is sending us first-class. Evvie's cab is also here, our plan being not to arrive in the same vehicle, since we are not supposed to know each other. Evvie is already having the driver store her fake Louis Vuitton suitcase in the taxi's trunk and modeling her traveling outfit and sophisticated hairdo for all our onlookers. Everything we have is new and we get lots of oohs and ahhs from the women.

Hy and Lola watch from their second-story balcony. Sol is walking around, kicking the Cadillac tires and doing other silly

148

things men do. He is followed by Denny, who imitates Sol's actions. The hood is open and they take turns examining the engine with knowing nods. Even a couple of the Canadian men have come out to stick their heads under the hood.

I am also dressed in my new duds and have also been to the hairdresser. The bystanders admire my new trappings, too, as I put my suitcase in the trunk of the Caddy. They look me up and down; this other member of the newly rich. The comments begin.

Hy calls down, "Fancy-schmancy. You sure you know how to drive a car manufactured later than 1950?"

"Hoo-ha," says Mary.

"How about a test drive?" Tessie leans over the upholstery while drinking hot chocolate with whipped cream. Evvie pulls her away. "Not bloody likely."

Hy can't resist it. "Ya really think you'll fool those rich dames?" His wife, Lola, punches him playfully. She of the mixed messages. *You shouldn't say such mean things, but you're so cute and clever doing it.* Talk about brainwashing.

"Don't worry about us, dahling," Evvie says. "Most of them started out as poor as we did."

Barbi and Casey come by, wearing tennis togs and carrying their rackets. They stop to catch the action.

"Very nice," says Barbi.

"Win the lottery?" Casey asks.

"New case," Hy answers for me.

"They're going undercover." Lola takes her turn after her husband. He always gets to speak first.

"Yeah," says Hy, "but what about visiting hours? We can pretend to be your poor relatives from the East Bronx looking for a handout. We'll even drive up in *your* car."

"There are *no* visiting hours!" Evvie is practically screeching. "Do *not* call. Just butt out!"

Hy and Lola nudge each other. They love to pull Evvie's chain.

With their expressions, Barbi and Casey send me a message. Call if you need us. I nod.

I am aware that my own girls are standing off to one side, saying nothing. Ida is pretending to read the ads from her mailbox. Sophie and Bella stare aimlessly. I suffer for them because they are feeling left out. But there's nothing I can do.

"How long will you be away?" Irving stands by Millie in her wheelchair.

"Yeah, I want to know, too." Sol stares lovingly at Evvie, who refuses to look at him. "Maybe we could have another go," he suggests.

There is smirking and giggling at that, since most of those standing here were witness to the Sol and Evvie breakfast debacle.

"Time to get moving," Evvie says briskly, looking at her waiting driver.

My girls look stricken. Sophie and Bella run over and hug us. Bella is near tears. "Hey," Evvie says, "we're not that far away and we'll be going back and forth a lot."

"If there are any new developments with the Peeper, please call and let us know," I say to my threesome. "We'll be in constant touch with our cell phones." For once, "progress" is coming in handy. Bella and Sophie beam at that.

Out of the corner of my eye I see Irving now getting into Denny's car with Millie and Yolie. Which surprises me since they hardly ever leave the premises. Twice in one week?

"And keep an eye on Irving and Millie. Something seems to be going on with them. Let me know."

"We will," both Sophie and Bella echo.

Evvie gets into her cab and they start to drive off.

I get into the Caddy and rev up as fast as

I can, not all that easy, what with having to try and figure out what all the fancy dials and whatnots are.

"Take your time," Evvie calls from the cab, waving to all like the grande dame she wants to be, basking in the glory of all those envious faces.

I get the Caddy moving, such a smooth ride compared to my old junker. Turn the corner from Lanai Gardens and don't look back.

I enter Wilmington House after having the Cadillac parked for me by a waiting attendant. No more parking behind the hired help with this hot item. I stand in the lobby, next to my suitcase, and look around. It's very quiet. A few residents look up from their books, newspapers, knitting, whatever. I smile. A few smile back. Some people are chatting, their voices low. I take a closer look at my new companions-to-be. Last time I was here, I didn't get the chance. Hmmm. Seems like a clone of Grecian Villas. Yet again, no shorts. No sundresses. No T-shirts. Women wearing pantsuits or skirts albeit cotton. Stockings and low heels. Men in sport shirts and slacks and sport jackets. Everyone looking very pressed. Is this a uniform for all the retirement facilities except ours?

Evvie arrives moments later with an attitude. This time just about everyone looks up.

"Thank you so much," she tells the cabdriver grandiosely, as he plants her suitcase not too far from where I am standing. She looks around the room, waving gaily to one and all. "Hi, there!"

Then she pretends to notice me. We play at looking each other over.

Evvie walks over to me, with her hand out. "Evelyn Markowitz."

I accept her handshake. "Gladys Gold."

Hope Watson rushes over to greet us with a fake smile. She takes both our hands in hers. "Welcome to Wilmington House. Most happy to see you."

She addresses the seated group. "These are our new tenants. I'll formally introduce them at dinner."

With that, the stylish ladies and gents go back to what they were doing.

Hope, hiding her hostility, asks, "Since you both arrived at the same time, you wouldn't mind my taking you up to your rooms together?"

"Of course not," Evvie ever-so-graciously agrees.

In the elevator, the phony smile disappears

and Ms. Watson's intense dislike of us takes over. She says nothing, so we say nothing as well.

When we reach the fifth floor, she leads us down the hall, walking on carpeting so soft one could sink into it. "Per your request, I was able to get you adjoining apartments with inside doors. You're lucky, because we don't have that many 'en suites.' "

"Thank you," I say.

"Has Philip Smythe moved in yet?" Evvie asks.

She bristles. She's not in the habit of discussing other residents, but she knows she has no choice in this odd situation. "He's due much later tonight."

She changes the subject quickly. "Since you weren't bringing any of your own furniture, we've furnished for you. I hope you find our choices satisfactory."

"I'm sure we will. Thank you again." My teeth hurt from all the polite smiles.

"Do not think I am pleased with this, but it was the board's decision."

"I promise we will not do anything to upset the other guests." I play pacifier. We need Hope's cooperation.

"I will hold you to that promise. Just give me your background information that I'm to use tonight when I introduce you."

Evvie takes a list out of her purse and hands it to Ms. Watson.

Hope opens both doors and hands us our keys. "Rules and regulations, as well as our weekly events schedule, will be found in the desk drawers. Breakfasts starts at seven. Lunch is at noon. Dinner is at six. Please be prompt."

With that, Hope marches quickly away from us.

We walk into our individual front doors. Before we even look around, we unlock the connected inner doors. Evvie looks gleefully at me through our private inside entrances. "Isn't this great!"

Still grinning, she turns and races away from me to inspect her apartment. I examine my own quarters, which I assume are similar to hers. How lovely. Spacious rooms, high ceilings with classic moldings. The décor, in keeping with the Art Deco downstairs, is exquisite, with softly muted colors and pleasant watercolors on the walls. We each have floor-to-ceiling windows as well as a private balcony and a beautiful view of the spacious grounds. My entire apartment back at Lanai Gardens would fit in the living room alone. I hear a noise and call into Evvie through her open door. "Are you all right? What's that noise?"

Evvie's joyful voice calls out to me. "That's me bouncing up and down on the bed. I don't ever want to go home again. Don't you just love it?"

I call back to her, agreeing.

She pokes her head into my place, all smiles. "Ready, get set, and go! I can't wait to see what our perp looks like. I wonder where Philip Smythe is right now?"

Seventeen:
The Mystery Man

It might have been a scene from a romantic movie. The place: Heathrow Airport. Morning. Slight rain, misty. An older gentleman, dashing, in his Burberry raincoat and matching peaked cap. A woman, a British Royal–class lady. Cashmere coat and matching wide-brimmed cashmere hat. Standing next to her Rolls-Royce, her driver waiting patiently and discreetly off to one side.

Their good-byes seem heartfelt, their kisses passionate. The script might have come from any vintage film.

"I wish you didn't have to jet back to the States this soon."

"I hate that I have to leave you. But you know, I must be back by the first."

"You'll call often, of course."

"Every spare moment I have."

She presses the familiar forest green Harrods gift bag into his hands. "So you'll remember me."

"How could I forget you, my dearest? It's been a most magical month. Now I must take my leave or I'll miss my flight."

She presses her handkerchief to her eyes to wipe the tears, then turns and indicates to her driver to open the door. "Until next August, my darling."

The driver helps her into the Rolls, as she continues to look back at her lover. They drive off. The man waves.

At the same time, nearby, a man in his forties bids good-bye to a pretty young woman leaving in a cab.

Both men turn and enter the same airport door, bumping into each other. They both apologize.

As they walk through the terminal, side by side, the younger man comments, "You look awfully pleased."

"I should be. I've just had a wonderful liaison with a lovely lady."

"I did, too."

"Then why do you look so irritable?"

"Because she wants marriage and I want amusement."

"Well, why not bed down only the ones without strings?"

"All of them have strings. Sex as a teaser, then, having shown their wares, marriage or no more sex. I don't want to be tied down, just to satisfy my normal male needs."

"If I may say so, that's your problem: Bedding down younger women. They place too high a price on what they have to offer. Take some advice from an old codger like me. It's the older women you want. They're so easy to get and so eager to please. So many are rich and ever so grateful. And they give you their all in gifts, in bed and out." He indicates his Harrods bag.

"Then how do you get rid of them when you tire of them?"

The elderly gentleman smiles. "That's never a problem. Old ladies have a way of dying."

They pause as each man is about to move toward a different airline.

"I'll keep that in mind. Thanks for the tip, Grandpa. Safe traveling."

"And to you, too, sir."

They nod at each other, two such men of the world, each recognizing a kindred spirit.

EIGHTEEN:
OUR DINNER WITH
THE RICH FOLK

At dinner, Evvie glances over to my table. Our eyes meet in satisfaction. How gorgeous everything is. The dining room shines with dazzling glass chandeliers, sparkling dinnerware, starched napkins — or *serviettes,* as the waiter pronounces it as he places one in my lap. Evvie is in heaven. She, too, is sparkling as she chats with her tablemates.

The people at Wilmington House take dressing for dinner fairly seriously. The women are all in cocktail dresses. The men wear suits and ties. The room is quiet except for very low conversation and soft elevator music playing in the background.

I look around my table. No one is smiling. The woman next to me introduces herself as Lorraine Sanders. She sits head high, body stiff, her lips pursed as if she's eaten something sour. In a matter of moments she informs me that her husband had lived here with her, but he died three years ago and she still misses him terribly. She points. "You're in his seat." With that, she touches the back of my chair as she gives me a resentful look.

As if I am sitting on his ghost. I wonder if she dusts it off every day. Oy.

Seymour Banks, tall, thin, not much hair, overly polite, in the next chair over, announces he lost his wife four years ago. He sighs long and hard.

Anna Kaplan, sweet-faced, shy, and somewhat heavy, says her husband died five years ago, but she informs me that doesn't mean she's gotten over it, either. With that, the hankie comes out of the pocket for many mournful sniffles.

I have the feeling they know one another's woeful stories by heart. I am aware they are all wearing dark colors as opposed to the brighter outfits all around the room. Lucky me. I guess they've put me at the bereavement table. And for a moment I suspect Hope Watson did that on purpose. I wouldn't put it past her.

After those pronouncements, my companions stop talking or even looking at one another and focus on their meals.

I glance over to Evvie's table, where she is smiling and animated in conversation. Leave it to her. Wherever she goes, she turns it into a party. Though I doubt even she would be able to warm up my lackluster group.

I am reminded of one of Evvie's and my favorite scenes in a much-loved Woody Allen movie, *Stardust Memories.* Woody is riding on a train filled with sad, drably dressed, pathetic-looking people. They are filmed all in black and white. A train passes theirs. It's filmed in color. Gorgeous, young, happy people drinking champagne and laughing. The expression on Woody's face says it all.

A marvelous cinematic moment, and I feel I'm living it now. Wait 'til I tell Evvie later. She'll get it immediately.

Hope Watson taps her fork gently against a glass and the room stills. "Good evening, everyone." Everyone parrots, "Good evening, Hope." I can't believe it. Sounds like kindergarten.

"Some of you have already met our latest arrivals. Let me formally introduce them to you. At table five is Evelyn Markowitz of New York City and Fort Lauderdale." Evvie is urged to stand up. She does and she receives polite applause. "Evelyn's hobbies are writing articles and attending movies, plays, and all forms of entertainment. I'm sure she will find much of that right here on our own campus. In fact, tonight we are showing a wonderful old classic, Spencer Tracy and Katharine Hepburn in *Adam's Rib*. Perhaps she'll do a movie review for us."

Evvie instantly responds, "You bet I will."

"Well, then, we'll be looking forward to that."

Evvie smiles broadly and sits down.

Hope turns to me. "At table three, meet Gladys Gold." I am urged to stand. "She is also formerly from New York, but then again, so many of you are." That gets polite laughs. "She has just recently arrived in Florida. I know she'll be happy not to see snow anymore. I hope you left your furs behind."

I smile the saccharine smile that Hope seems to bring out in me.

"Gladys enjoys reading and walks on the beach, and sometimes writes poetry." Again a smattering of applause. Evvie created my so-called bio. I just pray nobody asks me to recite a poem.

My tablemates acknowledge me briefly with little enthusiasm.

Hope is not through. "And before I forget, let me remind everyone of the monthly mixer this Saturday night. Ladies and gentlemen, get out your fabulous finery. It will be a gala evening for one and all." There is applause and murmuring at this announcement.

Whew. That's over, we're back to dinner. And what a meal it is. Gourmet, all the way. The chef comes from France, I'm told. I can't help but think of the girls back home. I hope they took a cab and went out for an early-bird special tonight. Then I wouldn't feel so guilty.

I make one more stab at dinner conversation. "Will you all be at the mixer?"

Anna continues eating as she speaks. "What for? My Harry won't be there for me to dance with." She sounds so pathetic. "Those others think they can still find love. When you're old, it's over."

"Ditto for me." Lorraine studies the dessert card. "We've already had our share of happiness. I stay in my room and put earplugs in so I won't hear the noise."

I'm afraid to ask Seymour. But he volunteers his response. He shrugs. "I come. I listen. I like the music. I don't dance."

Well, that was stimulating.

We are on our coffee and dessert when the dining room doors are suddenly flung open and a man appears. He stretches his arms out and says, "Oh, dear, I suppose I'm too late for dinner."

Everyone turns to look at him. Indeed, he is something to behold. For a man of seventy-five, he seems in excellent physical condition. He is about five foot ten, resplendent in a tuxedo and matching cape with a red lining and a black fedora. His glistening, dark, wavy hair is steel gray at the temples. His eyes are electric blue and for a man his age, he is utterly handsome.

He bows. In a plummy English accent, he says, "May I introduce myself? My name is Philip Smythe."

After dinner, as we are walking out of the dining room, Evvie purposely passes me, grinning. She whispers, "Wow. What an entrance. Smythe doesn't look like he could murder anybody, except maybe onstage. With that outfit he should be playing Dracula in summer stock."

"Dracula killed his women, don't forget," I whisper back.

Evvie laughs. "In books and onstage, Glad, make-believe stuff."

"I can see his appeal. Every woman in the place is gaping at him."

"Looks to me like this will be a whole lot of fun. I intend to enjoy myself. A lot!"

Evvie hurries to catch up to the other residents heading for the screening room.

"See ya at the movies!" she calls back to me.

Nineteen:
No Free Lunch

So much for not being here very long. Three days of *Hello, Mrs. Gold, how are you? Fine, and you, Mrs. Markowitz?* This pretending not to know each other is beginning to get tiresome.

After breakfast at our separate tables, I make an executive decision. I walk over to Evvie, who is just leaving the dining room. "Good morning, Evelyn."

Evvie is startled. I'm going out of character, but she's quick on the uptake. Nodding, she responds, "Gladys. Isn't it a lovely day?"

I pick up on her cue. "Nice day for a stroll." I indicate the patio doors.

"Why not."

And we go outside and out of earshot. "What's up?" she asks me.

"Nothing's up, sis. Let's become 'friends.' I'm tired of thinking up new ways to communicate. Then we can hang out together. Much simpler."

"Fine by me."

I smile. As the older sister by two years, Evvie does look up to me to be the leader. We've always made a good team. We think alike. I wish I could have found a way to make the girls understand that's why she was the right person for me to work with.

Together we scout the entire place. We check the grounds, the pool, the tennis courts, the bike path, and the walking trail around the lake. We cover the card room, the gym, the library, the TV room, the barbershop, the billiards room, the art room, and the snack bar.

Evvie gives up. "Where the heck is he? No sign of him anywhere."

Either he's skipped breakfast to sleep late or he left the premises. No sign of our guy. We've been trailing him since he got here. So far, nothing's been happening. He hangs around, socializes. Picking out his next prey?

We linger outside for a while. Evvie sits down on one of the cement benches that has the name of a rich contributor carved into its arm. "It's not going to be so easy keeping tabs on him."

"We need a different tactic." I sit down next to her and bend to touch the backs of my new Reeboks. They're rubbing against my ankles because they aren't broken in yet.

Come to think of it, all my new clothes feel uncomfortable. I don't feel like me. Like I'm not in my own skin. This is a strange new experience.

"For example?"

"One of us has to get closer to him. Make friends with him. But we have to be subtle. Maybe one of us can get assigned to his table and sit next to him at meals. Let's ask Hope Watson's help."

Evvie laughs. "Fat chance she'll accommodate us."

It's a tempting thought, though. To be away from my dreary tablemates. "At least she gave you a lively table."

"Some lively. All they talk about is the price of this and the price of that. Do you want to know the price of sable coats these days? Like they need them here. I really have to work hard to keep up with their assets."

"Smythe is taking his time picking out which old lady he wants for his next, maybe dangerous, love affair."

"Innocent love affair," Evvie comments. "Remember, innocent until proven guilty. Anyway, the longer he takes, the longer we get to stay here, which is fine with me."

"That, too."

We stretch out our legs and let the sun

bake our faces. "Mmm," says Evvie, "I could get used to this life."

"Well, don't. Because we aren't going to have it forever."

Evvie stands and pulls me up, too. "Then let's take in every advantage. Race you to the spa."

We've been in the Jacuzzi and the workout room. We went into the indoor pool and actually swam a few laps. Now we're in the "relaxation room," lying on adjoining tables with long towels covering our bodies and rejuvenating mud packs over our faces. The soft music lulls us. The aromatherapy session on our backs earlier makes us tingle pleasantly.

Suddenly I feel Evvie poke my arm. "Do you hear that?"

"What?" I mumble blissfully.

"Listen!" She pokes me again.

I hear voices coming toward us. They sound familiar. The door opens slightly and we hear Hope Watson whisper, "And this is where we have our delicious facials."

I take a peek from out of the corner of my eye mask. Hope moves back out of the doorway, remaining in the corridor while her little tour group tiptoes in.

"Mahvellus, absolutely *mahvellus,"* says

phony potential client Sophie Meyerbeer.

"Just too lovely for words," agrees sycophant Bella Fox.

Can Ida be far behind? "Perfect," says the third conspirator.

"Psst." I hiss at the three of them as I lift myself up from my padded table, holding my towel around me as best I can. Evvie does so, too. We glare at them.

"What the heck are you doing here?" Evvie whispers angrily.

The girls stare at us in horror. The mud is dripping down our faces.

"Who's there?" Bella is about to scream.

"What do you mean, who's there. It's us. Ev and Glad." We pull off our eye masks.

Bella grins. "I didn't recognize you with all that gunk on your face."

"What are *you* doing here?" Sophie is belligerent.

"You're supposed to be working," Ida sneers.

"We are working," Evvie sneers back.

Hope calls gaily from the hallway. "Ladies? There's so much more to show you."

"Meet us in the parking lot as soon as your 'tour' is over!" I demand.

"We're coming," Sophie trills toward Hope.

Bella sticks out her tongue at us as they

rush from the room.

We stand off to one side of the parking lot, behind some shrubbery, so no one can see us. It is a hot argument on both sides. We've been round it twenty times and everyone is still mad.

"How did you get here?" Evvie wants to know.

Sophie snarls. "We took two buses. Like you care?"

"What are we supposed to do? Let you have all the fun?" Ida is next.

"Yeah. Some work. Facials? I didn't see Romeo in the 'relaxation room.' " Bella's turn.

"We don't have to tell you how we do our job." Evvie is indignant.

"Days go by. You don't call," Ida chastises us.

Evvie snarls. "We've only been here three days!"

"If we had something to report, you'd hear from us." That's me.

"You could ruin our cover." Evvie is furious. "Just get yourselves home."

"What? And miss the free lunch? It's part of the tour." Sophie crosses her arms in protest.

Bella giggles. "We should visit every retirement place and get a free lunch every day. Let's do it."

Now I feel guilty. They are having such a good time and I'm spoiling it. What's the harm? I look at my watch and calm down. "Then get inside. Lunch is about to start."

"And don't you dare look at us or talk to us," Evvie demands.

Sophie is annoyed. "Yeah, we got it. We've never seen you before."

"Will you drive us home afterward? In the Caddy?" Bella pleads.

Suddenly a snazzy red Mercedes convertible whips past us.

"It's him!" Evvie whispers excitedly. "With three women!"

Almost as if on cue, we duck down behind our shrubbery. We are actually close enough to hear any conversation.

Philip opens the car doors for each of his passengers. The women pile out, pulling many shopping bags along with them, all bearing designer store logos. They've obviously been hitting Worth Avenue.

His passengers are practically drooling over Smythe.

A sixty-ish blonde, whose gray is showing, simpers, "Phil, you are such a darling to take us shopping. So patient."

"And the lunch at Bice was exquisite."

The others gurgle their syrupy thanks as well.

Philip doffs his Marlins baseball cap and bows. He's dressed in at least five hundred dollars or more of very casual wear. "My pleasure, pretty ladies." The parking attendant takes his car. Philip and the shoppers happily make their way inside.

A moment of silence, and then the girls and I all pile out of our silly hiding places.

"Hmph," Evvie sniffs. "Talk about corny acting."

"Wow!" says Sophie. "He can put his slippers under my bed anytime."

That about sums it up.

My cell phone rings as I am getting into my pajamas. I rush to get from the bedroom to the living room where I left it. For a moment I fantasize it's Jack calling. To apologize and make up.

"Hi, it's only me." Evvie laughs. "Just like home."

"I almost broke my neck running to answer. Why didn't you use the house phone or just walk through our adjoining door?"

"No reason. I like to respect your privacy. Want an update on tonight's mah-jongg?"

I shrug, trying to hide my disappointment that it wasn't Jack. But then again, if he did call, it would be on my home number and he'd get the machine. Jack doesn't know I have a cell. Damn him, I think. Foolish me. Why can't I admit it's over and stop tormenting myself?

Which makes me wonder — how am I going to get any of my messages from home? I still haven't learned how to access them.

"Why not? Your place or mine?" I say, without much enthusiasm.

"I'll come through." With that, Evvie enters from the interior door, carrying something wrapped in a napkin. "Leftover cookies from the game. Put on some tea."

I do so as she places the chocolate chip cookies on a plate and sits down to wait for the tea.

"Mah-jongg was a hoot. I can't get over how dressed up they get just to play games! Don't they ever relax around here? Anyway, remember the blonde from Philip's shopping spree? Well, she was at my table, and all the women wanted to know what Philip was like. Lucky she's a gusher. She went on and on about how cute he is, how gallant, how patient, as he schlepped them from store to store. Where they shopped. What new gowns they bought to wear for the mixer."

"He didn't pay for their stuff, did he?"

"No, but everyone was impressed that he treated them to a very expensive lunch. At a very expensive restaurant."

"Did she mention if he said anything personal about himself? This was a good opportunity to do some sleuthing."

"I tried asking direct questions, but she was all about adjectives. How dashing, how clever, how sweet, blah-blah-blah. She's obviously set her cap for him."

Now her eyes light up. "And guess what? A little later Philip walked by where we were playing. He smiled at everyone. Kibitzed a bit. You know — stuff like, How come you beautiful gals don't have dates tonight? Talk about a line of jazz. And then he wandered away. Probably to flirt with the bingo players, too. Women are such suckers. Everyone was so sappy, making goo-goo eyes at him. When he looked back, I could swear he winked at me."

I pour the tea. Evvie chomps away at the cookies.

"How can you be hungry after all the food we eat around here? You're going to blow up like a blimp." I'm grumpy and I can't help it. Cut it out, I tell myself.

Evvie stops eating the cookies. "This is all so exciting. It's gonna be some competition to capture the only lively guy in the place.

176

This sure beats having to do stakeouts in the car."

She gets up, yawns. "Well, time for beddy-bye. One thing Betty, the blonde, did comment on, was that he carried a wad of money in his wallet. She figured he was filthy rich."

"So what? So is everyone else around here."

"Except us." Evvie sighs as she puts her cup in the sink and throws the napkin in the trash. "Why did I have to go and marry Joe? If I'd married a rich guy, I could have ended up living in a place like this. Where I really belong."

"Woulda, coulda, shoulda." I remind her of one of our favorite phrases.

As she goes through her door, she grins. "Tomorrow night's the big mixer. I can hardly wait to catch the action. Wanna bet he makes his move? Some lucky gal is gonna get a shot at romance with Romeo."

TWENTY: THE MIXER

I wait downstairs for Evvie to finish dressing and join the group. We're all in the clubhouse. What a difference from the one we have at Lanai Gardens. This looks like a large, fancy nightclub. And they have a band, a real live band. We're lucky if we can get someone to spin records. If I thought the women in this place were always dressed — well, it was nothing like what I'm seeing tonight. Much fancier cocktail dresses and evening gowns. Subtle colors, obviously very expensive. The men aren't in tuxedos, but I'll bet they are wearing their best suits and ties. I am in basic black. Figure that would fit in anywhere. I've dressed it up with a scarf and earrings. I look pretty good. Actually it's fun to have an excuse to dress up.

Every woman's been to the beauty salon. I've now learned the hard way, when it's mixer night you call way ahead for an appointment. Or go into town for a do, or it's hot rollers in your own bathroom. Evvie managed to snag the last appointment on the premises. I haven't seen her since I spotted her walking into the shop at three.

A bar with champagne cocktails is being set up by a bartender. Such an air of excitement. Even the rather staid men seem to have perked up. Since it's not a holiday, there's no theme, but the entertainment committee put up balloons, colored streamers, and whirling lights to make it festive.

The band plays the music of our youth: Benny Goodman, Frank Sinatra, Artie Shaw. I have to admit, it's lovely. There must be rules of behavior, since all the men take turns dancing, then changing partners.

I have been watching Philip Smythe cruise the room. His method seems to be that he makes a point of dancing with every woman who is single. Not hard, since every one of them is eagerly waiting her turn. It's amusing to note that the men are putting a stiff upper lip on it, but they are visibly jealous. This new guy's cramping their style. Not only that, he's an excellent dancer, he looks great in his tuxedo (the only man wearing one), and his energy is making the others try harder, something I think they aren't used to.

There is a buzzing sound from the crowd

near the door. I turn around. And there's my Evvie making one heck of a grand entrance. She's wearing the low-cut scarlet red cocktail dress and matching boa from our thrift shop shopping spree. Her hair — now colored back to its original auburn — and makeup are stunning. And, oh, my, she's wearing the dazzling fake diamond necklace.

Well, well, Evvie, look at you.

The other women are wearing jewelry, but nothing as startling as hers. And Evvie is carrying it off, behaving as if a person with her demeanor would only wear real jewelry. Even I'm amazed and impressed with my sister. She is noticed, by one and all, as she enters the ballroom.

The next song is a waltz. I am actually surprised. Seymour Banks, my dinner tablemate, leaves the edge of the room where he has been playing wallflower, bows, and asks me to dance.

To my unasked question, he tells me why. "Because you sit at my table."

As if that makes us members of the same not-so-glee club. Nevertheless, I get up and he gracefully whirls me around. He's not too bad.

"It's like falling off a bicycle," he tells me, spinning me again.

Lo and behold, Philip has Evvie in his arms. He didn't waste any time. Put a redhead before the bull? Or something like that. They are breathtaking to watch. I had forgotten how good a dancer Evvie was. All those years of lessons she made Papa pay for so she could become a star.

Every so often, as Seymour and I clumsily dip and turn, I catch the tiniest snatch of conversation from Evvie as she is dazzling Philip.

"Did anyone ever tell you that you look like a movie star?" Evvie says.

"My dear, you flatter me."

I can't help but smile. The woman who would be Doris Day now has the role she's waited for all her life. I hope she gets Smythe to reveal something that will help our case.

Seymour actually tries to engage me in conversation. He speaks yet again about his dead wife. Believe me, I'm sympathetic. How well I remember the rut that widows and widowers find so hard to get out of. Myself included. Playing grief over and over again, as if that could make it come out differently. I want to repeat the oldest and truest of all clichés — this, too, shall pass. But he isn't ready to hear it. Who am I to preach — did I ever get over my own loss?

Right now, though, I want to get closer in order to hear everything Evvie and Philip are saying. I find myself leading poor Seymour. And here we are again, spinning our way around dancers to get to the most popular couple on the floor. There isn't a woman on the floor who isn't watching them.

Evvie's hand moves up his back to touch the black and silvery hair. "Oh, yes, Philip dear, I'm a widow."

Philip, *dear?* A widow? Her very alive ex-husband, Joe, would have a fit if he heard that.

Another turn, as she swirls her red skirts sexily and bats her fake eyelashes. "Poor little me. I'm all alone in the world."

As we nearly collide at the bar area, on purpose I might add, I try to poke her. Evvie ignores me as she manages crocodile tears for dear Philip. She lowers her voice, but I hear her anyway. ". . . six months to live, but oh, how I intend to enjoy them . . ."

Oh, Evvie, what are you doing? Our plan was to see which woman he picks so we can study his M.O.: it's not supposed to be you!

The waltz is over. Seymour says something to me, but I don't hear him. I can't stop staring at the magic couple. Philip is not leaving Evvie's side. She continues to talk and smile and flirt outrageously. He takes her by the arm and picks up another glass of champagne for her at the bar. She smiles endearingly up at him. He whispers something to her. She nods. They walk out onto the terrace. I swear, every woman's eyes still follow them. The emotions range from curiosity to prurient interest to downright jealousy. The die is cast. No doubt about it. Romeo has picked his Juliet.

I'm going to kill my sister when we get back upstairs.

Twenty-One:
On the Terrace

We're Ginger Rogers and Fred Astaire, Evvie thinks, as she looks around the terrace. The two of them dressed in glamorous evening wear, a full glorious moon, and the weather, Florida's best, balmy and soft. The kind of night for falling in love.

"Don't move." Philip stands with his arms outstretched. "I want to remember you just the way you are. My lady in red."

"I was just imagining Fred Astaire. That's the kind of beautiful thing he would say to Ginger."

"And rightly so. This is indeed a cinematic moment. Remember in *Top Hat* they danced on such a set as this?"

"You like movies?"

"I am a devotee. I'm mad about them."

"Then you are a man after my own heart. I'm crazy about them, too."

His voice lowers. "I hope so. That I am a man after your heart." He steps toward her.

"Do you have any idea how beautiful you are?" He reaches out and takes each end of the scarlet boa and pulls her slowly toward him, sliding his hands up the boa until he brings her close enough to kiss her.

Taking her gently into his arms, Philip leads her into a fox-trot.

"There's no music," Evvie says.

"We don't need any music."

Is this me? Evvie thinks. This poor girl from the Bronx? Who went to movies as a child to drink in the beauty of how other people lived? To dream of how life could be if her parents hadn't been poor immigrants, hardly able to speak the language of this country they so luckily adopted?

"Beautiful lady in red," Philip murmurs in her ear, and she shudders with pleasure.

Is this gorgeous man holding me? Is this the man of my dreams? Can a girl fall in love at first sight like they do in the movies?

"Yes, dear?" she murmurs.

He whispers in her ear, "I'm Philip."

"I'm Evelyn," she whispers back.

He begins to sing. " 'I never will forget the way you look tonight . . . My lady in red.' "

TWENTY-TWO: WHEN THE LOVE BUG BITES

It's midnight and I've been pacing, seems like forever. Finally, I hear the key turn in the lock. I listen at the front door. I hear two voices mumbling in the hallway. Then the door closes. Is she alone?

A moment later, Evvie pounds on our adjoining door and comes prancing in.

"Bingo," she says, whirling me around. "We're in."

I force her to let go of me. "Where have you been?"

She looks at me strangely. "What are you — my mother?"

"I've been waiting for hours."

"And I've been on the job."

"Really? What have you learned about our alleged, possibly dangerous, killer?"

She grins. "That he loves champagne. He loves to dance. He simply *loooves* beautiful women." She preens, satisfied with herself. "Did I look gorgeous tonight, or what?"

"That's it? Nothing about his back-ground?"

"Give me a break. I've only just begun." She hums the once-popular song those words came from.

I grimace.

"Lighten up. Isn't this what we planned? We needed to get closer to him. Well, babe" — she whirls herself around — "I'm as close as we can get."

I cross my arms against my chest. "Not quite. And how much closer are you willing to *get?*"

Evvie is puzzled. Obviously she hasn't considered the next step.

She kicks off her heels and flops down on the couch. "What are you talking about?"

"You know darn well what I mean. He's not looking for a buddy." I imitate Ida as best I can. "He's going to want sex."

Evvie jumps back off the couch and heads for the adjoining doors. She flings them open. "Boy, that's gratitude!"

With that, she enters her own apartment and slams the door behind her.

I have this sudden memory of Evvie coming home with a date when she was sixteen. My mother and father didn't trust this boy. After they interrogated her — Where did she go? What did she do? — hot-tempered

Evvie ran from the room saying she was old enough to think for herself and nobody was going to tell her what to do. So, now I've become our judgmental mother? Part of me has always respected Evvie's independence. But I still can't resist calling after her.

"You forgot your glass slippers, Cinderella."

When I lift my head off my pillow and squint to read my little clock on the side table, it's only seven a.m. I can hear Evvie's radio on next door. Why is she up so early? I feel bad about being so hard on her last night. Maybe we'll have a cup of coffee together and clear the air before we go down to breakfast. I put my robe on and hurry across the bedroom and through the living room. I'm still not used to the size of this apartment. It's so far to go from one room to the other.

I knock on her adjoining door. To my surprise, when she answers, I see she's already dressed. In a stylish jogging outfit. And wearing makeup, with her hair smartly combed. I still can't get over the auburn color. My gray suddenly feels very old to me. "Good morning," I say. "You're up early."

"Yes." Her voice is cool.

"How about we have coffee together before we go downstairs?"

"No time." She looks at her fake Cartier watch. "Philip is meeting me. We're going jogging."

"Jogging," I sputter. "Since when have you ever jogged?"

"I have no time for this. He's waiting."

"Let me throw some clothes on and I'll join you. I'll walk, though."

"What for? I don't need a chaperone."

"Excuse me, I thought we were partners."

"Hello? Don't you get it? I don't need you. I am perfectly capable of doing this job alone."

Who is this stranger standing before me, coiffed and perfumed and haughty? Her nail polish perfect. When and where did she buy that outfit? In the downstairs boutique at those exorbitant prices? On Ferguson's expense account, no doubt. After one night of dancing, she's actually convinced herself she's one of them, these rich ladies of leisure?

"Evvie, what are you doing?"

She doesn't answer me. She checks herself out in the mirror of her compact. In all the years we've been in Florida, she's never owned a compact.

I blurt, childlike, "What am I supposed to

do while you're on the job?"

"Really, Glad, you're being thick. There's plenty to do around here. Find something."

With that, she turns and walks out her front door.

I call softly after her, "Don't break a leg, Miss Doris Day."

Twenty-Three:
In the Garden

How clear the sky is. How fresh the air. Even colors look brighter to her on this beautiful day. Flowers toss out their delicious scents as she passes one bed after another. The pond glistens as she and Philip jog around it. Evvie can't remember the last time she felt like this. If ever.

She still treats me like the baby sister. Evvie bristles, thinking of her spat with Gladdy. She's only two years older, for goodness' sake, but she acts as if she's the only one who behaves responsibly. She thinks she's in charge of our friends just because she's the only one who still drives, and now she thinks she's in charge of me, too! What about all those years I helped raise her little Emily when she was forced to work after Jack was killed? Granted, I love her daughter as much as I do my own Martha, but that's gratitude for you.

Philip turns his head to look at her and Evvie giggles. Slow walking with the girls around

Lanai Gardens didn't prepare her for this. She keeps up with him as best she can.

"Am I moving too quickly?" he asks with a look of concern.

"Just fine. I can keep up."

"I know you can." But he slows slightly anyway.

A couple of women jog past them. The women grin widely at Philip, flirting outright, ignoring Evvie. Philip grins back.

"You're quite the ladies' man, aren't you?"

"I plead guilty. Women are the much nicer sex. They're so soft and pliant. Are you soft and pliant, *mon amour?*"

Evvie blushes. "You're a fast worker."

"At our age, I should go slow?"

With that, they both break out laughing.

Philip is serious now. "Let me tell you something about me. I was raised by an elderly aunt after my parents died. She was the only family I had left. She gave me so much love, and when she became terminally ill, I was devastated. I was only thirteen at the time. But I knew it was up to me to take care of her. It took so long for her to find peace. It was a blessing when she finally died."

"You mean, as a thirteen-year-old, you took care of her alone?"

"Not quite alone. Auntie was very rich. Our whole family had been rich. We had servants to do everything. But I was the one who nursed her."

Evvie stops to sit on a bench for a short rest. She can't take her eyes off him. She's never heard a man speak so gently and so kindly.

"So, you see, as a very wealthy man, I could spend my time as I wanted. I traveled, even dallied with work for some years, but once I reached a certain age, I knew I had a mission. I owed it to my beloved aunt Dorothy. I wanted to ease the pain of older women. I wanted to be with them, do whatever they needed until . . . they needed me no more."

"And this is why you're attracted to me? Because of my illness?"

He sits down next to her and takes her hand. "In this case my attraction is much more than that."

Evvie's heart flutters in her chest, and she suddenly regrets having lied to Philip about being ill. Her job was to find out if he was guilty. But what's she's sensing in this lovely man makes her want to blurt out the truth. That she's here under false pretenses. But something stops her.

Philip kisses her hand and looks deeply into her eyes. "It would break my heart to lose you."

TWENTY-FOUR:
BACK TO LANAI
GARDENS

Breakfast is a nightmare. I feel at a total loss. Everyone is talking about Evvie and Phil, even my moribund group. For a change they're not kvetching about their dead spouses and sad lives. Today it's "Who is she — that hussy in red?" "She's only here a couple of days and she acts like she owns the place."

And from the eager babbling of people at other tables, all of whom by now have noticed the absence of the new twosome, I conclude that they are the sole topic of breakfast conversation.

And we promised Hope Watson we would keep a low profile. Wait until the gossip mill reaches her ear; she's going to have a fit. I eat quickly and excuse myself. Since my sister has made it clear I'm not needed, I'm heading back to Lanai Gardens to check on my girls.

I park in a guest spot, since my old Chevy is in its own space, and head for the entrance to my building. I'll check the mail and then I'll listen to my answering machine. Maybe Jack called, I think, but in my heart I don't believe it.

"She's not there, she's here, stop dialing." I hear my cell phone ring just as I spy Bella hanging over the rail of her floor. Bella waves agitatedly to me. Then I see Ida come out of Bella's apartment. "Come up, hurry."

I cross the courtyard to the building opposite mine, where Evvie and Bella have their apartments, and hurry up the stairs. I'm too nervous to wait for the elevator.

Hy and Lola, who live next door to Bella, pop out of their place as soon as they hear our voices. Mister Buttinsky has to stick his two cents in. He announces excitedly, "Sophie's gone nutsoid." He whirls his finger around his head to make the point.

"What happened?" I ask the girls.

Hy insists on answering for them. "She called nine-one-one in the middle of the night."

Ida shakes a fist at him. "Shut up, yenta."

He shrugs. "I was only trying to be neighborly." With an injured last glance, he pushes Lola back into their apartment and slams the door behind him.

"That man," Ida says. "I wanna string him up from the lamppost."

"Never mind him. Tell me."

Bella is quivering. "We're just about to go to the hospital to visit her. Denny said he'd drive us."

"Well, I'm here, I'll drive. Let's go." As we hurry to the elevator, I say, "Talk."

Ida catches me up. "She called for an ambulance at two a.m. We didn't know. We didn't hear anything. When we got up everybody was phoning or knocking on our doors. We called the hospital. They said she was resting. She's not in intensive care, so they said we could come at visiting hours."

Denny is standing by his car. I thank him but tell him I'm driving over. He is as caring as ever. "I hope Miss Sophie is okay."

I indicate that Bella and Ida should get into my Chevy. It's closer than the Caddy.

"Where's Evvie?" Bella asks as I start to drive.

"She's very busy being a detective," I say in a very cool voice.

Ida is sharp. "You both met Philip?"

"You could put it that way. I'm here and she isn't. The red dress and boa did the trick. Get it?"

Ida's eyebrows rise. "I think so."

196

Bella looks puzzled but I don't bother to explain.

"Fill me in. What's been going on?" I ask.

Bella looks to Ida to do the explaining. "Where do I begin? A couple of days ago we all went for a walk. We get to that stop sign on the corner near Phase Three? And Sophie stops. We start to cross the street and she won't go. We tell her it's safe, no cars coming."

"She won't move. Like she was digging her heels into the cement."

"We ask her why," Ida continues. "She says she's waiting for the light to change. I had to tell her twice that it was a stop sign, not a light."

"How bizarre," I say, now really beginning to worry. I don't want to begin to think about how serious this might be.

Bella gets more excited. "Tell her about the ants. You know how Sophie hates ants in her kitchen. Or any bugs."

Ida shakes her head. "I get a hysterical phone call from her. She's screaming, 'Ants!' Bella was with me."

"We were playing gin rummy," Bella interrupts.

"We rush over to her apartment and she's standing in the corner of the kitchen whimpering and swatting newspapers at the walls.

"She kept telling us there were ants everywhere, but there weren't any."

Ida's eyes tear up. "It can't be the onset of . . ." She can't even say the word. *Alzheimer's.*

Since the hospital is literally across the street, we are there in one minute. We could have walked it, but with Bella and her arthritis, it would have taken twenty minutes. We hurriedly find out Sophie's room number, get visitor badges, and rush to her side as quickly as we can.

Sophie is not the put-together woman we know. She looks bedraggled and frightened. And suddenly old. She is trussed up to IVs and other paraphernalia.

"Why didn't you call us?" Ida demands. "We would have come with you."

Sophie starts to cry. "I don't know. I suddenly didn't remember your phone numbers."

Bella and Ida move closer, each taking a hand to hold.

I kiss her gently on the forehead. "Tell us what happened, why you called for help."

"I just woke up and I felt really bad."

"Where? Your heart?"

"I don't know. Everywhere. I just didn't feel like me. I thought I was going to pass out. Everything in my body was wrong, I

198

don't know! I was scared I was going to die. I didn't want to be alone." She starts to cry again, deep gasping sobs. I've never seen her like this before.

"Well, well, what have we here?" In struts her beloved doctor, Dr. Friendly, the one we call Dr. Strangelove behind his back. He gives me the creeps. He is short and humped and wears large round glasses with black frames. And he always looks like he needs a shave. He's mostly bald, but what few hairs he has left, he strings across the top of his head. What I hate the most is his smarmy smile. We move back from the bed, out of his way.

"Sorry I'm so late. Emergencies happen all the time around here."

With you as their doctor, I don't wonder. "What's wrong with her?"

"Well, we won't know until we take some more tests, will we?" He listens to her heartbeat, takes her blood pressure.

Oh yes, lots of tests, lots of expensive tests. "But what are her symptoms?"

"She doesn't seem to have any that I can tell. But I'm sure we'll get her back in shape, presto majesto, won't we, darling?" He smiles at Sophie and she tries a small brave smile back. "Meanwhile, I'm giving you a little anxiety reliever," he tells her as he makes another notation on her chart. "I don't want my big girl to be worried."

That's some great idea, I think, something to mask the real symptoms.

"She already takes ten pills every day," Ida says, with some anxiety of her own. "What's really wrong with her?"

"We're still working on that little mystery, aren't we? We have our cholesterol and our arrhythmia and our blood pressure and our weak bladder, our osteo, and our restless leg syndrome under control. Now let's see what's new."

He studies Sophie's face and asks, "What's this rash?" He checks her arms as he *tsk-tsk*s under his breath.

He briskly makes another notation on her chart and then pats Sophie's cheek. "We might add an antibiotic while we're at it."

She smiles wanly at him.

"Gotta go, others need me." With that, he trots out of the room like the white rabbit on his way to the Mad Hatter's tea party.

As soon as he leaves, Sophie's pathetic smile disappears and she sits there softly sobbing, clutching our hands, not wanting to let go.

"We have to call Jerome."

Ida agrees with me, but Bella shakes her

head back and forth. "She will be so mad if you bother him."

We are sitting in my kitchen having breakfast. When I arrived last night I quickly checked my messages. None from Evvie. I was hoping she'd realize I'd gone and she'd call.

Sophie's son, Jerome, the jeweler in Brooklyn, has always seemed self-centered to me. The few times she has asked for something from him, he gave it grudgingly or not at all. He never comes to visit, but sends flowers on her birthday and syrupy Mother's Day cards. Why am I sure he gets his wife to do it? "But he should know about this. Something is very wrong. Sophie has never been like this before. She seems so fragile."

"Maybe Dr. Strangelove is poisoning her," Ida snaps.

"What — and lose all the money she can still spend on him? I doubt he'd want to kill the fatted calf."

"You two are terrible," Bella says. "You are so disrespectful. Besides, Sophie is not fat."

"He doesn't deserve our respect. I still believe Jerome should be told."

Ida is worried. "Let's think this through. He might come down here and decide Soph should move up north to some assisted-living facility. He'll dump her in some awful place and forget about her. We'll never see her again."

This stops us. Finally Ida scribbles on a piece of paper. "Glad, you call him, and if he mentions most of these words I've written, then we're wasting our time."

I glance at the paper. She's written "Too busy to talk, maybe he should look into assisted living," "Can't get down right now, busy season," and "Keep an eye on her, call me later."

I look up Jerome's store number. Bella pours more tea and finds some stale Oreo cookies to give us strength.

I dial the number. Jerome answers. "Jerome, it's Gladdy Gold. I'm calling because your mom's in the hospital." I listen. "No, it doesn't seem too serious, but your mother needs some help. Perhaps you could come down for a few days and assess the situation." I nod at Ida and repeat what he's saying: "Oh, it's your busy season." Ida holds up one finger. "I think she needs a little support from her family." Again I repeat his answer for them: "You think she should be in assisted living?" Ida scowls and holds up two fingers. "But you can't be sure of that unless you come and see her. Oh, it's not possible for you to talk right now; we should just keep an eye on her. Yes, we certainly will do that."

I shrug and hang up. Ida holds up three fingers, wiggling them now. Bella is amazed. "You must have ESP," she tells her.

"No, I just know a lazy good-for-nothing son when I see one." Ida speaks from experience. Unfortunately.

The ball is back in our court. "We have to figure out what's wrong."

"What can we do?"

"First, give her lots of love and attention. And then, maybe we'll come up with something by ourselves."

Ida says, "We always do, don't we? After all, we only have one another."

TWENTY-FIVE:
TROUBLES

Conchetta and I sit in a cool spot behind the library on a couple of old patio chairs that have been there forever. It's her lunch break and we're catching up. She shakes her head as I tell her about Sophie and Dr. Strangelove. Sophie is home from the hospital now, but she doesn't seem like her old self. More head shaking as I tell Conchetta about Evvie becoming one of the rich people overnight and taking up with a potential murderer.

"Incredible." Her head is still shaking as I tell her that Jack and I no longer see each other. Jack's choice.

"No, not Jack! He loves you."

"Maybe so, but he's out of my life."

"*Madre mia!* And all that's happened this week?" she marvels as we sip water and fan ourselves with back-issue magazines left on the small patio. "Bet things were never this interesting in the years when you were a librarian."

"That's for sure," I say. "The plots were always in the books, not in my life. How's your family?"

"Pretty dull compared to your comings and goings. My sister, Nina, is pregnant again. The family is hoping for a boy after three girls."

"That's great."

"Never mind me. You seem so unhappy, *amiga.*"

"I'm miserable. I'm so tired of trying to take care of everyone and their problems. I guess I need somebody for me to lean on."

She angles her ample shoulder toward me. "This one's available."

I take her up on her offer. I lean into her and we sit that way quietly for a few moments, listening to the sounds of ducks in the near distance. All the houses in this neighborhood back onto canals. And ducks are ever-present.

Conchetta breaks the silence. "Let me quote my uncle Paco. No matter what's wrong, he always says get a second opinion. The car won't work, the mechanic wants to bill you five hundred bucks for a valve job. Paco's advice: Get another opinion. Sophie's doctor is a quack at best, so get . . ."

I finish it for her. "Another opinion."

"Yes. And this case of yours, ditto. Evvie is not thinking clearly right now. Discuss it with someone who's not emotionally involved."

"You're on a roll. And Jack?"

"That's a puzzle. I think you need to wait until you see him again. And you will. He's a good man. He wouldn't want to make you unhappy."

"He already has. Guess there's no statute of limitations on getting dumped no matter how old you are."

More sitting quietly. A gaily colored kite appears, flying lazily above us. Then it disappears over the palm trees. "Conchetta, lately I've been thinking of our old group. When Francie was still alive, when Millie didn't have Alzheimer's. Sandy and Joan hadn't moved back north. You were always the baby in the group among us old bags. Remember the fun we had?"

"Sure do. The concerts we went to, the lectures, the crazy Bollywood movies from India that we loved."

"What I liked best about them is the way hundreds of people would just appear and sing and dance regardless of the plot."

I'm starting to feel better already. I start to giggle.

"And the wild parties we had for the

Oscars when we dressed up as characters from the nominated movies. Remember when you came as Darth Vader and your pants dropped off when you and Sandy were having a sword fight?"

Now Conchetta is giggling as well.

"Oh, what about election nights? The screaming and throwing popcorn at the TV set every time you-know-who captured a state."

She hits me playfully on the shoulder. I hit back.

"Please don't remind me. Millie, Sandy and Joan, and Francie tap-dancing to that song they wrote called 'Chads: Dimples, Hanging, and Preggy.' Silliness like that. Don't get me started on stuffing ballot boxes."

I laugh out loud. It's the first time in a while. How nice to be spending a relaxing time with a friend. "We don't have much fun anymore. No, I shouldn't say that. You and your family still laugh a lot."

"You don't hear us when we discuss Cuba."

"I feel discombobulated. I want to go back when we were all together."

"Not going to happen, *pobrecita.* You have to make do with what is. As you very well know."

"Remember Francie always saying carpe diem? Seize the day!"

"Yeah, and she was right. Take every day and make it count."

"And she did. Every day was to be lived to the fullest for Francie. Now she's gone —"

Barney pops out of the back door. "School bus with a zillion noisy teenagers. Help!" He hurries back inside.

We get up, stretch. "I feel like I'm one hundred years old," I say.

"Me, too, and I'm only thirty-eight."

We laugh and hug each other and I feel a little better.

That afternoon I drive back to Wilmington House in Alvin's Caddy. I feel like a yo-yo. I almost forgot to change cars. Can you imagine the looks I'd get from the attendants if I accidentally drove the old Chevy up to the entrance?

Ida will keep an eye on Sophie and report to me. This is difficult. I feel I need to be in both places and it's not possible. My priority right now is finding out what Evvie is up to.

Of course, that might not be so easy. When I go upstairs, Evvie is not in her room. Where has my sister gone now?

Twenty-Six:
The Pond

They are the only ones near the pond. Philip has picked out a solitary spot where they won't be seen easily from the path. Evvie sits on the grass at the edge, letting her bare feet dangle in the cool water. Philip is at her side, holding her hand. She wears a lovely pale yellow, strapless sundress. Her matching sandals lie nearby. As she leans toward him, a small bottle of pills drop out of the pocket of her dress. He quickly reaches for them before they roll down into the water.

"Oh, goodness, I forgot my pills."

He hands her a bottle of water and then examines the medications container. "There's no label."

Gently pulling the container away from him, she thinks quickly. She could tell him the truth, that the pills are vitamins, but then why carry those, when she supposedly has a life-threatening illness? "I always carry them in a small bottle instead of dragging the larger one they came in."

"What are you taking?" She hesitates. He smiles and reaches into his jacket and pulls out a bottle as well. He winks. "You tell me yours, I'll tell you mine."

Evvie tries to remember what Sophie takes for her heart. "Dijoxin." She takes one pill out and swallows it with water, then puts the bottle back in her pocket. Playfully, she reaches for his bottle. She has to divert him. She hopes he doesn't know that Sophie's pill is white and quite small, unlike the large gray vitamin.

"It's Vicodin."

"I've heard of it. What's it for?"

"Migraines. I've had them all my life."

"Oh, you poor dear, they must be painful."

"Yes, they are." He lookes at her bottle again. "Is that all you take? Just the one? What exactly is your condition?"

Her mind is working as fast as it can. "I have my other pills in the morning." She reaches for his hand again. "It's such a beautiful day; let's not waste it on depressing subjects. We'll start to sound like really old people who only want to talk about their illnesses."

"You are right, my dear." He kisses her hand, and looking deep into her eyes, he recites, " 'Dost thou love life? Then do not squander time, for that's the stuff life is made of.' Ben Franklin."

Evvie rallies. She can handle this. "How about, 'Gather ye rosebuds while ye may. Old Time is still a-flying.' Robert Herrick."

He continues it. " 'And this same flower that smiles today, tomorrow will be dying.' "

It's a strange moment. Evvie is sorry she chose that poem; she had forgotten those next chilling lines, yet Philip seems pleased. How charming that he loves poetry as much as she does. It was poetry that got her through the lonely years at school when she felt so awkward and unattractive. And when she wasn't reading poetry, she was acting. Her shy, real self would disappear while playing the wonderful parts onstage. Cruel queens, famous heroines, and gorgeous debutantes: that's when Evvie came alive. On the stage. But it all came to nothing, Evvie thinks bitterly. Her parents had forbidden her to pursue a theater career. She was expected to pick some neighborhood boy and get married.

Philip leans closer to her, his lips nearly touching hers again. She pulls away slightly. Being outdoors makes her nervous. What if someone should come along? She has to change the mood. "You have such a beautiful voice, Philip. Did you ever have professional training?"

"No, my dear, these are the affectations of English private schools. Or as they call them, public schools." This time he kisses her lips gently.

Footsteps crunch along the nearby path and Evvie instinctively pulls away.

Twenty-Seven: The Busybody

It takes me a while, but finally I find Evvie sitting on the grass next to the pond. I hurry toward her, and then stop when I realize she is not alone. She is with Philip. They are holding hands and looking longingly at each other. Evvie is wearing another expensive-looking new outfit, something sexier than the clothes we originally bought.

I hesitate. Part of me doesn't want to intrude. The more sensible part says this is a job and I'd better check up on my assistant. I pretend to be strolling and just happen to see the happy couple. Now I get to play the hypocrite.

"Evelyn. Philip. Hello, there." My voice is an octave higher than normal. I am fairly trilling. Evvie startles and, caught off guard, throws me a dirty look. Philip immediately stands up, dusts his pants, and breaks out the charm.

"Gladys Gold," I say quickly, before he

realizes he's never seen me before. "We met Saturday night. At the mixer."

Naturally, he won't admit he doesn't recognize me. "But of course," he says. "Though it was rather crowded."

"Yes, wasn't it? But such fun."

He gazes down at Evvie. "It certainly was."

Luckily there is a bench right next to them, so I perch at the edge. If I sat down on the grass, I'd never be able to pull myself up. I indicate Philip should sit again, but he doesn't. "Don't let me disturb you," I babble on. "I didn't have a chance to tell you when we spoke that night, we had something in common."

"Really?" He is losing interest, but what I'm about to say should grab his attention.

"Oh, really?" Evvie adds, her voice like ice.

You, too, sister dear. This ought to teach you not to be so smart. "Yes, my niece, Myra, works at Grecian Villas. You know, she works for Mrs. Gordon, the manager? Myra told me so much about you."

There is the slightest twitch in his eyes, but he pretends delight. "Yes, of course I remember her. A lovely lady. Very kind."

My dear sister is sizzling. I can always tell when she is angry because her earlobes turn red. Evvie reaches out to Philip. "Philip, dear, we have to leave."

He gallantly helps her stand as I glare at Evvie from behind his back. *Don't you dare,* I mouth to her angrily.

Evvie, spiting me, puts her arm through his and starts to lead him away. "So sorry. We have an appointment," she says to me, ever so sweetly.

"Yes, we must hurry," Philip agrees.

As Evvie pulls him along, I stand and grab on to his other arm. "Yes, I must also. I'll walk back with you." Without missing a beat, I say, "So tragic about poor Mrs. Ferguson, wasn't it?"

His step falters momentarily. "Yes, indeed. She was a lovely lady."

He has a one-track mind, this Romeo. Everyone's such a lovely lady.

Philip picks up the pace. I wonder why. Can it be he doesn't want to discuss lovely, dead Esther Ferguson?

We reach the lobby. "Which way are you going, Gladys?" he asks. Whatever makes me think that if I say right, he'll be going left? "Oh, toward my room." I point with my right hand.

"Well, then we'll have to take leave of you." He fairly pushes Evvie toward the left. I grip his arm a little tighter and glare at Evvie.

"Have you ever seen that darling TV show where Donald Trump tries to hire an assistant?" Evvie knows it very well. She loves that show. "Isn't it funny when he looks straight at the poor loser and says real loud, 'You're fired'?"

Get it, *Evelyn*? You're fired.

With that I let go of Philip's arm. That should leave them both reeling. I wonder what lies he'll tell Evvie about Grecian Villas. Assuming she'll speak to me again and let me know what he said. I've learned one thing about him. He doesn't want anyone to know about his past. If he is really guilty, he must assume no one has figured it out or they'd be after him by now. Lighting this match under him should get some results. He'll be very wary of me. We'll see.

And hey, sis — I hope you got my message.

Twenty-Eight:
Sophie

Back again. Caddy to Chevy-land to check on how Sophie is doing and maybe see if there's anything new on the Peeper situation. Who am I kidding? After that awful scene with Evvie and Philip yesterday, I need to go to my own home once more. I need to be where I feel I am myself and not some interloper.

I quickly check my machine for messages. Nothing, as usual, from Jack. I sigh. So near and yet so far. I won't leave a message for him. I cannot bring myself to call and be rejected again.

In fact, there is only one message. From Alvin Ferguson. From earlier today.

I call him back. Unfortunately, he's not home and I get Shirley.

"Hi, Mrs. Ferguson," I say cheerily. "Alvin called. What's going on?"

Her tone is colder than an ice pick at the North Pole. "We checked online. Quite a few charges you've already piled up on your house account. You must like that fancy hotel we're keeping you in. Living high off the hog, are we?"

I suddenly have a picture in my mind of Evvie's new clothes. I try to bluff. "I thought we were keeping expenses down."

"Well, the boutique at Wilmington House certainly likes your business. Couldn't you find a less expensive place to shop? Like Wal-Mart? Or Cheap Haircuts?"

I gulp. "We did buy most of our outfits at a thrift shop."

"Three hundred and fifty dollars for a yellow cotton sundress? Matching sandals, one hundred and five. Jogging outfit, one hundred and twenty-five. And there's more. Thank goodness you only bought one of each. And what about that expensive hair coloring?"

I'm dancing as fast as I can. "Look, these items were bought because we needed them in a hurry. I assure you" — another gulp — "that won't happen again."

"I certainly hope not. My husband isn't made of money, you know. He just acts like it. And what progress have you made?"

I try to be polite. Not easy with that scratchy smoker's voice grating like chalk on a blackboard. "Quite a bit. We've hardly been there a week, but we are in constant contact with Philip Smythe." No lie here, I think. "We're trying to work our way into his confidence."

That's for sure. At least one of us is.

"Just remember. No more big-ticket items." With that, Shirley hangs up on me.

Thanks a lot, Evvie.

I fill Ida and Bella in on the latest news over dinner in Ida's apartment. Sophie is too tired and listless to join us. I don't elaborate on Evvie's behavior toward me. I keep it light. "Since Evvie's made the first contact, she's the one who's taking the first steps with Philip."

Ida is no fool. "Yes, I'm sure that red dress and the boa made quite a splash. Tell me more about that. And what do you do while she's interrogating Philip?"

"Not too much," I admit.

I feel I need to protect Evvie. Ida, sensing my reluctance, doesn't ask any more questions. Bella only wants to know all about the fancy clothes everybody wears. I neglect to tell her that our Evvie is wearing some of the most expensive items of all.

Neither one of them mentions one word about Jack. Either they're being tactful or nothing's going around on the grapevine, like maybe that Jack's been seen with another woman? Stop that, I tell myself.

I spend a restless night back in my own condo. I can't stand the idea of being at Wilmington House right now. I am in no mood to keep playing rich widow. I'd rather be in my own home where I belong, yet I want to know what's going on back there with my badly behaving sister. And this case that's turning sour. My sister has upset me so much, I can't think clearly. She's blurred our plans by getting involved with Philip directly. Is she onto something with Philip, or is she thoughtlessly just having a fling? I want to tell Evvie about Sophie, but I will not call her. Let her realize I'm gone and she'll phone me at some point.

Or will she? I'm a wreck. Somehow everything's gone bad since we took the Ferguson job. I'd like to call Alvin Ferguson up and quit. Shirley would be happy, I'll bet.

Instead, I try to catch up on my crossword puzzles until my eyes close. I can't remember the last time I felt so stressed.

I wake up to the bell ringing and a pounding on my door. My clock tells me it's only seven a.m. I want to pull the pillow over my head. I had a terrible sleepless night, but I know I have to answer.

Ida and Bella peer through my screen door. They look frantic.

"What?"

"It's Sophie. Throw something on and get over there. Quick."

We each have keys to one another's doors in case of emergencies. I hurry to Sophie's apartment. Ida and Bella remain outside, which surprises me.

From inside, I hear singing — or is it shrieking?

" 'Some enchanted eveninggggg . . .' "

"That's Sophie?"

Bella nods. "I called this morning to find out how she was feeling. No answer. I knocked on the door. And heard strange noises. So I used my key. What I saw made me hurry back out again."

"What's going on?"

" 'Youuuu might meet a strangerrrr . . .' "

"Wait," says Ida. "You need to see for yourself."

We walk into Sophie's apartment to find her in the kitchen. She wears a pink bra and panties and black socks. And a cowboy hat. I have no idea where she got that hat from.

She sees us and gives us a big grin, a rather bizzare sight considering that she is stuffing her mouth with food. The refrigerator door is wide open. The small dinette table next to her is covered. Potato chips. Cookies. Rice Krispies. Ding Dongs. Doughnuts. Crackers and much more. Most of the packages are open.

Coyly, as if we were playing a game, she giggles and scampers away from us. We follow her into her bedroom. And watch incredulously as she jumps onto her bed and starts hopping up and down, singing again at the top of her voice. In between giggling. And falling and then picking herself up.

" 'Home, hooooome on the range. Where the deer and the buffalo roooooam,' " belts Sophie.

Her immaculate bedroom is a mess. Pillows and blankets on the floor. Clothes tossed out of her closet. And more opened packages of food on her bed. Looks like all her shoes are lined up along one wall. Lined up, I notice, by color.

"What is she doing?" Bella clings to Ida's arm.

Ida shakes her head. "I have no idea."

Sophie waves to us. "Jump in. The water's fine."

"Are you all right?" Actually, I don't know what to ask her. She seems very happy. And energetic. And crazy.

"Of course I'm all right." She plops down

on the mattress, legs splayed and a dopey expression on her face. I swear she looks like she's drunk. I don't see any liquor or wine bottles around. And besides, Sophie never drinks.

New song. " 'Oh, I danced with a dolleeee with a hole in her stockin' . . .' " She becomes confused. "What's the next line?"

Bella actually answers. " 'And her toes kept a-rockin . . .' "

Now Sophie and Bella are doing a duet. " 'And her knees kept a-knockin'.' "

Ida punches Bella. She shuts up, mortified.

I search Sophie's bedside table. "Check all the medications."

Ida moves to her dresser. Bella goes into her bathroom.

Sophie thinks it's a new game and she hops off the bed and tiptoes behind Ida. Ida looks at her, shaking her head in wonder.

"Here's her Lasix and her Zocur." Ida lifts them up. Sophie tries to grab them. Ida is faster and slips them into her pocket. Sophie sulks. Then she tiptoes into the bathroom after Bella.

In her side table drawer, I find her Sular and Cipro.

Bella reports from the bathroom. "Here's Requip and Cannibals."

"Give me that," Sophie yelps.

Cannibals?

Sophie runs after Bella as she hurries out of the bathroom waving the pills up high. Sophie is pulling on Bella's T-shirt.

Ida looks at the frantic Bella. "Did you say cannibals?"

"Help me," Bella cries as she throws the pill bottles at us before Sophie can reach them.

I catch one. Ida, the other. Sophie starts toward me. "Sophie. Sit!" I demand.

She immediately drops down to the rug, pouting. She turns her back on us and faces her lined-up shoes, muttering at them.

I am astounded. It's an unmarked bottle with only the label *Cannabis* on it. "She's got cannabis!"

"I knew a cannibal couldn't fit in that little bottle. What's that?" Bella asks.

"Pot! Marijuana! She's stoned!"

Bella is surprised at my knowledge. "How do you know stuff like that?"

Ida, droll, answers her. "Gladdy reads a lot of books."

I sit on the floor next to her. "Sophie, honey, where did you get these pills?"

She is pointing and naming her shoes. "Blackie. Brownie. Whitie, Reddie . . ."

I gently take hold of her arms to get her

224

attention. "Who gave this to you?"

She squints to see the word, then smiles. "Dr. Friendly."

Why am I not surprised? "But there's no pharmacy label."

She grins lopsidedly. "That's because he gave me his samples. 'Cause I'm his favorite patient. And I like it so much, I used them *all* up."

Ida looks puzzled. "I didn't know pot was legal as medicine in Florida."

"It's not. As far as I can recall."

Sophie leans over and puts her head in my lap. " 'Cause he likes me." She grins up at me. "He says the laws are stupid. He knows better."

Ida is furious. "He should be arrested."

Bella is worried. "Is Soph a drug addict?"

"Sophie. Look at me." It's not easy keeping her attention. Her head is weaving back and forth. "Why did he give you these pills?"

"For glaucoma."

"You don't have glaucoma."

"I told him my eyes were burning."

Ida paces in a frenzy. "That's it. That quack is going down! He's a dead duck. No more Sophie in his stable."

The metaphors are mixed, but she's got the right idea. "First question is — how do we get her down from her high?"

Ida has an idea. "We call Eddie at the pharmacy." Our local pharmacist is a whiz at answering medical questions when we can't reach our doctors. Which is usually the case.

Much later, when Sophie is back to herself, more or less (we leave her looking at her lineup of shoes, perplexed), we decide we have to do something now. It's time to get her to a new doctor. And fast.

We each have doctors we like and respect.

Ida suggests we call all of them up. "First one who will see us, gets us."

TWENTY-NINE:
DOCTORS, GAMES,
GRIEF, AND HOPE

Ida won. She managed to get us an appointment with her doctor for two days after she called. Unheard of. Though she did say it was a personal emergency that had to be dealt with immediately.

The four of us sit in Dr. Reich's waiting room in his office on University Avenue. I am running on fumes with so little sleep last night; we've all been taking turns watching Sophie since she came down from her high. But Ida is perky and determined. She has a cause and it's invigorating her.

Bella was reluctant to come with us because she'd seen enough doctors, thank you, she didn't need to look at another one. But then she decided it was right that she help solve Sophie's problem.

Sophie looks disoriented. And sullen. She doesn't know where she is but she suspects it will not please her. Apparently she also had tranquilizers in her kitchen drawer. Our pharmacist looked up her record and he's the one who knew about them. He suggested she take one. It's calmed her down, but she still seems in a daze over what's happened to her.

When the doctor finally enters, I am surprised at Ida's choice. Dr. Reich is young, thin, and sprightly. She explains he took over when her original doctor died and she has no complaints, pun intended. He is good enough.

Dr. Reich is pleased to see Ida. And surprised, since she had her annual checkup two months ago. She would not tell his nurse when she made the appointment why she was coming to see him. And he is further surprised to see that she arrived with three other women.

"The situation was too complicated to explain on the phone," Ida says as she introduces us to him and we all take seats in his private office. "We're here on behalf of our friend, Sophie here, who is in serious medical trouble."

Sophie here scowls with displeasure.

"She doesn't have a doctor of her own?"

"Yes, I do." Her voice is whiny to say the least.

I take over, hoping I can be tactful enough. "She does, but her doctor doesn't seem to be helping, and she's getting worse."

Dr. Reich tries to stop me. "This isn't quite ethical."

I interrupt him. "Please just hear us out —"

Bella jumps in. "We're not even talking lawsuits."

Ida pleads, "It will never go further than this room. We need your help."

For a moment he shifts his eyes from us and looks over at the very agitated Sophie while he toys with a letter opener on his desk. We wait. Finally he looks back at us and nods.

I continue, "Every time she sees him, he orders batteries of tests and comes up with a new disease and new drugs. Right now she is being treated for high blood pressure, high cholesterol, arrhythmia, restless leg syndrome, tension, glaucoma, and a rash, to name just a few."

Bella nudges Ida. "Show him the medications."

Dr. Reich holds up his hands, a stopping gesture. "Ida, I'm not comfortable with this."

"We won't be here long enough to make you too uncomfortable. Honest." Ida reminds him that she's never been a complainer before.

Bella puts her two cents in. "We're uncomfortable enough for you. So you don't have to be."

Maybe a little too dramatically, Ida upends her purse and all the pill bottles drop out. I take the list out of my pocket and read, "Vasotec, Lasix, Coreg, Plavix, Zocur, Klonopin, Dijoxin, Sular, Cipro, Requip, and amoxicillin."

Bella chimes in. "And her leg isn't restless anymore, but her whole body is a nervous wreck."

Ida adds, "And the rash went away the next day so it probably had been a heat rash or just nervousness, but he still insists she keep taking the antibiotic."

By now we have the doctor's full attention. He reads the dosage from each bottle, making notes on his pad. His brow is furrowing up a storm. "Rather alarmingly high dosages."

And now I get dramatic. I hold the bottle up. "Oh, and her cannabis."

His eyes widen. I hand him the bottle. "You know this is against the law?"

Ida nods. "Yes, we do."

"We think she needs a new doctor," I add.

Sophie moans. "I do not."

Dr. Reich takes a book from his desk and looks something up. Then he leans over to

Sophie, who cringes. He speaks quietly and kindly. "Mrs. Meyerbeer, you should stop the Cipro and the Requip. They are fighting each other and may be causing some of the problems you are having. I suggest you get in touch with a psychopharmacologist to help you with those dosages. You keep on like this, there can be liver damage."

Sophie refuses to listen; she shakes her head from side to side in denial.

I add, "She had a terrible reaction to the cannabis last night."

"I'm not surprised. Especially with every-thing else she's taking." He doesn't take his eyes off Sophie, who glares at him.

Ida is furious. "That doctor should be disbarred."

Sophie jumps up. "Don't you dare tell him his name. You'll get him in trouble!"

Dr. Reich stands and gently takes her hands in his. "Mrs. Meyerbeer, listen. I truly believe you need a second opinion about what is wrong with you and what medica-tions you need to take. It doesn't have to be me. I can give you a list of doctors to choose from. But you must see someone else."

Ida piles all the pills back in her purse, but Dr. Reich keeps the pot. "I don't think you need these."

Bella giggles. Everyone glances toward

her. "But she was funny when she was on them."

Dr. Reich opens his door. Sophie rushes out like the devil is after her. Ida shakes the doctor's hand. "Thanks, Dr. Reich. Don't worry. We've never been here."

His answer is a shake of the head and a cynical smile. We say our good-byes and hurry to catch up with Sophie.

On the drive home, Sophie keeps smacking the back of my seat. "I won't."

Ida says, "You will."

Sophie says, "I won't."

Bella says, "You better or we won't talk to you anymore."

Sophie scrunches up her eyes. "Why won't you talk to me anymore?"

"Because you'll be dead. Because your liver will shrivel up and turn into chopped liver. And after you're gone I'll take all your clothes and keep them because you won't need them where you're going." Bella sits back, satisfied with her reasoning.

There is silence for a moment, and then Sophie sighs. "All right. I'll go see another doctor. But you stay away from my closet."

That's one fire put out. Hopefully we'll get a break in the Peeper case soon. I have the feeling the answer is right in front of my nose? And I'm just not seeing it!

■ ■ ■ ■

The next day, once again this yo-yo heads back up north for yet another hourly drive. Ida and Bella have Sophie well in hand; it's time I head back to Rich People Land and see what my dear sister has been up to. Good thing Alvin Ferguson is the one paying those high gas prices for his Caddy, and not me.

THIRTY:
PLAYTIME AT THE POOL

Evvie smiles, seeing the mob scene at the pool. Although the pool is Olympic-sized and exquisitely and expensively tiled, it is a rare occurrence when more than a dozen or so people use it.

Today is different, Evvie thinks gleefully. The Most Watched Couple — Philip and Evvie — is making an appearance, jauntily dressed in matching swimsuits and sun hats. They've kept to themselves the past couple of days, and among the catty remarks they've heard made by some jealous women is that they are antisocial. Philip insists they make friends. Evvie would rather stay by themselves, but he has a point. Better to get them on our side, she thinks.

So today they're at the pool. They take off their matching tops, kick off their matching flip-flops, and wade in. Philip splashes and Evvie giggles — like teenagers in love.

Word goes around fast and soon there are

other swimmers hopping into the pool. And more sightseers turn up to catch the action.

Evvie glances up and sees Hope Watson at her office window, watching the tableau unfolding before her, her eyes like slits as she gnashes her teeth. Eat your heart out, Hope, she wants to say.

Leaders that they are, Philip and Evvie get the swimmers involved in the kids' game of Marco Polo, in which whoever is "it" closes his or her eyes and tries to catch players by the sound of their voices. There is much splashing and laughing, making everyone feel young again. And there's plenty of kibitzing from the observers who have gathered around the pool.

A thought pops into Evvie's head. She remembers Myra and Mrs. Gordon commenting that Philip made friends with all the women at Grecian Villas and Esther Ferguson wasn't jealous. But Evvie shrugs it off; that has nothing to do with her.

The women may be envious, but they recognize that being in Philip and Evvie's shadow adds excitement to their lives.

Fun, yes. And scandal, too. For when Philip is "it" and he hears Evvie call out, he manages to grab her and pull her under the water for a tad too long. When they come up for air they're grinning sheepishly.

Evvie looks up again just in time to see Hope Watson pulling her blinds closed. The expression on her face is one of obvious disgust. Evvie laughs out loud. It's what I've always dreamed of, Evvie admits to herself. I'm finally the star!

THIRTY-ONE: MORE GRIEF

After the Wilmington House attendant takes the Caddy, I am heading inside when I encounter Anna Kaplan, Lorraine Sanders, and Seymour Banks, my dining room companions, coming out. A vintage Lincoln is waiting with the door open. I guess it belongs to one of them.

"Where are you going? To a funeral?" I ask, noting their black outfits.

They look at me, chagrined.

Seymour answers. "We're going to the cemetery to visit our spouses."

Oops. That was a faux pas. "Sorry. The clothes threw me off."

Lorraine gives me a disdainful look. "To show our respect."

I am curious. "How often do you visit?" I say it reverently, hoping that will get me past my nosiness.

"Once a month," she tells me.

"What do you do when you come back?"

Anna is annoyed. "Why are you asking these questions?"

I backtrack. "I'm a widow, too. What you do interests me."

Anna is somewhat mollified. "We don't do anything. We have our meals and then the rest of our time we stay in our rooms. The day is spent in mourning." Her eyes tear up.

With that, Seymour helps the sad-faced women into the Lincoln.

As they drive off, I hear Lorraine say, "What nerve!"

I deserve that. But it gives me an idea.

I can't find Evvie anywhere, so I decide to chat with Hope Watson about my ideas for my tablemates. I find her in her office reading reports.

At the sight of me, she is even cooler than usual, if that's possible. Her arms immediately cross.

I won't dawdle. I get right to the point before she throws me out. "Listen, Hope, I am sitting with three people at my table who are still in mourning for their spouses after a very long time. They seem very sad and very lonely. I would like to help them somehow. I know you include medical services. Do you use any out-of-house psychological clinic that does grief therapy? It's so wasteful that they don't allow any joy in their lives."

I wait a moment as Hope looks at me incredulously. "*This* is what you came to talk to me about? About people you hardly know, who mean nothing to you? Not about your so-called case? I cannot believe you stand there and want to play social worker. You want to talk about grief? I'll give you grief."

Uh-oh, here it comes. I brace myself.

"Let's talk about your sister. And her outrageous behavior." Her hands move as if they have a life of their own. She rearranges folders on her desk. Moves pens around. Lines up papers. "What about your promises?" She mimics Evvie. " 'We'll be like little mice,' said your promiscuous sister. 'You'll hardly even know we're here'!"

She laughs harshly. "Hah! She's turned our lovely home into a circus. Everyone's in turmoil."

It's better than sitting around half-dead. I think it but don't say it.

"Blatantly carrying on with that man."

"*Blatantly* is a harsh word, Hope. Surely you exaggerate?"

"You call hugging and kissing in front of everyone not blatant? Or playing hide-and-seek, running around the lobby like naughty children? Or sitting at the piano, with him singing love songs to her, and touching each other."

He can play the piano and touch? Very ambidextrous. Frankly, I'm as mortified as she is, but I have to defend my sister.

"Hope, don't forget we're undercover here. She's playing a part."

Hope stands and fidgets with her collar as if it were choking her. "Undercover! Yes, indeed, under the *covers with him.* Disgraceful. Ladies don't behave that way."

She walks me to the door and opens it. "Your sister is a slut! What have you got to say now, Mrs. Gold?"

Oy. There's only one way out for me. "So, what about it, Hope? Any psychologists you can recommend for bereavement counseling?"

Her mouth drops open. She's speechless. She hurries to her desk and pulls a card from her Rolodex. And shoves it at me. Then shuts the door in my face. There is one thing I've learned about people like Hope Watson: startle her, shock her, and she withers away into submission.

When this is over, my sister is going to owe me big.

■ ■ ■ ■

It's a few hours later, and I've been pacing in the hallway outside my apartment. From a window I see Philip loading two small suitcases into his trunk. Can Evvie be far behind? I race down the flight of stairs and hurry outside. And there she is, putting a small makeup bag in the trunk. And wearing yet another new outfit. Yikes! I have to stop her before she buys out that shop. Single-handedly she's supporting the boutique. Their number-one customer.

Evvie is obviously startled to see me.

"Hi, Philip. Hi, Evelyn. Going on a trip?"

At least she has the decency to blush.

"Just a short one." Evvie busies herself by spreading her new cashmere sweater over the passenger seat.

I assume my annoying, seemingly clueless, simpering persona. "North, east, south, or west?"

Philip closes the trunk. "Can't tell. It's a surprise."

I glare at Evvie. "How nice for you. May I have a private moment?"

She wants a private moment like she wants the heartbreak of psoriasis. But she does step away. Not too far, in case she

241

needs to beat a hasty retreat.

I run my fingers over the shoulder of the gorgeous two-piece beige linen dress she's wearing. "Lovely, simply lovely," I say for Philip's benefit. Then I whisper in her ear. "Shirley Ferguson is having a conniption about how much you're spending on clothes. So cut it out! This is not a Hollywood movie. You don't get to keep the wardrobe."

She pulls away from me and whispers, "All right, but keep your voice down."

"There's a lot going on at home. Don't you even want to know about your friends? Sophie, especially."

"Of course I do, but not now." She can barely stand next to me. She wants desperately to move away. I try to hold her with my stare.

"When?"

"I don't know."

Philip beckons her. "We have a bit of a time pressure here," he calls out.

Evvie starts to move, but I grab her wrist. "Do you know what you're doing, sis?"

"More than I ever did in my whole damn life." She looks at me defiantly.

I'm trying to keep my voice down, but it isn't easy. "You are way far out of line."

Evvie pulls away. "Nice chatting with you,

Gladys. See you around."

She sprints away from me and gets into the scarlet red Mercedes convertible. She ties a scarf around her hair and beams a large toothy smile at her Romeo. Still working on the case, is she? And off they go, who knows where. Am I just a wee bit jealous? You bet I am. I was once on a surprise trip. Was it only about a month ago? And I blew it.

I decide to have lunch, because right now I don't know what else to do. There aren't many people in the dining room. Not for lunches. Residents usually take day trips or eat in their compact kitchenettes in their apartment suites.

However, my erstwhile eating companions are present. Drenched in their usual gloomy silence. They each have a book propped up in front of them. Don't they ever have a conversation about anything? I sit down and greet them. They murmur back.

"So, what's everyone reading?"

Seymour holds his paperback up. *Organizing Your Garage.*

Hmmm. Perfect reading for someone who no longer has a garage.

"Anna?"

"It's a cookbook." *Recipes for Eating Alone.*

For someone who eats with a mob every day, but might as well be eating alone, for all she notices. "Lorraine?"

"*The Fungus Among Us*. As if it's any of your business. Why do you insist on interrogating us? You some kind of spy or something?"

Good guess, Lorraine. I almost start to laugh at that one, but her face remains serious. I hope the book isn't about foot diseases. "Really, what's it about?"

"Searching for mushrooms in forests."

Wow. Talk about not living in the here and now. How can they stand the excitement? This won't get me anywhere. I make another attempt. "Seen any good movies lately?" I'm almost afraid of what they'll come up with.

Seymour answers without looking up. "They showed the Hepburn-Tracy one the other night. But I saw it when it played originally. So, I didn't bother."

"I don't go to romance movies. They always make me cry," Anna contributes.

Lorraine ignores me this time.

I play with my roll, pinching it into tiny pieces, as I think of an approach to this grim threesome. I try to read their personalities. It isn't easy. They don't talk all that much unless it's about missing their dead spouses.

I look over to Evvie's table. Of course she

244

isn't there. I try not to wonder where she and Philip have gone.

Suddenly I remember a TV movie some years back called *Queen of the Stardust Ballroom*. I decide to try that tack. I ask if anyone remembers it. "With that lovely actress Maureen Stapleton."

Lorraine, annoyed, shakes her head. Seymour says its sounds like a female-type movie; he never saw those, only his wife watched.

Not surprisingly, Anna did. "Isn't that the one about the woman who goes dancing in that famous dance hall in New York and wins a contest?"

Success. "Yes, that's the one. She was a widow just hanging around feeling sorry for herself, and someone suggested that she should go dancing." I smile meaningfully. "And she meets a man and falls in love again. They have a wonderful time dancing. And together they win a contest and she is named queen of that ballroom."

Lorraine looks up from her book. "Now I remember. She goes home that night and drops dead of a heart attack." She smirks.

Oops. I forgot that part. "But she dies happy," I say lamely. Since I have their attention for a moment, I don't intend to lose it. "That wasn't the point. She realized that as long as she was still alive, there was a life to lead. New adventures. New feelings. Isn't it better than shutting oneself off, just letting time go by and not getting the most out of one's life?"

Losing them again. New tack. I guess it's time to get personal. "I was widowed, too. I lost so much time when I was wrapped up in my own grief. I wasted all those years and I'm sorry now that I did."

That holds their interest, somewhat. I reach into my purse and take out the card Hope Watson gave me and place it on the table. "I have the name of a grief therapist nearby. Maybe it's something the three of you should consider."

That really gets their attention. And with it, finally, emotions. Though not what I might wish for. They react as if I tossed a rattlesnake on the table.

"What?" Seymour looks confused, his eyes darting every which way, as if he should make a run for an exit.

Anna's eyes widen. "What has this got to do with me?"

Lorraine slams her book shut. "You are so nosy! What business is it of yours how we spend our time?"

"I'm sorry. I know I'm intruding, but I just hate seeing you sad and living in the past. You're still here and you hopefully have many years more; why not enjoy them? Surely you don't think your loved ones would want you to mourn away the rest of your lives? They'd want you to be happy."

Oh, boy, I am not handling this right. The three of them freeze. Confusion from Seymour, fear from Anna, anger from Lorraine.

Finally, their strongest member, Lorraine, says with a voice of steel, "I think you might consider changing tables. Perhaps you'll find personalities more suitable to yours elsewhere."

Dead silence. I've only had my salad, and I *was* looking forward to the lamb cassoulet, but I think I've overstayed my welcome. My presence is no longer desired. And frankly, I've had it with them. I get up. "I'm truly sorry. I was only trying to help."

As I leave the dining room, I glance back at my now former table. I can't believe my eyes. They are having a heated discussion. Actually talking to one another. Well, maybe fury is better than boredom. Maybe getting mad at me put some excitement into their day.

I remind myself of that comic strip character from many years ago, Mary Worth, who stuck her nose in everybody's business. An irritating, sappy bore who spoke only in clichés and platitudes. Like me. Today.

Boy, did I hate her.

So what am I supposed to do around here if my "case" has left the premises?

Well, I know one thing I don't want to do is imagine what Evvie and "Romeo" are up to.

THIRTY-TWO:
FALLING IN LOVE
AGAIN

Evvie can't believe her luck. What a glorious day. And she's doing something she's never done before, even though she's lived in Florida for more than twenty years. She glances over at Philip, standing at the wheel of this obviously expensive yacht he's rented. He looks windswept and gorgeous as they glide down the Intracoastal Waterways — the ICW, as Philip calls them. The water seems like jade velvet. It couldn't be more perfect.

They pass one awesome waterfront mansion after another. Her jaw drops. It's amazing, the differences in the way people live in this state. Will she ever be content going back to Lanai Gardens after all this? A line from an old song flashes into her head: "How ya gonna keep 'em down on the farm, after they've seen Paree." Perhaps everything is going to change forever, now that Philip is in her life. For one brief moment, Evvie lets herself remember she's supposed to be on a case, that this man is suspected of murder. But she's sure now. She's spent enough time with him. He's kind and loving and cares about other people. She's watched for the red flag to come up and warn her, but he hasn't made a false move. This man could never hurt anyone. Alvin Ferguson is wrong. Now, all she has to do is convince Gladdy. Yes, she's been selfish and self-involved. But surely Gladdy can understand what it's like to be caught up in passion? She'll make it up to her once Gladdy understands that this man is a good man. A man Evvie now dreams she might spend the rest of her life with.

What a romantic. There's champagne; dinner is already on board, waiting to be heated later. Maybe much later, she grins to herself. We don't have to leave the ship, Philip tells her with a sexy, knowing look. It's as if she's living a dream. Seventy-three years old and she's never known such happiness before. And what feelings of love and passion! Never did she think she deserved such joy. From her lowly beginnings to this — she's come so far.

Philip smiles and waves to her. She waves back as she lounges in her deck chair sipping the champagne. Soon, she thinks languidly, soon, she'll be in his arms. With the waves rocking them into careless abandon.

She can hardly wait.

I can die after this, Evvie thinks to herself, and it would be all right. She is finally living the life she'd always dreamt of.

She shakes herself and laughs. What a silly, morbid thought.

Philip makes his way toward her. "Want to do some sightseeing? We could really play hooky and head down to the Keys. Maybe pull into a slip at the Ocean Reef Club near Key Largo."

She reaches up for his lips. "I don't need to see anything but the look in your eyes."

He pulls her close. "Ditto." He kisses her, hard. Breathless, they come up for air. "Evelyn, dearest, I can't wait any longer."

"Neither can I."

She feels as if she were in heaven already.

Thirty-Three: Grief Therapy

I can't believe this is happening to me. Here I am sitting in the car with — you'll never guess — three people who I didn't think would ever speak to me again. The gloomy threesome from dining room table number three.

I'm in Seymour's classic Lincoln and all four of us are on our way to our first Bereavement Group session. How did this happen? Amazingly, I did get through to them. Apparently, after some arguing and crying and insisting — how I would love to have been a fly on that wall — they decided I was right. Maybe they needed help. Maybe the old busybody had a point. They weren't having any fun.

But, as they told me, it was under one condition. Since I was also a widow, I had to go, too. Or else they wouldn't. For a moment, I was tempted to say I am not going and who cares, anyway, whether you do or not. But after all my hard work playing the insipid Mary Worth, it had worked. And after they acted upon my suggestion so fast, what else could I do? There was an opening the next day and they grabbed it. So, here I am, a very unwilling participant.

I remind myself that no good deed goes unpunished.

The therapy session is held in an ordinary room in a community center not far from town. Just plain wooden chairs in a circle. A wooden table holding tissues and water bottles. A chalkboard. On the board, these words are written:

NUMBNESS. DENIAL. ANGER. DEPRESSION. ACCEPTANCE.

The participants are all prowling the room like a pack of coyotes sniffing the air for garbage. No one looks anyone else in the eyes. I am the only one sitting.

Finally, a young woman walks in. A very young one. She looks about twelve in her bland clothes, rimless glasses, and mousy hair. She takes a deep breath. Pats her notebook for security. Why do I have the feeling this is her first group? Right out of college textbook time. "Hi, everybody. Let's all sit down. Okay?"

They take their time choosing seats. Measuring who will be seated on either side of them. My threesome sits next to one another. Misery loves company? Or safety in numbers? Our leader sits down next to me. No one else comes near us.

She smiles, a little nervously, I think. When everyone is settled, she begins. "Good morning. My name is Heather. I am your group leader. But you can call me Hetty."

Tight smiles appear at that. I almost expect her to say, *My name is Hetty. I am your server. And what do you want for breakfast?* Or maybe, *My name is Hetty. I am an alcoholic.*

"Let me share a few thoughts with you. First of all, this is a newly formed group, so we'll all be starting from the same point. I can imagine what pain you might be feeling, pain you suffer alone, but you'll find sometimes it's easier to talk to strangers.

"Always remember: You are not alone. You'll be sharing similar experiences and you'll find new friends here who become your support group. And the most important thing to know is everything said in this room is private. What we reveal to one another stays here."

A fifty-ish, husky man in a brown polyester

leisure suit with flamingoes on his shirt raises his hand. "Just like Vegas, huh?"

Slight laughter. Here we go. There's always one comedian in every bunch.

Brown Leisure Suit apologizes by making a zipping motion across his lips. There is busy straightening of chairs, a few coughs, and finally silence.

"Just a few ground rules before we start. Take turns. Don't interrupt. Be supportive and pay attention by using eye contact."

With that, everyone seriously looks around the room, making eye contact.

"Let's begin by introducing ourselves." She points to Anna. "Will you start?"

Need I say that my threesome is all dressed in black for the occasion?

Anna looks around like the kid in the class who hates to be called on first. She blurts it out fast. "My name is Anna. And my dead husband was Harry." She clamps her mouth shut and her eyes tear up.

Seymour, sitting next to her, assumes that's the pattern. "My name is Seymour and my dead wife was Sally."

Lorraine, stiff as ever, recites. "Lorraine. Jim."

Next to Lorraine is a rather large lady, redheaded, maybe in her sixties, wearing a bright green dress a tad too tight for her.

She sits with her hands cradled in her lap. "I'm Brenda. I lost my darling Arnold not three months ago." And the tears begin. The box of tissues is passed to her.

Leisure suit speaks up. "Frank. My loss was Gary."

There is a shifting of eyes. Embarrassed, but respectful. Hoping to show a nonjudgmental attitude — gay people can love, too.

Last and as far as I'm concerned least is me. What am I doing here? This is crazy. "Gladys. My husband's name was Jack." And what about the loss of my other love? My other Jack? Do I say Jack twice? Jack. Jack? Who shall I say I'm mourning? I feel so foolish here.

"Well done," says Hetty. "That was the easy part. What we want to do now is reach deep inside ourselves and speak out about our loved ones, identify our feelings toward them." She gets up and walks to the chalkboard. "These are the phases of grief you will go through." She points to the words already on the board. She repeats them: "Numbness, then Denial. Anger. Depression. And finally, Acceptance."

She looks at each of us to make sure we got that. "Our goal is to open up and share. So take a few moments and revisit your memories, and our next step will be to verbalize our feelings through our memories. I'd like us to create an atmosphere of trust, where we can relate our stories without fear."

Silence as revisiting takes place. I can't bring myself to think about Jack. Either Jack. But I do, despite myself.

Anna seems to surprise herself as she raises her hand first. "I was married to Harry for forty-five years. We had two children, Stevie and Stanley. He was a good provider. We lived in Boca. He was a dentist. Both my sons are dentists. We all had very good dental plans. I never had to worry about a single cavity." She stops, dabs at her teary eyes. Takes the box of tissues from Brenda. Then looks up at Hetty, as if waiting to hear if she got a good grade.

Hetty smiles encouragingly. "Very nice, Anna. But tell us your feelings. What about losing Harry? Tell us what upsets you the most."

Anna thinks for a moment. She seems at a total loss. "That I don't like anybody else touching my teeth? Not even my boys?"

Swell. Unclear on the concept. This is going to be a long two hours.

Hetty shakes her head. "Seymour? May we hear from you?"

Seymour smiles shyly. "My story is similar."

Oy, I hope not. I lean back in my uncomfortable chair.

Seymour leans forward. "Sally kept a nice house. Miami. Kids. Good job."

Hetty stops him. "Feelings, Harry, feelings." She gives him a hint. "What were your thoughts at your wife's gravesite? Start with that."

Seymour looks a little puzzled. "I wasn't there."

Anna is surprised. This is news to her. "You weren't there? Where were you?"

"I was here. She was buried in Teaneck, New Jersey."

Now Lorraine is fascinated. "What was she doing in New Jersey?"

Seymour looks sheepish. "She ran away with my accountant seventeen years, three months, and five days ago. That's where they moved to. To get a fresh start."

His story was similar? Did I say I was bored? Oh, my. Those three spend all their time with one another and are clueless?

Young Hetty seems nonplussed. College didn't tell her how to handle situations like this? She tries for some retort. "And you're feeling anger about what happened."

"No." He shrugs. "I guess the better man won."

The group stares at Seymour, astonished. I, along with them. There's a smattering of restless movement as we wait for our leader to remember she is still in charge.

"Wait a minute." Lorraine just got it. "So who's in the grave you visit with us?"

Seymour blushes. "It's just a stone I put up. It's not like I could go to Teaneck every month."

His friends stare, shocked and chagrined.

"Can I take my turn? I'm ready." Brenda has her hand up. "I am definitely in touch with my feelings. I loved my Arnold. He went everywhere I went. He slept with me. He rode in the car with me. He ate off my plate when he was extra hungry." She smiles shyly. "He even followed me into the bathroom. We were inseparable. I miss him every minute, every second of every day. You want emotions?" She glances at the chalkboard. "I'm numb and in denial and angry and depressed, but I'll never accept the loss of the love of my life." She sobs. And grabs the tissues back from Anna.

For a moment there is silence. Then Brenda cradles her arms in her lap again, as if caressing something. "He fit right here, right in the center of my chakras."

There is much mumbling. She was married to a midget?

Lorraine is furious. "You're talking about a cat? Or a dog?"

Brenda bravely lifts her head. "They don't call them man's best friend for nothing. I dare you to find someone as wonderful as my Lhasa apso!"

Seymour is confused. "What about your husband?"

Brenda huffs. "He's dead, too."

It's beginning to feel like a circus in here, with the keeper losing control and the animals about to run wild. Hetty is speechless.

Lorraine starts to address the group. For a moment we don't know it is she. Her head is down, her voice is low. "You want to talk about an emotion? How about hate? I hated the way he cut his toenails and let the bits fly across the bed. I hated the way he picked his teeth in public. I hated the way he snored and mucus dribbled out his nose. I hated the way he treated our children. I hated the way he told stupid jokes at parties. I hated his mustache. And his beard. In fact, I hated his whole damn face. And his body wasn't much either. I hated the way he lay on top of me and grunted. And never giving me an orgasm." She stops. We all stare at her.

I wonder if our leader might like to take a break. Maybe she needs time out. Maybe to go outside and phone *her* therapist.

Frank jumps out of his chair. "My emotions are running over. I need to talk about Gary." He paces the room, all eyes following him. "We met at the country club. I was so young, such a novice. He taught me everything I know. I was naïve; he had to lead me through every step. He could have had others more experienced. But no, he chose me. He wanted to be my mentor. How he made me keep up! Going to the gym, working out. Keeping the body a well-oiled machine. Every morning, noon, and night, practicing 'til I got better at it. And he was always so patient when I was so clumsy."

Anna throws her arms up as if to push him away. "Stop it," she cries. "I can't listen to this."

Lorraine jumps in. "These are not things one should confess to a mixed audience."

And talking about her non-orgasms is?

Even Seymour professes embarrassment.

Brenda says she can handle it.

Frank is angry. "When Gary died, my game went to hell. I couldn't putt worth a damn. My swing turned to crap. I had a right to cry when my golf pro dropped dead on the ninth hole. You'd cry too if you'd spent three thousand dollars trying for a halfway decent score!"

He sits down. Utter silence. He's crying over losing his golf pro?

"You have a wife?" Anna finally manages to squeak out.

He bats his hand as if to swat her away. "You mean my wife the hooker?"

Is he still talking golf or is he talking sex? Nobody's about to touch that line.

"Time's about up," Hetty whispers, wide-eyed, without looking at her watch. "But before we finish, I'd like to say, we've made some progress . . ." The group stands and begins to disperse.

Suddenly there is the sound of hysterical laughter.

Everyone turns. To me. I am the one laughing. And crying and laughing. I am hysterical. "What about my turn? I want to tell you about my two Jacks. I lost them both. One of them was murdered and the other stopped loving me."

One by one they sit back down and listen to me.

"There is something powerful about not allowing yourself to give up your pain when you lose someone. There is comfort in holding it close. It warms you. It keep you from ever letting yourself take risks again. No matter who or what you loved. It lives forever inside you. I say to myself over and over again, I got over my husband. After all, it was over forty years ago. Ridiculous. No one mourns that long. Try telling that to someone who survived the Holocaust. You look at yourself — this outside shell of you. You seem to be functioning in a real world. You get on with your life. You have children to raise. And friends who are there for you. You even have a career. But there is always that piece that is missing. Once you admit the truth, that it can never be filled again, you start to heal. Something similar might take its place. But it will never be the same. Your only hope is to try to make peace with that part that will haunt you forever."

I get up. I start for the door. Suddenly this motley collection of strangers engulfs me and hugs me. I hug them back. Lots of tears and tissues being handed out.

Lots of smiling and *See ya next time* and *Take it easy* and off they go.

Anna shakes Hetty's hand. "Thank you," she says. "I really got a lot out of this."

At dinner that night, I can't believe my eyes. There are my tablemates waving eagerly to

263

me as I enter. They are dressed, dare I say, colorfully?

When I reach the table, I am hardly seated when Anna makes an announcement. "I say. I say," she begins, raising a glass of champagne. "We have so much to talk about. Here's to us, the new Four Musketeers."

What have I unleashed?

And what will they think when I suddenly disappear one day when the case is over and I no longer show up at Group? Will they wonder if I'll ever solve the Jack-not-loving-me case of my own? I wonder, too.

They might miss me. And I actually might miss them.

THIRTY-FOUR:
CRISIS

I am running so fast, my heart is pounding and I am breathless. I feel a stitch in my side, but I keep going. The phone call put me in a panic. Will I get there too late? Will she be dead by then?

The hospital seems so quiet, but then again it's a Saturday night. When the elevator finally gets up to the ICU, I see so many friends waiting. Ida and Bella are leaning over Irving, trying to comfort the distraught man. Mary sits next to him on the couch, holding his hand. Tessie sits in a chair across from him. His best friend, Sol, paces, unable to hide his fear. Yolie and Denny stand huddled in a corner, hugging each other. The two of them are crying. Enya is praying, and even a couple of the Canadians are there as well. Finally, I see Sophie. She is seated away from them, near a window, sobbing.

By the number of empty coffee cups, I get

the feeling they've been here quite a while. They look weary and worried.

Ida hurries to meet me halfway.

I have to ask it. "Millie. Is she . . . gone?"

"No. But she may be in a coma. Somebody mentioned putting her in a hospice. But no one's told us anything definite yet."

"Oh, God, what happened?"

Ida and I move away from the others. "If it wasn't for Mary, she'd be dead. Thank God, even in his fright, Irving had the sense to call her right after calling nine-one-one. He actually remembered she once was a nurse. She ran over. When she saw that Millie had been vomiting and was choking to death, she knew what to do." Ida tries to hold back her tears. "It may be too late anyway. Mary told us she even had a seizure."

"What caused all this?"

"Brace yourself: Sophie. Remember when she announced, when we were doing our quilting, that her doctor had a cure for Alzheimer's?"

"Oh, no."

"Yes. Irving would have tried anything to save Millie. Sophie encouraged him to go. From what we could piece together, he took Millie to Dr. Friendly, who gave her an experimental drug."

There seems to be a mild commotion. Irving is yelling at a nurse and everyone surrounds them. We hurry back.

Irving tries to pull away. He is shrieking. "No, no, I won't. I can't." He is near hysteria.

I turn to Mary. "What's happening?"

"They have a form that Millie filled out a long time ago. To pull the plug and not resuscitate her if the doctors feel she is beyond care. But Irving won't sign it."

"Let me go to her. I have to be with her. Let me!" Irving is wailing. It is heartbreaking.

"All right," the nurse tells him. "But only for a few minutes."

Sweet, gentle Irving shouts, "I'll stay as long as I want!"

The nurse leads him out. I am aware of Sophie staring at his back. She can't bear it and turns away. Ida and I exchange glances. Bella sees us. We all three head over to where she now stands.

"Sophie —" I start.

"No, go away." She won't face us. "Leave me alone. I mean it. Go away!"

Ida gently pats her on the back. She winces. We leave her standing there.

Hours later, some of us are still there. We have been taking turns waiting. Irving had his way. He's still with Millie. We're sitting in a circle of chairs and couches. Ida, Bella, Mary, Enya, Yolie, Denny, and me. Enya leads us in prayer.

"The Lord is my shepherd; I shall not want . . ."

Sophie still won't join us. I feel terrible for her suffering. But I can see her lips moving with ours.

It is near midnight when Irving comes back to us. We've been sleeping or dozing or reading, but we are still there. He looks exhausted, but there is a small smile. We look to him expectantly.

"She is out of the coma. She will live."

We all run to him and embrace him. He tells us to go home and rest, but he is staying.

As everyone picks up books and newspapers, sweaters, preparing to go home, Irving walks over to Sophie.

"I'm so sorry," she sobs. She can't look him in the face. "It's all my fault. I'm so sorry."

He puts his arms around her and holds her. "Please don't blame yourself. Millie wouldn't want you to." He kisses her gently on the forehead.

We are all in a puddle of tears.

We stand outside for a few moments, breathing the cool nighttime air. Yolie and Denny tell us they will walk back home.

"Tell them, Denny." Yolie insists, pulling at his shirt.

His head is bowed. "Yolanda wanted me to tell you about us taking Irving and Millie to that awful doctor. But I didn't listen to her." He cannot look at us.

Mary tries to comfort them. "Millie was in very bad shape. You knew that. She was near the end. Irving wanted to try anything — maybe it would have helped. But you mustn't blame yourself."

Yolie asks, "What happens to her now? Will she come home?"

Mary answers. "I doubt it. I believe she will have to go to an Alzheimer's facility. She will need much more care than you can give her."

"What about Mr. Irving?"

Ida answers that one. "He'll need all the help all of us can give him. Maybe you'll stay with him?"

She cries with joy. "I will never leave him alone." Denny hugs her.

They walk on, clutching each other. Mary

drives Enya home.

The rest of us pile into my car.

As we drive across the street to where we live, Sophie tells us she's made a decision. "I'm gonna call the AMA and tell them about Dr. Friendly."

We nod, though in the dark of the car she can't see that. It doesn't matter. She knows we are on her side and support whatever she wants to do.

We continue to hold vigil most of Sunday. There is no change in Millie.

Finally, utterly exhausted, back in my apartment, I notice that I have a message on my cell phone. It's from Hope Watson. Apparently the prodigals have just come home from their weekend trip. She thought I'd like to know that and maybe do something about my sister.

Monday afternoon I'm back at Wilmington House, yet again. I look around for her. Evvie is nowhere to be found. I make discreet inquiries, since everyone seems to be on an Evelyn and Philip watch. Not seen today at all. Not at lunch. Or breakfast. But, I am told with snickering, there are hints from kitchen staff that meals are being served by room service. In Philip's room. Maids report there has been a Do Not

Disturb sign on all day. Even the staff is in on the excitement. No wonder Hope gives me a dirty look as I pass her in the lobby. I move away quickly before she starts asking questions. I ponder what to do. Go upstairs and knock on his door? And make a fool of myself? No way.

I try Evvie's apartment first. I knock, but no answer. I open our adjoining doors and enter, but there's nothing to see but the usual spotlessly clean rooms left by the daily maid. I stand listlessly in the middle of her living room.

I don't remember the last time I felt this unsure. What do I do now?

THIRTY-FIVE:
NIGHT GAMES

"Hit me." Evvie indicates her cards. She's showing a three and a deuce.

Philip deals. It's a ten. Evvie groans. She turns over her card. Also a ten. Phil singsongs, "Take it off. Take it off."

It's midnight. They are in Philip's apartment, straddling his king-size bed. Two bottles of champagne sit in their buckets, one empty, one with only a quarter left. They're drunk and by now everything's funny.

Evvie sits on her knees and struggles to unbutton her blouse. Too drunk to manage it, she tries to pull it over her head. It isn't easy since she's purposely put on as many pieces of clothing as she could. She can't stop laughing. Neither can Philip.

Alongside the deck of cards lay the already discarded strip poker items. A sun hat — Evvie's. Sunglasses — Evvie's. One beach robe — Evvie's. One sweatshirt — ditto. The only item on Philip's pile are a pair of socks.

She mumbles, almost incoherently, "Not fair." The blouse is now stuck over her nose. She giggles.

He reaches over. "And it's also not fair you put on twice as many clothes as I did. Here, let me help you." He gently tries to pull it off, but she keeps trying also, which causes them both to fall sideways as the blouse rips. She is down to a T-shirt and bra. For a moment they look intensely at each other, their faces very close. He reaches out and gently smooths her hair.

Her lips are close to his. She whispers, "You must be cheating."

"How can I be cheating? You see what I deal." His breath blows wisps of air into her ear. She shudders, deliciously.

They both manage to pull themselves back up. Evvie hiccups, and then giggles. "Well, you better not be." She reaches for the cards and starts dealing, clumsily dropping many of the cards.

"So, go back to what you were telling me," Philip urges.

"I was singing at this club in the village. It was my big chance. The joint was filled with servicemen on leave. I was good. I know I was."

She deals him a six. He indicates wanting another. She deals him a king. He turns his card over. Another picture.

"Gotcha." Evvie is gleeful.

Philip reaches for the tie that hangs lopsided around his neck. She leans over to help him pull it off. And falls against him. He holds on to her.

"I was good. I coulda been the next Doris Day. I know it."

He nuzzles her hair. "I'm sure you could." He moves her so she'll be seated in his lap. Her face is in his neck; she makes little hic-cupping sounds.

"So what happened, Evelyn dear?"

"I met a soldier that night. I was dumb enough to marry him and that was the end of my career." She starts to cry.

He rocks her gently in his arms.

Her voice is slippery. "You coulda been a star, too, with your golden voice."

"I dabbled a bit in the arts. I acted for a while."

That interests Evvie, but she is too immobile to respond with any energy. She mutters. "Would I know you? Where would I have seen you?"

He stops her with his lips and kisses her long and hard. He pulls away. "Not important." He indicates the cards. "You lost again."

She looks confused. "Were we playing?" She doesn't remember the cards being dealt;

they were all in a jumble.

"We never stopped, and you lost again," he says as he lifts her T-shirt and slowly removes it. He looks at her. "You're beautiful." He pulls the straps of her bra down and gently kisses her breasts. She moans.

"Now help me." He lifts her hands to help him take off his shirt. She stares at his naked chest.

"You're beautiful, too."

"Even the band is beautiful."

She laughs, knowing the reference. *"Cabaret."*

"Life is a cabaret, dearest Evelyn. And we shall live it to the fullest."

He lays her down on the bed and lowers his body onto hers.

Thirty-Six:
The Showdown

I had dozed off on Evvie's couch. I'm wakened by the sound of the key turning in her lock. I glance at my watch. It's four a.m. I stand and face the door as it opens. Evvie is startled to see me. Her face is blotchy, her hair and makeup a mess. For a moment neither one of us speaks.

Evvie drops the small overnight bag she's carrying. "Run out of sugar?"

Uh-oh, she's on the defensive. "More like run out of patience."

She walks past me into her kitchen and puts some water in the kettle.

I follow her. "You might want to know that Millie nearly died last night."

She has the decency to look upset. "Is she all right?"

"That's a long conversation for another time, but I will say she's never coming home again."

She pales. I can see that Evvie is trying

not to react. She seems determined to deal only with right now. Evvie puts cups out for both of us. "Join me in a cup of tea?"

"Whatever. You've avoided me long enough. We have to talk."

"There's nothing to talk about."

"You can look me in the eye and say that? Evvie, your behavior with Philip has destroyed any possibility of keeping you on this case." God, how stuffy I sound.

The kettle whistles. She pours the tea and looks straight at me. "See? I'm looking you in the eye. I don't give a damn about this case. Call Ferguson and tell him: case solved. Phil is no murderer!"

"And how do you know this for sure?"

Her hand shakes as she lifts the cup. "Because I know how wonderful he is. Because I love him!"

I sigh. "Oh, Evvie." I feel myself trembling. I didn't expect this. "What happened to playing a role and getting at the truth?"

Now Evvie drops all pretense of wanting tea. Her eyes open wide. If she could breathe fire, she would. "I am telling you the truth. And don't you 'oh, Evvie' me. Don't you use that condescending tone. What do you think — you have a monopoly on falling in love?"

"You actually believe you fell in love at

first sight?"

She mimics me. "Yes, I actually did. I fell madly in love with him the moment I saw him. And he fell for me as well."

"Please let's sit down and discuss this." I can't stop sounding stiff and formal, but this is an Evvie I don't know anymore. I thought I knew my sister, but this throws me. All our years of closeness and I could read her as well as she could read me. All this time, I thought she was playacting. How could I have been so blind?

"No, I don't want to. Your disappointment is like a black cloud fouling the room. I'm happy and I won't have you raining on my parade."

I try to say something but she won't let me.

"And don't give me this bull about our case. I don't give a damn about it." She takes a sip of her tea, grimaces, and then pours it down the sink. "You know how many years I've waited for the right man to come along? Only all my life. I thought I might get a second chance after Joe dumped me. But what was out there? Drips." She laughs.

"*Drips* — there's an out-of-date word. How about losers. Deadbeats. Schmucks. I told myself it would never happen. All the good men were taken. Not that I had the right man in the first place. Joe was a dud. I fell in love with a soldier's uniform and the romance of war. I married him because he came back alive. But he was never the one, Gladdy. You know that. You've seen me through all the pain of that marriage. Once the kids had come, the trap was sprung. No way out."

I try to say something but she stops me with her hand. There's a hell of a lot she's got to get off her chest. I listen. What else can I do?

"Then you come down here to live near me and I think, this is good, we have each other. We'll grow old together, we don't really need men, and that's that. But, no, you get to meet Jack. And both of you fall in love. You'd already had a great marriage the first time. Now you get a chance for another happy marriage. I will never have what you had twice. What will happen to me? I get to shrivel up all alone."

All these sad years, I think. I thought we were close, but she never talked about this before. She kept it all in. And my happy marriage? The one that lasted eleven years before my husband was murdered and my life ruined. What's happened to her sensitivity about that? "Evvie. We see a pattern in

Philip. He goes from one retirement community to another and picks a woman —"

"Shut up! He's a good man. He was kind to Esther Ferguson. He knew she'd die soon and he gave her comfort. He let her think it was love. He explained that to me."

I hate to say it, but I have to. "He thinks *you're* going to die soon. You told him that because you knew that would attract him."

For a moment, Evvie stares at me. I feel the white heat of her rage. "You dare to think this is pity? This is different!"

"How is it different? He thinks you're rich. He thinks you'll die. He will comfort you, too. He's out to get something from you. We don't know what it is yet . . ."

"How little faith you have in me. How arrogant of you. You think you're the only one who would recognize a good man? Well, Philip *is* a good man. You're wrong about him. He's kind and loving. The man I deserve to have."

"Yes. He's a saint."

She runs out of the kitchen, toward her bedroom, shouting at me. "Get out of here. You just stay away from him!" With that, she shuts herself in.

I walk to her bedroom and stand there talking to a closed door. "Please, Evvie, don't do this."

She flings the door open. I haven't seen her like this since she was a child having tantrums. Her face is livid. "You're just jealous. You've lost Jack because of your stupid stubbornness. You won't even sleep with him! You think I didn't know what was going on? Or should I say what wasn't going on? Well, I'm not making your mistake, sister dear. I know how to please a man even if you don't! I am having the best and only good sex I've ever had in my entire life and I'm not going to let you spoil it for me. Now, get out of my apartment!"

I drag my weary way through our adjoining doors back to my own apartment. For a moment I stand unmoving, as if I've lost my bearings.

My sister hates me. I no longer have a sister.

Philip is almost asleep when he hears the frantic knocking. He opens the door slightly so as not to reveal his nakedness.

Evvie stands in the hallway, sobbing. He pulls her inside. "What is it? What's wrong?"

"I had a fight. A terrible fight."

"With whom? Where did you meet someone at this hour to fight with?"

Evvie's eyes widen and she steps back from him. "It was my next-door neighbor. She saw me coming in late, looking disheveled. She called me names —"

"Who is it? I'll go now." He reaches for his robe.

She grabs his arms. "It's not important." Evvie suddenly realizes he has nothing on. She stops, startled. Sober now.

He pulls her close to him. She trembles from the bareness of his skin against her.

"Stay with me. All night."

"I shouldn't."

"Of course you should. I'll protect you."

He wraps her arms around his nude body. "Stay with me forever. Evelyn, I've waited for you all my life, dearest love."

His skin feels hot to her touch. Yet she shivers.

"When was the last time you felt like this?"

She moans. "Never."

He lifts her up and carries her to the bed. Evvie feels as if she were sinking into a golden pool of quicksand.

Thirty-Seven:
Aftermath

I hear noise coming from somewhere close. It wakes me. My head aches. Another dreadful night. I didn't drop off until about seven a.m. I am beginning to feel sleep-deprived. I lift my head and look at the clock. Eleven-thirty a.m. Dragging my sluggish self out of bed, I get into the shower and pour water, as hot as I can stand it, over my aching body.

Evvie's words have reverberated in my head all night. In her hurt, my sister called me a failure. My fault that Jack left me. Those words said in anger will hurt forever. She says she's in love, so why does she have so much rage? Because she doesn't want me to spoil her happiness? But she knows I would always want her to be happy. Because another part of her knows she is wrong? And she is in denial?

Or am I wrong? I am no longer sure of what I feel or what I think. My head spins and I feel a throbbing headache coming on.

I get dressed to go downstairs. But what for? What's the point of my being here now? Should I call Alvin Ferguson and give up the case? It's tainted now.

As I walk out into the hall, I see Evvie's front door is open. People are moving about inside. This is odd. Usually there is only the one daily maid. I glance in and see Evvie's suitcase on a trolley. Along with clothes on hangers on a rack. A porter is about to wheel everything out.

"What's going on?" I ask.

The porter reaches me. "Mrs. Markowitz will be residing in another apartment. She has given up this apartment." I can see by his smirk that he's up on the gossip, too.

I'm stunned. She's moving in with Philip. So fast? Because of our fight? Things are happening too quickly. She musn't move in with him. What if he is a killer! Is there any way to stop this? But how?

I am going back to Lanai Gardens. I have to tell the girls what's happening. Oh, how I wish Jack was here. I need his level head.

When I reach the main lobby I see the backs of a large group of people. They're laughing at something. I walk over, curious.

Evvie and Philip are standing in front of this large assembly of avid listeners. Evvie is reading as Philip, at her side, gazes adoringly at her. What is she saying? I move closer. Feeling like an idiot, I use the large palm trees as cover and I listen in.

Then I realize what she's doing. Evvie is reading her new review of the movie they played here, *Adam's Rib*.

"And so the lines are drawn. Kate Hepburn has taken on Judy Holliday's case. And Spencer defends the ugly husband. And every night they fight over it and always nearby is that silly neighbor. I can still hear that song he writes for Kate, called 'Farewell, Amanda.' He is always trying to break up their love, but love always conquers all. This is a romance and romance is always wonderful." Here she glows at Philip. "And, of course, they live happily ever after."

Evvie bows and all the new sycophants applaud. Evvie has transferred her role as Lanai Gardens' resident critic into her fantasy life. She and Philip are the new god and goddess. I back away and head for the door. Let me out of here.

Not only is my sister under the spell of this lothario, her review is awful.

The girls stare at me, distressed, as I tell them of Evvie's enchantment. "I don't know what to do," I admit to them.

285

We are in my apartment, shades drawn. I feel like I'm in mourning. Nobody has even asked for something to eat; it is that serious.

Bella shakes her head. "I can't believe she was so mean to you. She loves you."

And I can't believe I am betraying my sister by saying cruel things behind her back, something I have never done before.

"We've got to get her out of there," Ida insists.

I shrug hopelessly. "There's no way to do that."

"Kidnap her," suggests Sophie.

Bella is not convinced. "That won't work. We're too old and weak to carry her out of there."

Ida suggests, "We can drug her and drag her out."

"No matter what we do, she'll hate us for interfering." I feel helpless. I have no idea what action to take.

Ida stands up and crosses her arms. "There's only one way. We have to prove he's a killer. Then she'll come to her senses and come home."

"But what if he isn't a killer and this is real love?" Sophie finally starts rummaging through my fridge in search of a snack.

"But what if he is? How can we take that chance?" I ask.

Bella looks at Ida questioningly. "So, do we have a plan?"

Ida instinctively takes charge. She senses my helplessness. "I think we should consult with Barbi and Casey. Maybe their computers will come up with something. They helped us last time; maybe they can again. They're out of town on some convention, but only for a few days."

"Yes," Bella says eagerly. "I'll go, as long as I don't have to drink any more of their weird chai."

They look to me for my decision. I am desperate for any help. Whatever I do, I'm afraid Evvie will never forgive me.

With a heavy heart I give her my okay.

The girls and I have dinner together. It's a somber affair. We're worried about Evvie and light conversation seems too difficult to manage. Sophie sees our glum faces and tries. "Ya know, when I was on pot, I had a vision."

We all stare at her. Sophie is back to her old happy self and that's good news indeed.

"I saw a building that circles round and round like a merry-go-round and Sol falling madly in love with Evvie and Evvie falling in love in a red dress and the killer falling in love with everybody and they're all jumping

287

out windows. Falling."

I fairly choke with laughter at that. So does Ida. Bella beams. This sounds like fun.

I can't resist asking, "So what does your drug-induced epiphany mean?"

Sophie takes a quick bite of her stuffed cabbage and says, "Well, I don't know what a *piffany* means, but in my vision Evvie is in the mood to fall in love. That's why she dated Sol."

Bella giggles. "Yeah and see how that turned out."

Sophie continues, "And Sol is desperate to fall in love and have sex. Remember how he tried to get her up to his apartment?"

"Who could forget?" Ida chuckles.

Sophie continues with a logic all her own. "Well, Evvie isn't interested in Sol. She goes speed dating and jumps from chair to chair and the killer jumps from luxury hotel to luxury hotel and Sol, and Sol . . ." She loses her train of thought.

Bella claps her hands. "I get it. And Sol jumps from window to window!"

The two of them high-five each other.

Ida and I exchange amazed glances. "Are you thinking what I am?" she asks me. "Is Sophie's subconscious under drug abuse giving us the clue we've needed all along?"

"Sol is the Peeper?" I ask.

We stare at one another. It all fits. Desperate Sol, who can never take his eyes off women's bodies, is the Peeper!

I announce, "Tomorrow we have a serious talk with Mr. Sol Spankowitz. Good work, Soph."

Sophie beams, proud of her accomplishment. "So what's for dessert?"

Thirty-Eight:
Exit the Peeper

It's early morning and we are drawn to a big crowd gathering at S building. There's a lot of yelling.

As the girls and I get nearer, I'm aware of a number of our Canadian renters standing in some kind of circle. Some of the other neighbors have come out and are watching intently, many still in their bathrobes. Hy and Lola are there, too. No surprise. They never miss anything that goes on at Lanai Gardens. And Irving. Irving? It's his third day at home since he left Millie in the hospital, and he is part of this crowd? Yolie, as always, is at his side. He looks tired, but seemingly involved. Dora Dooley is there. Dora? Why?

"Leave me alone! Get your paws off me."

I know that voice. It's Sol Spankowitz. He is dressed all in black. A Superman Halloween mask hangs around his neck.

"We're too late," I say to my girls. They

nod. Looks like someone else unmasked the Peeper — literally — before we could.

"Don't hit him. Please." This is from a very frightened Irving, Sol's only real friend. He shakes his head back and forth.

One of the Canadian women, I think her name is Alice, points at Sol. "You disgusting creature!" Her husband, Jim, has his arm around her, protectively.

Now Tessie hurries over, belting her bathrobe, and joins in. "What's all the noise around here?"

Jim tells us. "There's your Peeper! My wife caught him with his nose against our window. She woke me and I ran out after him."

Another of the Canadians adds, "I was picking up my newspaper from my front step when I saw Sol run past. I see Jim coming after him and Jim yells for me to stop him. So I do."

Sol is in tears. "I'm innocent, I tell you."

"Liar," Alice says. "I saw you good and clear."

"How could you see me? I wore a mask —" Sol stops, realizing he's just convicted himself.

Hy has to put his two cents in. "I always suspected the butcher."

"Yeah, sure," says Tessie, shoving him.

"You always know everything."

"Should I call the police?" one of the S building residents calls down from the second-floor balcony.

At that, Sol begins to crumple.

"Not so fast." Tessie moves into the inner circle where Sol stands, quivering. She holds him up with her hefty arms. "He's got a right to defend himself."

"Not here. In court, when he's on trial for lewd and lascivious behavior." Alice must watch a lot of lawyer shows.

"All I want is a little love — is that so much to ask?" Sol raises his arms beseechingly to the crowd.

Hy chuckles. "With your weenie sticking out? That's what you call love?"

Now the laughter begins.

"I call that sex," Alice says.

"I call that perversion." Alice's husband is close to grabbing Sol. Tessie places her large body protectively in front of him.

"My wife is dead, but a man still got needs." Sol is practically on his knees. "I should have thrown myself on her coffin and died with her."

Hy gives advice. "You got two hands, don't you? And a VCR?" More chuckles and sneers.

Sol shakes his head. "That's not love." He

looks around, appealing to his enemies. "I'm not what you call a handsome man."

"That's for sure." Even Ida is rallying with the mob. I elbow her. She gives me a dirty look.

"I'm not very good with women."

Hy looks around. "Where's Evvie? She can testify to that."

"I'm shy. I don't know what else to do, so I just look. I don't mean no harm. I'm a worshipper of lovely ladies' bodies."

This cracks Hy up. "The schmuck needs glasses. He peeps on old ugly broads and calls them lovely bodies? Pathetic."

Alice's husband walks over to Hy and glowers down at him. "Don't make disparaging remarks about my wife."

Hy backs off. "I mean all the other old broads he peeped."

Lola pinches his arm, warning him to shut up.

A bevy of women arrive. The news is traveling fast. May Levine, Eileen O'Donnell, and Edna Willis come barreling down the path. They push their way through the crowd and start pummeling Sol. Tessie tries to ward them off. These are women Sol peeped and they want revenge. Dora Dooley applauds. Revenge is sweet.

May steps out of the circle and smacks

Hy. "I heard what you said. Old broads! You should talk, you dirty-minded, ugly *putz*."

"Stop that," says Lola, pushing May away from her adored husband.

Now Jane gets a shot at Sol. Sol covers his head with his hands as she hits his bald head over and over. Tessie pulls her away but Eileen and May get at him.

"I could use a little help in here," Tessie shouts.

Little Irving, though terrified and utterly embarrassed, enters the circle to help. He timidly reaches out to stop May but she shoves him away.

The audience is hooting and cheering and making side bets.

Sol pleads his case. "What's a man supposed to do? Do I spend the rest of my life itching and scratching? Where is the justice? I see the married men and their wives. I am so jealous, I can't stand it. Night after night I cry in my lonely bedroom. So what should I do? Somebody shoot me and put me out of my misery."

"Why don't you just get married and shut up?" says Jim.

Sol sees a breath of hope. "Who would marry me?"

Tessie lifts him up in her powerful arms. "I would, snookums. And I'll give you all the sex you want. A woman has needs, too."

"You want to marry me?" Sol is clearly terrified of being dropped by this Amazon of a woman.

"I do!" With that she lifts him high in the air, triumphantly. "Name the date, pussycat."

Sol turns at the sound of many sighs. The women are smiling. Even the peeped ladies forgive. Women do like a good romance. Especially Dora. The men applaud. Except for Hy, who's disgusted. Irving shakes his head sadly and walks away.

"Got any of those cute little blue pills?" Tessie asks Sol. "Ya know — wink, wink — Viagra?"

Sol looks down at his grinning new fiancée and shudders.

Sophie is disappointed. "We shoulda been the ones to nab him."

"Yeah," adds Bella.

"We coulda got him last night."

"Never mind," adds Ida. "He made his bed and now he's gotta lie in it!"

I shake my head in disbelief. Thus ends the case of the Peeper.

THIRTY-NINE:
GOSSIP REVISITED

It still seems strange to me that our condo neighbors, the seemingly very sophisticated Barbi and Casey, work out of an inexpensive minimall in a store that used to sell shoes. Their research business name, Gossip, is the only word seen on the blackened outside windows. In very small letters at that. And their office, so to speak, is a huge work space done up almost totally in white. White floors, white walls, white furniture, except for their moveable desk chairs, which are black. When we walk in we automatically feel we should whisper as if we were in some hospital. Last time we were there, they offered us spicy chai, so this time Bella came prepared with her own Lipton's tea bag.

Some exchange of hellos, and then from Casey, "Where's the fifth musketeer? How come Evvie isn't with you? You girls are always joined at the hips."

The girls look nervously toward me. I toss

out an answer. "New job. She's at a retirement complex keeping her eye on our perp." Well, it really isn't much of a stretch. One could certainly say she's doing just that.

"We did hear some rumors as to a new gig," Barbi comments.

"First we discuss price," I say.

Casey laughs. "I thought that was supposed to be our line." Barbi puts her arm around Casey's shoulder and giggles.

Sophie has a suggestion. "What about a senior discount?"

"Look," Barbi says, "we know you can't afford us. Can we barter?"

"Barter? You mean trade for services?" Ida asks.

"Precisely," says Casey. The two of them are wearing their wedding rings again, rings they do not wear around the condo. I get the feeling they wore them last time as a test, to see how we would react. We must have passed the test. Considering the fact that my girls can't keep a secret about anything, they never said a word to anyone. And yes, Casey's in masculine clothes — a shirt and pants — and Barbi's wearing a long, flowing skirt. I'm waiting for one of them to address the other as husband or wife, and then all bets are off. The girls will spread that piece of news like cream cheese on a bagel.

"What have we got that you would want?" Sophie asks in surprise.

Barbi smiles. "Ida makes the best pecan pie in Florida."

Ida beams. "Anytime you want one, just give me an hour's notice."

"What else?" Bella wants to know.

"That's it," says Casey.

The girls think for a moment.

Bella says, "I sew very good. As long as I can use a magnifying glass."

"You don't really have to throw that in," says Barbi. "However, thanks. Anything that needs repair we'll come to you."

"I make a great matzo ball chicken soup," adds Sophie. "The secret is that you have to use parsnips."

"I didn't know that. Sure, add that to the pot," Casey says, laughing at her pun.

"I suppose I should contribute something, but I don't know what," I say.

Barbi shakes her head. "We're good. Chicken soup, pecan pie, and free sewing work. Sold."

Casey adds, "However, we'd be interested in hearing how you solved the last case and played bingo at the same time."

"Dinner and the story. My apartment at your convenience," I say.

"Great," says Casey. "Negotiations finalized." She is now all business. "What can we do for you today?"

Ida, stepping easily into Evvie's position, reports, "As Gladdy mentioned, we have a new case." She fills them in about Alvin Ferguson, his mother, Esther, and Romeo — a.k.a. Philip Smythe — living at Grecian Villas in Fort Lauderdale.

Barbi and Casey listen avidly.

"So the son thinks Romeo could be a killer?" Casey rubs her hands in anticipation.

Ida adds, "His wife doesn't think so. There's no motive. He gets nothing from Esther's dying."

"I'm not sure." I shudder, thinking of Evvie alone with him.

"Start with a couple of facts. When did Philip meet Esther?"

"The manager, Rosalie Gordon, and her assistant, Myra, at Grecian Villas said they lived together three months. They met the first week after he arrived in May."

"When did Mrs. Esther Ferguson die?"

I look at my notes from our meeting with Alvin and Shirley Ferguson. "July twenty-seventh."

"And he moved out when?"

"July thirty-first. Apparently, he was too

heartbroken to stay any longer."

"What do you know about him?"

I relate how popular he was wherever he went.

"Name of the last residence before Grecian Villas?"

"Seaside Cliffs. Sarasota."

"And where he is now."

"Wilmington House. Palm Beach."

And they're off, sliding their moveable chairs across the room to their individual computers. They type and type and type. Then exchange information with each other, talking a kind of high-tech jargon, as we sit and share the one Lipton's tea bag at the little white table at the side of the room.

The two of them finally turn and grin at each other and do high fives. "Yes!" they say in tandem. They slide back, beaming.

"Easy," says Casey.

"Piece of cake," says Barbi.

Casey starts. "We checked this year. All three of the facilities you mentioned are within this year. Here's something interesting."

Barbi continues. "Three months at each residence. One month off to get installed in the next place and maybe time for a little vacation." Barbi whips a sheet of actual paper (the first I've seen here — white, of

300

course) out of the printer and hands it to us.

We read. January through March, Smythe was at Seaside Cliffs in Sarasota. April he took off. And seemingly traveled. No actual address. Then May through July he was at Grecian Villas. No known address in August, but he showed up at Wilmington House on September first.

"What does it mean?" I ask.

"Yeah," says Ida. "I don't get it.

"A very organized man, this Mr. Smythe," says Barbi. "It looks like he's following a plan. Three months in one place, then he uses the next month to resettle. Then three months in the next, etc."

"In other words he's planning ahead to leave regardless of how good his life is there? How very odd." I am surprised.

"That's what it looks like," says Casey. "Let's take a giant leap here."

Barbi speaks. "You tell us he met Esther at the beginning of May and she died at the end of July."

"You aren't saying . . . ?" Ida looks stricken.

"How do you feel about coincidences?" Casey grins. "Any bets on his having done it the same way the previous time as well?"

Sophie and Bella shake their heads vigorously.

Casey's back at the computer. "Okay. Point one. Esther Ferguson died July twenty-seventh. Give or take a day for funeral arrangements and good-byes."

"Right on schedule." This from Barbi.

"Well, we know two things about this man already. He is compulsive about keeping to a schedule. And he plans everything in advance."

"But what's he really up to?" I wonder.

"Up to no good, I would guess." Casey leans back on her desk chair, relaxing. "Interesting case you guys have."

"Okay. What about Seaside Cliffs?"

"All we know is he had a lady friend named Elsie Rogers. When she died of natural causes, he moved again."

"Any bets on the dates?" Barbi asks sarcastically. Barbi slides back to her desk and types once more. After a few moments she turns. "He met Elsie in January. She died at the end of March. He left right afterward, and one might guess, crying crocodile tears. Off on another month's vacation. A mourning period, hey? This man is some piece of work. Let's go back even further. Let's try last year."

Again the typing. Casey reports. "Roman

302

Villas, Tallahassee. September, October, November, last year. And again December off for good behavior. Hmm. Nobody died. He had an affair with a Pearl Mosher, but that's all it says."

Ida is perturbed. "How can your machines tell you that?"

Barbi answers for her. They like to take turns. "If it's in writing somewhere, we can pick it up. The retirement communities have in-house newspapers. Just check the gossip columns."

Now Casey again. "Before that, Savannah, Georgia, then Macon, Georgia. Our boy has been moving his way down south."

"And no doubt the same pattern," says Barbi. "Wonder why nobody ever checked all the other retirement communities before they let him in?"

I stare at the sheet of paper in my hand, more and more worried. "Because, as I've said, he's charming, and because he had the money to get in. As long as he had no police record, why not take him in? He always gets great recommendations from the previous facility. After all, they describe him as a 'saint.' "

Casey asks, "In Wilmington House, has he picked a new lady friend yet?"

I say, choking on it, "Yes, he has."

"Anyone wanna place bets that he'll be out of there by November thirtieth?" says Barbi to Casey. They laugh.

I shudder. Will it be Evvie who dies of an "accident" before the end of November? Ida is thinking the same thing. She looks at me, eyes wide in fright. But then, it's still early September, I think; she's still safe. They only just met.

"Wow!" All this time Barbi continues typing. She turns and faces us. "Wow!"

"What?" Casey says, "Spit it out."

"He's followed exactly the same pattern for ten years previously, plus this year, making it eleven. And . . ."

We all react nervously to her excitement. "And what?" I ask.

Barbi looks at us with an expression of disbelief on her face. "Before that, there is no residence for a Philip Smythe. As far as I can tell — there is no record anywhere of this man named Philip Smythe."

FORTY:
TEARS IN THE
GARDEN

It was one of those days when wise people stayed indoors. Seniors especially didn't dare venture out. The heat in Tallahassee was oppressive, the humidity breaking records. But for the Cuban laborers excavating dirt for the new swimming pool, the weather didn't matter; a job was a job. Roman Villas, a sister to the more southern Grecian Villas, was putting in a lap pool. Their gardens, which lay at the extreme border of their property, were considered a waste. Nobody bothered to walk that far just to smell the flowers. And over the years their questionnaire asking "What would you like added" yielded many requests for a lap pool. Business was good; Roman Villas could use the tax break. Thus the new pool.

The laborers dug. Beautiful flower beds were being transferred by wheelbarrows to other areas. The clods of dirt spewed dust into the workers' nostrils.

Pedro Reyes angled his shovel deeper

down below the hydrangeas he had just lifted out. The shovel was stopped by something odd. Surprised, he bent down to check it out. His shovel had hit plastic sheeting. His eyes suddenly met other eyes, Dead eyes. Attached to a body. A dead body, seeming to stare accusingly at him through the plastic covering. Pedro jumped up and gasped, his shovel flying through the air. "Madre mia, es muerto!" He moved hurriedly from the offending sight and crossed himself.

Immediately the other workers ran to see for themselves. Ninety-year-old Pearl Mosher, who had been a chaste woman all her life, was now stared at by workers horrified at seeing what was left of her dead, naked body.

FORTY-ONE:
AT THE MOVIES

They sit in the last row of the theater so they won't disturb anyone else — or be seen, for that matter. They eat popcorn sloppily and whisper and giggle and kiss and touch each other playfully.

"We're behaving like teenagers." Evvie feeds Philip a handful of popcorn. She has never had so much fun with a man before, she thinks. Every day she falls more in love with him.

"Did you ever behave like this as a teenager?"

"No."

"Well, it's about time."

"We should be ashamed of ourselves."

He nuzzles her neck. "No, we shouldn't. We're making up for all we missed in the past, and besides, we're more fun than the movie."

They are watching a romantic French classic, *Belle de Jour.*

She pushes him playfully. "Stop it. I can't

read the subtitles."

He nuzzles her again. "You want to know what they're saying? *Je t'aime, je t'aime, je t'aime.*" Each word punctuated with a tiny kiss.

The "client" in the brothel on screen puts his hand on Catherine Deneuve's breast. Philip does the same to Evvie.

She smacks his hand. "You're shameless."

"I'm only following the plot, step by step."

"You are so naughty." Evvie looks around, worried someone is watching them, but it's the late show and few people are in the audience. She even hears snoring wafting from somewhere down below.

"Okay," she says. "Pay attention. I've got one. *A Kiss Before Dying.* Author?"

"Ira Levin, from his novel of the same name."

"Actress? The original, not the remake."

"Joanne Woodward."

"Leading man?"

Philip hesitates. "You got me. I forgot."

"Robert Wagner. I win."

"And this is your reward, Miss Smartypants." He kisses her, hard, leaving her breathless.

"We're going to be arrested for indecent exposure. We'll be disgraced in front of everybody."

"Who cares. My turn. *A Place in the Sun.* Author."

"Theodore Dreiser."

"Original title?"

"An American Tragedy."

"Female lead?"

"Elizabeth Taylor."

"Male lead?"

"Montgomery Clift."

"Other female lead?"

"Shelley Winters."

"Director?"

Evvie is stumped. "No fair, only four questions allowed."

"George Stevens. You lose. My pleasure."

Evvie throws the rest of her popcorn at him.

"Come on." He takes her hand and places it on his knee.

"How come you only choose movies where innocent women are murdered?"

He moves her hand up his leg, slowly.

Evvie gets with it, teasing him with light touches. He moans.

Suddenly, Philip pushes her away, his whole body shaking as he cries out in pain.

"What is it? Are you all right?"

His hands move to his head.

"You look like you're in pain. What is it?"

"It's these damn migraines." Philip presses his left hand against his temple as if to push the pain away. Then he reaches his other hand in his pocket and pulls out his medication. He's trembling so hard, he can hardly open the container. Finally he manages to shake out two pills. Evvie quickly pulls the cap off their water bottle and hands it to him.

Philip leans his head back against the seat, his eyes closed, his body shuddering. He moans quietly for a few minutes, then he opens his eyes again.

"Are you all right, my darling?" She is frightened for him.

"Forgive me, Evelyn, my dearest. For a moment I wasn't myself."

With that he closes his eyes again as Evvie gently wipes his sweating face.

FORTY-TWO:
FRIENDS AND SISTERS

Ida tries to console me. I have been trying to reach Evvie ever since we got home from Barbi and Casey's Gossip meeting. She doesn't return my calls. Ida and I go for a walk to help me calm my nerves. When we get back there's a message on the machine. From Evvie. For a moment, I have hope. I listen, then rewind it and listen again.

"Stop calling. There is nothing you can say that I would want to hear. I am very happy. Leave me alone."

I start to rewind again, but Ida takes my hand. "Glad, enough. Stop torturing yourself."

"I know. It's just so hard to let her go."

"In all the time I've known you two, I've never seen her like this before."

"It's because she hasn't wanted anything badly enough. Believe me, when she really wants something she'll do anything to have it. Like when she was a kid, she was always

311

jealous of me. She couldn't get it through her head I got things before her because I was the older one. When I got the two-wheeler bike first, she wanted one, too, and right away. Mom would tell her that in two years it would be her turn. She'd throw a tantrum. You can imagine how she behaved when I brought home my first boyfriend. She did everything she could to sabotage us."

"Good old sibling rivalry. I only have a brother and we always hated each other's guts, but we never wanted what the other one got."

"My favorite memory is when Evvie found a dead mouse and put it under the couch where my boyfriend and I were sitting. The smell drove him home."

Ida grins. And I do, too.

I can't keep my eyes off the answering machine. Ida shakes her head. "Don't even think about it."

"But she's in real danger."

"If you insist on trying to interfere with Evvie and her obsession with Philip, you'll only make her dig deeper in. You can't reach her that way. I know that for a fact." Ida turns to the window, her back to me. "That's how I lost my son. Andy was going with Sheila, and they broke up. I made the mistake of telling him I never liked her, and I listed all her awful qualities. When they made up again and got married, neither of them wanted anything more to do with me."

It's been years since Ida mentioned the rift in her family. But she never told me why they never write, why they don't let her visit her grandchildren.

"I tried to apologize. They weren't interested. She turned my weak-willed son totally against me."

I put my hand on her shoulder. "I'm so sorry."

She nods, through tears. Her voice is hesitant, as if she's choosing her words carefully. "I guess I've always wanted to tell somebody. It would have been you, but you and Evvie were so close . . ."

"I wish you had. How did you keep all this in without cracking?"

She smiles wryly. "Maybe by becoming a bitch?"

I reach out and hug her. I remember when Ida moved in. It was fifteen years ago or so. She came alone. She wasn't interested in making friends and stayed by herself a lot. But slowly, I am guessing, when she felt safe, she started joining in the activities around here. She never spoke of her family except to mention her son and his family in

California. But she said very little. And we were always aware she wrote them letters but they weren't answered. She had no family pictures hanging anywhere in her apartment. But why do I feel she is still leaving something out?

Briskly, Ida changes the subject. "I know this is different. It could be a matter of life and death."

"I have to warn Evvie."

"She won't believe you. But you can't get through to her by bad-mouthing Philip. Not yet, anyway. We have to wait for the right opportunity."

"You're a wise old owl," I say, hugging her. We both shed a few tears and feel better. "Let's try and concentrate on something happier. Like the upcoming Tessie-Sol marriage."

Ida starts to laugh. "Did you see the expression on his face when Tessie saved his ass by proposing to him?"

"I had the feeling he'd rather have been hauled off to jail." Now I'm laughing.

"I bet he'll lose that sex urge for good the minute she gets naked."

"And then he'll have to go back to being the Peeper."

Laughing hard feels so good.

I lie on the couch. Ida went home hours ago. I am so tired, but I can't sleep. I miss my partner, my sister. She was always my other half. What I didn't know, Evvie usually did. Her insights were sharp. They complemented mine. If I saw something one way, she'd figure out the other angle. We should be sitting next to each other right now, excitedly firing away our thoughts. We'd put our heads together and come up with the solution. I still can't believe she's not here.

All along, even when I was worried about her playing the role of a widow, I felt she had good instincts about Philip. But that was before she fell under his spell.

I close my eyes and try to recall the things she said. My mind conjures up our first meeting with the Fergusons. When Evvie heard Philip's name, what was her comment? After a few moments it comes to me. She said what a la-di-da name. As if he was already sounding phony.

I sit up. I'm getting excited. Evvie, dear, you were onto him and you didn't know it. I try to remember the next comment she made about him. But first, I raid the fridge.

A few cookies with lots of sugar might help. Nervous eating is called for.

Then when Smythe made his grand entrance at Wilmington House, Evvie said he could play Dracula in summer stock. Even then he seemed unreal to her.

I think about the parking lot, the time we were giving the girls hell for sneaking in, pretending to take a tour. Philip drove up with those women in the car, and Evvie said — now I pace, trying to recall her words. Evvie said, "Talk about corny acting."

Now I'm pacing faster, and stuffing more cookies down my throat. I'll be sorry tomorrow. When she started dancing with him at the mixer, the first thing she said to him was, "Did anyone ever tell you that you look like a movie star?" I assumed she was handing him a line. She was. But there are a million other lines she could have used. Yet every time she's commented about him . . . yes!

And when he interrupted the canasta game she was playing, he flirted with all the women, giving them all a line.

Evvie, you did it! You nailed him. You've seen just about every movie you possibly could, every TV show as well. You didn't realize it at the time, but your subconscious recognized him. You'd seen him as an actor!

An actor using a stage name. Not his real name at all.

So eleven years ago an actor took on his character's name, Philip Smythe — and began a secret life. Why?

Suddenly it's as if a weight is lifted. Evvie and I are doing what we do best. Working together. Figuring things out. As if she were sitting here with me right now, I can almost feel her presence in the room. Thanks, sis.

Now I'm anxious again. I called my friend Conchetta at home a while ago and filled her in on all the latest developments. She said she'd look up Philip Smythe's name on her home computer.

A few minutes later, she calls back.

"Any luck?" I ask.

"No," she answers. "I Googled the name but nothing came up. I assume if it was a famous character name, it would have appeared. I also tried theater, TV, and movies on the Internet Movie Database. If they don't have it, it's either nonexistent or not important enough to make the cut. Sorry."

I'm disappointed, but I try to hide it. "Well, thanks for trying. I know I interrupted you and your family's evening entertainment."

"Not to worry. We taped this week's

episode of *Lost;* our family's hooked on it. I hope you can get Evvie out of there soon. Keep me informed."

"I will. Thanks again, Conchetta. I'll see you at the library soon, I hope. When we can get this thing wrapped up."

More pacing. And thinking.

So not in movies, theater, or TV. Through my tears of frustration, I finally smile. Maybe not nighttime TV, but daytime? Who was it told me about a show where the characters all had stuffy names? Of course. Now I know just the person who might be able to tell me who played the part of Philip Smythe.

I can hardly wait until morning.

Forty-Three: Dora Knows Her Showbiz

It is a beautiful September day, not a breeze in the air, just gentle warmth caressing the body. Everything seems so different with Evvie being away. The girls step out of their doors this morning expecting we'd go back into exercise mode, now that I'm staying home for a while. I still can't make up my mind. Remain here until I hear from Evvie, or go back to Wilmington House, where I can keep an eye on her even if I can't protect her? At the moment it feels right to stay. I can think better in my own surroundings. While we were away, Ida was trying to keep the girls on our usual schedule, but without us, it faltered. But even though the girls are expecting it, I'm not adhering to our old schedule. The girls are befuddled.

They watch me walk away from my building. Ida tentatively calls out, "Want company?"

I shake my head and continue on. I walk

briskly to Phase Six. My head is full of last night's realizations. Was Evvie's subconscious right? Am I correct in thinking so? It's a long shot, but I'll know soon enough.

Before I knock on Dora Dooley's door, I can't help but glance up at Jack's apartment. Has he been around since I ran into him last time? Or is he still off somewhere? Does he think of me at all? Or am I out of sight, out of mind? I shake my head. Stop it, that's not why you're here.

Dora Dooley takes a while to answer her door. I remember she first has to climb out of her bulky recliner. Okay, she's at the door. Now for a short interrogation.

"Who's there?"

"Gladdy Gold."

"Who?"

She doesn't have her hearing aid on. I repeat it. Louder.

"Wadda ya want?"

"May I come in and talk to you?"

"Why?"

I need a shortcut or I'll be standing out here forever. "I want to talk to you about your favorite soap opera."

The two locks unlock quickly. Open sesame.

As I walk in the door Dora peers at me closely. "I know you. Well, he isn't home."

She continues talking as she turns and makes her way back to her sunroom. "Jackie Langford is my only good neighbor. Nobody else takes out my garbage. You think the rest of them would help an old lady out." She's now climbed back up into her recliner.

This time I seat myself on the tiny, rickety chair, the only one in the small, stifling room. The recliner takes up most of the space and the TV set takes up the rest. A game show is on, at high volume. I wait for the commercial; I already know Dora's rules.

The commercial comes on.

"Is it possible to put the TV on mute? I really need to talk to you."

"What's mute?"

I get up and reach for the clicker. Her eyes show panic as I gently take her most important possession from her hand. "I'll give it back, I promise." I find the mute button and press it. Blessed silence. She looks at the soundless screen and then back at me fearfully, as if I were a voodoo witch. Probably terrified I won't turn it back on again.

Before she can complain, I talk fast. "I want to talk about your favorite soap opera, *World of Our Dreams.*" A show she told me was filled with stuffy character names. I can't believe I remembered it, but I'm thankful the brain cells were with me this time.

Once again I've said the magic words. Her eyes light up. "Did you know Penelope was pregnant and Sean isn't the real father?" She cackles. "While Sean was boffing Elizabeth, Penelope was kicking up her heels with Percy."

"No!" I say pretending surprise. "How shocking!"

"Just wait 'til Sebastian finds out. He's Penelope's father. There's a shotgun in his hall closet." She grins, toothlessly, happy to be sharing her favorite show with someone. Anyone. I ponder yet again about how lonely people deal with their days and nights. For Dora, the characters on *World of Our Dreams* are her kinfolk, a family she can visit with every day. Always available. Always loyal. Willing to share all their secrets.

"I want to ask you about Philip Smythe."

Dora looks at me, confused. "Who?"

I feel panic setting in. Was I wrong? It would have been too easy if this had been the show.

"Philip?" Dora asks, interrupting my mental anxiety attack. Then she breaks out in a big smile. "But he left the show years ago."

Thank you, God.

"Really? Tell me what happened."

Now Dora's eyes sparkle. She might not remember what she had for breakfast, but ask her about *World of Our Dreams* for all the years it's been on . . .

"It must be years ago, ten, maybe fifteen. Philip Smythe had a nervous breakdown."

I don't dare interrupt. Is she talking about the character on the show? Or the actor? Or both? I need to hear everything she knows.

"Oh, at first it was a great story line. Audiences were thrilled and chilled. Eighty-year-old wealthy Moira Atherton was drowned in her gold-plated bathtub, while sexy, wealthy Philip, calling himself Romeo, read her Shakespeare. He made it look like an accident. And Romeo wasn't suspected because he had no motive. But it was murder."

Bingo! I can hardly catch my breath.

"Then someone else on the show was killed. He just wouldn't stop. He needed to kill. More and more. Philip was turning into a serial killer. So the producer fired him. That's Glory Hill — boy, was she uppity. She's producing some new show now. Anyway, the serial killer plot was scaring the viewers. I was never scared. Philip was so gorgeous." She stops, satisfied.

Now I'm confused. "This was a part an actor played on the show. The character's name was Philip Smythe?"

"That's right."

"He was killing older women on the show? Other characters?"

"Right. Oh, those piercing eyes. I would have gladly let him kill me."

"So why was the actor fired? Couldn't they just stop playing the murder stories? I mean, if he was so gorgeous, why take him off the show?"

"Here's the skinny. He and Glory Hill had a big fight. You see, he was also one of the writers of the show. He wanted to keep his character killing, and she didn't want him killing off all her good stars. And the stars were complaining, too. They were afraid to open their new scripts, in case they were Philip's next victim. I read that in a TV magazine."

"He was also one of the writers? What was his name, this actor-writer?" I hold my breath.

"Writers. Writers. Who ever remembers writers?" For a moment she thinks, then smacks her forehead. "What a dummy. I can't remember the writer, but I remember the actor."

I feel like smacking my own head, I'm getting such a headache. "Okay, so tell me the name of the actor, who was also the writer, who made up the character of Philip Smythe, also played by this actor? Have I got it right?"

She grins. "I'm glad you're paying attention. Ray Sullivan."

Ray Sullivan. At last.

Gotcha.

On my gleeful way out of the apartment, after thanking Dora profusely and after telling her I can't stay until the show comes on in two hours, she calls after me, "While you're here, you could take out the garbage?"

Walking home from Phase Six I suddenly see a familiar car. It's Jack's. It's coming toward me and instinctively I hide behind the nearest palm tree. I see four people in the car. Another man and two women. He's on a double date?

I can't stand it. I am miserable. He's going to have to move out of Lanai Gardens. Or maybe I will.

Don't think about him. You've just figured out the real name of Romeo/Philip Smythe. You've just solved a murder case. Be happy about that. And I am.

FORTY-FOUR: BACK TO GRECIAN VILLAS

Ida and I get out of my car and head for Rosalie Gordon's office at Grecian Villas. She called me fifteen minutes ago, and there's no doubt she has something very important to tell us. From Mrs. Gordon's tone of voice, I know it's about Philip. We told her we'd hurry right over.

I've already filled Ida and the girls in on our big break, thanks to Dora Dooley and her soaps. There's no doubt in anyone's mind now. Philip Smythe, née Ray Sullivan, is a killer. We are more than shocked even though we suspected him. It was one thing to feel sure he killed Esther Ferguson. But after hearing what Casey and Barbi told us, it's the enormity of his crimes. We must believe he is a serial killer. God knows how many women he's murdered.

I'm aching to rush over to Wilmington House and rip Evvie away from her killer-lover's arms. I have this fantasy I will face him and call him by his real name and he will fold. Evvie will see the truth and the good guys win. But he is a murderer; who knows what he's capable of? I will do nothing, not before I have a chance to fill Morrie in and get the police on our side. Which I will do this afternoon. Believe me, I'm not looking forward to this. He has to know his father and I are kaput.

My instincts tell me to go slow. Stay away from Wilmington House until Morrie tells me how to handle this. According to Casey and Barbi's calculations, Evvie should be safe for another couple of months. That doesn't allay my fears. Evvie has a strong personality. In her emotional feelings for Philip she might admit who and what we are and why we are at Wilmington House. She could accidentally set him off. I can't take that chance. Until Evvie is out of there, I won't be able to rest for a moment.

Ida, bless her, has stepped into Evvie's shoes. She is amazing. She assures me that as soon as Evvie returns from the Twilight Zone, as she keeps calling it, she, Ida, will move back to position number three. I could have kissed her for saying that. In the midst of this trauma, there's been an unexpected blessing. With Evvie being away, Ida and I have become closer and I've learned more about her than I've ever known.

It doesn't take long for Rosalie Gordon and her assistant to fill us in. They are obviously terrified and insist we speak behind locked doors. That's how we learn that something terrible happened in Tallahassee at their sister business, Roman Villas. Worse. A missing resident, Pearl Mosher, was found dead and buried in their backyard. Something must have gone wrong and Philip must have been forced to kill his lover ahead of time. It must have driven him crazy to have his schedule spoiled. How arrogant of him to have moved down south and later on stayed at another branch of the Villas. Only a madman would take such a chance.

"Can you help us?" Rosalie asks timidly.

"We're on our way to see the police today. We have a lot to tell them, and your news is vital."

"There's much more than you know." Ida tries to reassure her. "There will be a strong case against Philip Smythe very soon."

"But what should we do?" She wrings her hands. Myra stands behind her, equally tense.

"Nothing," I tell them. "Just wait and we'll keep you informed. I know it will be hard, but reassure your partners up north and try to keep things calm — business as usual.

Discuss this with no one else unless you feel you must talk to your lawyer."

"But can you keep us out of the spotlight?"

"I don't know. I'll ask Detective Langford to do what he can to protect you. Your coming to us will be considered very helpful. Detective Langford is very kind. So don't be afraid when he calls on you."

I take down the Tallahassee information, including the name of the detective in charge.

They walk us to the door. The elegant lobby is full as usual. Almost everyone looks up as we appear.

Ida, my mensch, shakes Rosalie's hand. "Thank you for the tour," she says grandly. "You have a lovely place. You'll be hearing from us soon."

With that, the lobby sitters go back about their own business.

Rosalie manages a small smile and we leave.

I can't wait to get to Morrie. Is he in for a big surprise.

I call Morrie from our cell phone. I hear the reluctance in his voice. He's afraid I'm calling about his father.

"Morrie. Listen. I'd like to come in and

discuss a murder. It's a case we're on."

"Where is this?" he asks guardedly.

"In Fort Lauderdale. But it's more complicated than that. I'm concerned he will kill again where we are in Palm Beach."

Morrie must have his hand over the phone. I doubt that he paid any attention. I can barely hear him talking to someone in his office. Then he's back to me. "Listen, Gladdy, we're very busy over here and that's out of our jurisdiction. Call the police up there."

"No, you don't understand."

He cuts me off. "I really can't talk now." And he hangs up.

Thanks for nothing. Morrie still has this annoying habit of not taking me seriously.

I dial the police station again. You don't get rid of me that easily, I think. I make an appointment to come in and see him.

FORTY-FIVE:
MORRIE AND GLADDY
AND OZ

Morrie is finishing up a call. Cops walk by his open door, recognize me sitting there, and wave and smile. I don't know whether it's because they think I might become his stepmother or whether I'm considered that weird old broad who thinks she's Agatha Christie and solves crimes. Not that they know who Dame Agatha is, so maybe I'm seen as just that neighborhood busybody. Ida was dying to come with me, but she'd promised Sophie she'd go to her new doctor with her. It's her first real visit with Dr. Reich, so Ida said she'd accompany her.

A terrific-looking guy comes by in a very flashy plaid jacket, stops, sees Morrie on the phone, and walks in. He's about forty, medium height, light chocolate brown skin with very short-cropped black hair; he looks like he works out in the gym a lot and has a smile that could make strong women weak. He walks over to me and shakes my hand.

What a firm handshake. He introduces himself. "Hi, I'm Oz Washington, or even Ozzie. Really Oswald, but please never call me by that name. I was Morrie's former patrol partner. Now we're both detectives."

Oy, is he a charmer. "Oz, like in wizard of?"

He grins. "Yeah, I get that a lot. I've heard about you."

Morrie finishes his call and walks toward us.

I address this at him. "Seems everybody around here knows who I am. Morrie must be some chatterbox."

"I resent that," Morrie says, as he joins us. Now I have two gorgeous men hovering over me. Oh, to be forty years younger.

Oz laughs. "We actually see you as the one who solves most of his cases. He'd be lost without you."

Morrie hits him playfully on the shoulder. "Funny."

I say, "The Peeper case is closed."

"That's good news. Anybody we know?"

"Sol Spankowitz, who is in desperate need of a wife. And Tessie will marry him. And nobody's pressing charges."

He thinks about that for a moment and smiles. "So why are you here?" He's already forgotten my phone call.

Oz asks, "Have you another case you've already solved for him to take credit for?"

"You're pushing your luck, feller."

"Mind if I sit in? I might learn something. That is, if Mrs. Gold will let me."

Ask me anything, *bubbala;* you only have to blink those long eyelashes. "Sure, why not."

Morrie reiterates with sarcasm. "Sure, why not, you need to learn *something.* Even if it's only manners."

The guys grin at each other. Cop banter. Actually I think Morrie is relieved. Does he really think I would bring up the subject of his father? Never again. I have my pride. I take a sheet of paper out of my purse.

"I wrote it all down so I wouldn't forget. I'm on a case that now needs the police to get involved. Namely, you, Morrie, I mean Morgan." Maybe he's more formal around here.

"We're all ears," says his former partner, gleefully.

I read from my list. "A Mr. Alvin Ferguson hired us to check on a man named Philip Smythe who lived with Alvin's mother until she drowned in her bathtub. Mrs. Esther Ferguson was ninety-five. Mr. Smythe is seventy-five. They shared an apartment at a retirement complex, Fort Lauderdale's

Grecian Villas. Mrs. Shirley Ferguson, Alvin's wife, told us Philip adored Esther, had no motive to kill her. He was not after her money. Yet her husband, Alvin, insists on believing Philip Smythe murdered his mother.

"We find out Philip Smythe moved from Grecian Villas immediately after Esther died and is now living in Palm Beach at Wilmington House. My sister Evvie and I went undercover to see what we could find out about him. She's still there."

Don't think I miss the sniggering exchange of glances as the two hardened detectives think of us old dames undercover. But I persevere.

"Further investigation on our part led us to the surprising news that Philip has spent the last eleven years going from one retirement community to another, staying the exact same amount of time in each place, following an identical schedule. Three months there. Finding a lover, and leaving on exactly the same date each time. I might add, at that point, the woman he had been sleeping with" — I see their eyebrows go up at my naughty words — "had conveniently died of seemingly natural causes."

By now I'm aware that other police staff have been entering the room and standing in the back quietly listening in. I also see something glitter in Oz's eyes, but I can't figure out what he might be thinking.

"Investigation now indicates that Philip Smythe is a false name. He leaves an eleven-year-old trail, which ends abruptly at that time. He doesn't seem to have existed before that."

I keep expecting one of them to interrupt, but they stay very still, paying attention. So I soldier on.

"Further investigation leads me to learn his real name is Raymond, or Ray, Sullivan, and that he was an actor and writer on a daytime soap opera in New York City for many years. Until he was fired — eleven years ago! As a writer, Ray Sullivan came up with the story line of a man who keeps murdering older women in retirement complexes. As the actor, Ray played the part of Philip Smythe, the serial killer. Putting one and one together: Right after being fired, he began acting out his TV role in real life.

"Which brings us up to this very morning. I have only just learned that a year ago, last September, in Roman Villas, a retirement complex in Tallahassee, Philip romanced a lady named Pearl Mosher. She ostensibly had a fight with him, and it was presumed she left the premises in the middle of the night. Her murdered body turned up this week in the gardens on said property."

I pause and take out another sheet of paper. "Here is the list of every retirement facility in which Philip Smythe, a.k.a. Ray Sullivan, lived, and the names of all his dead lovers. I also have the names of all the managers of these places. I also have the name and number of the investigating officer in Tallahassee. He is awaiting your call. Oh, and tomorrow I'm going to be checking in with some showbiz types. The rest of the answer lies there."

There is a very long silence. Morrie looks flummoxed. Oz is grinning. Suddenly there is a burst of applause from everyone in the room. Except Morrie.

Oz shakes my hand. "Have you thought of enrolling in our police academy? We need detectives like you."

He winks at Morrie. "Take over, champ. This senior citizen here needs your help desperately." With that, he exits the room, laughing out loud.

The others file out with last admiring looks at me and amused glances at Morrie, who is still in mild shock. The room is at last empty.

Morrie is mortified. "You could have told me all this without an audience, you know."

"I tried." I blush. I look around, making sure we are alone now.

"Morrie, I must tell you something very important." I pause. This is hard to say.

"What is it, Gladdy?"

"It's Evvie. She's become involved with this man. She believes he's innocent. I'm afraid she is in great danger."

He returns my serious look. "Got it.

"We'll take over now. But you have to promise me you'll stay away from the case from now on. Do not talk to another person. This man is obviously dangerous. Stay out of it now. Do you hear me, Gladdy?"

I nod, but my fingers are crossed behind my back.

It is only after I leave the building that I feel remorse for what I did to poor Morrie. It wasn't nice of me to take my frustration out on Jack's son. But I sure feel better.

FORTY-SIX:
TASK FORCE

We are in my kitchen discussing my meeting with Morrie.

"I wish we could get to Evvie and warn her," Sophie says for about the fifth time in ten minutes.

"Yeah," Bella agrees.

Everyone is repeating their fears as if, in the retelling, they'll vanish.

Ida changes the subject. "Are you really going to see those people, even though Morrie said no?"

"Yes. His men won't have time to do everything. I think I'll handle it better. I really need to see this case through."

The phone rings. Bella jumps. Everyone's on edge, terrified of hearing bad news. It's Morrie. I immediately switch on the speakerphone, so the girls can listen in. Another of the devices Jack talked me into. Jack . . . Never mind — no use thinking about him now. Mr. Double Date.

"Hi, Gladdy. How you?"

"Fine. How are you?"

"Still a little shaken after that bomb you set off in my office. I guess you are well beyond finding purses in Kmart."

"Guess so."

"Just want to give you a heads-up on what's happening. We're in touch with all the precincts in every city he's lived in. A task force has already been set up. We're waiting for the autopsy report on Mrs. Mosher. Maybe we'll get lucky and pick up some DNA."

"Good." About time he took me seriously.

"So far, it's all circumstantial. We have no proof yet. I just want to warn you. Everybody, keep quiet. I mean all you girls."

"We hear you," chorus Bella and Sophie. Ida nods grimly.

"Talk to no one about any of this. Keep away from Evvie. We don't want Smythe to get suspicious and run. Or even worse, become dangerous to Evvie and maybe others in that place."

"But —" I try to get a word in.

"Listen." He interrupts me. "The Palm Beach police have arranged for someone to move into Wilmington House as a new resident. One of their retired officers. Someone who'll keep his eye on the dangerous Mr. Smythe."

"I am so relieved to hear that. But Smythe can be tricky —"

"Yes, Gladdy . . ."

There's that condescending voice again. "Just make sure he's very watchful."

"I'm sure he will be. I've already spoken to Ms. Watson and she is expecting a Mr. Donald Kincaid to arrive today."

"How did she take it?"

"Somewhat upset."

"I'll call her, see if I can calm her down."

"Good idea."

"Okay, but you better promise to keep in touch with me on my cell phone."

I can almost see the smile. "Gladdy Gold, you have a cell? I thought you hated progress."

"Never mind that. Just do it." I give him my number.

"Gladdy . . . I'm sorry about you and Dad." His voice is concerned, but cautious.

I choke up. "Thanks," I manage to say.

Not five minutes later, my cell rings. It's Hope Watson sounding like she's on the verge of hysteria. "Is it true? They know for sure he's a killer?"

"I'm afraid so."

"How soon will they pick him up?"

"I don't know yet. It will take careful planning. I know what you're going to say next. Don't tell anyone."

"But what about my board? I have to answer to them."

"The more people who know, the more dangerous it could be."

"I must at least tell the president of the board."

"Do what you need to, but it mustn't leak."

I can hear Hope Watson is close to tears.

I continue, "Hope, you must keep everything as normal as you can."

"All right." She can barely speak.

No more subterfuge — I need to know. "How is my sister?"

She sounds startled. "She and Philip are having a wonderful time." She can't hide her sarcasm. "They're everywhere. They're the fun couple. Everyone wants to be part of their clique."

"Good. In fact, try to add some activities that keep them surrounded by people as much as possible. I don't want anything to upset the status quo. The less they are alone, the better."

"I can't believe this is happening to us."

"You'll feel better having a policeman on the premises at all times."

"When are you coming back?"

341

"I don't know. Soon, I think."

I don't intend to tell her about the ladies at the Roman Villas dealing with a dead body found on their premises. It's bad enough, her having the killer living in her own establishment.

I pray all these delicate manager ladies won't fall apart.

Forty-Seven:
The New Man

"Ladies and gentlemen, may I have your attention?" She taps a spoon on a glass. The eating stops momentarily as Hope Watson addresses the dining room group. She smiles a little too brightly.

Evvie is only half listening; her attention is on Philip chatting with the woman on the other side of him.

"We have a new resident, Mr. Donald Kincaid. He tells us he's formerly from Brooklyn."

Donald Kincaid stands and bows. Evvie glances up. This new man is the picture of a jolly roly-poly sixty-year-old, dressed in a rather loud checkered jacket. He gives the impression of an easygoing guy with no worries. "Thanks, Hope. Just to let ya know, I'm single and available. And a good dancer."

There is some tittering at that from some of the ladies. Even Evvie smiles.

"I also spent years as a security guard at Wal-Mart. And I even got to play Santa Claus at Christmas. Lucky I have rich kids who can afford to send me here."

More laughter. Evvie notes that he's coming across as a likable guy. Yet, there's something about him . . . She goes back to her meal and joins Philip in his chat with other people at their table.

"So," continues cheery, blustery Donald, "if any of you ladies feel like you're in trouble or something, I have a great big gun, so just dial my extension, five-oh-five. I will be at your apartment in a flash."

The seemingly sexual innuendo receives a lot of laughs. Hope pretends to be shocked.

Evvie looks up from her Dover sole. She's startled to see Donald Kincaid looking directly at her. "Remember, five-oh-five, if you need me." He winks, and then quickly glances away.

Did I imagine it? Evvie thinks. Was he talking to me?

Evvie wakes up. She imagines she heard something. Something in the hallway. She glances at the clock. One-fifteen a.m. Philip is sleeping, although restlessly. She tiptoes to the door and looks through the peephole. She is surprised to see Hope Watson and the new resident, Donald somebody, who just moved in. The man she imagined had winked at her.

They are talking softly. And looking at Phil-

344

ip's door. What does it mean? She and Philip are being watched? Why? The man, Donald, what was it about him? He said he had been a security guard? But he looks like a cop. A real cop. Something in the way he stands there. At attention. Ready for what? Is Watson going to throw them out for misbehavior? Something's wrong . . .

She is pulled back into the room by the sounds of moaning. Philip is thrashing about, trapping himself in the sheets, seemingly deep in some nightmare.

He's mumbling, becoming more and more agitated. "No . . . go back . . . you can't come out . . . No!" As Evvie leans close to him, his arm whips out, hitting her.

"Phil! Wake up!"

His arms flail. "Get back. I didn't say you could come out . . . My head . . . my head . . ."

She hears more mumbling, but she can't make out the words. Once he cries out, "Ray!" and then, " 'To sleep perchance to dream . . .' "

And suddenly it's over. Philip is sound asleep.

Forty-Eight:
Mister Ten Percent

I take the rickety elevator up to the third floor. The building is old and smells of decay, and it is in a warehouse part of Miami I've never been to before.

I walk down the dreary hallway lit by very low wattage. I'd be afraid to walk it at night. I'm not that comfortable during the day, either.

I enter the office of Herbie Feldkin and Associates, on time for my ten a.m. Monday appointment. I don't see any associates. I don't even see Herbie Feldkin. I do look around. It's a one-man office with a lot of very old furniture and very old faded black-and-white photos on the dingy walls, along with a number of movie posters, equally from long ago. It seems at one time Herbie had a few fairly well-known actors in his stable.

And there he is, in an old glossy black-and-white: Ray Sullivan, a.k.a. Philip

Smythe. I have to touch it to believe it. Next to a photo of a famous movie star.

"When they make it big, they leave." Herbie Feldkin, I presume — late sixties, short, bald, and stubby — enters carrying a brown bag. "That's the nature of the business."

He takes out two hot plastic cups of coffee and a couple of Danish and by removing a messy stack of *Hollywood Reporter*s and *Variety*s, he makes room on a table already decorated with discolored circles from years of hot coffee cups.

"Cream and sugar?" He indicates the little packets.

"Thank you, that's very thoughtful." I help myself.

"Don't get a lot of company, as maybe you already guessed. But I used to be a contenda," he says imitating Marlon Brando. Evvie would love this guy. They could talk movies forever. With the thought of Evvie, I grow cold. I must get this over with and get home. I feel a clock ticking in my head.

He sits down behind his scarred desk. I sit in front of him.

"This is really a set."

"What?"

He indicates the furniture. "I bought the original set of *The Maltese Falcon*. Actually I'm very rich and retired and live on Fisher

347

Island, but it amuses me to come in once in a while."

I don't know whether to believe him or not, but I like him. He doesn't take himself seriously. Maybe the shabby suit he wears came from the wardrobe of the same picture.

"So, Mrs. Gold. You tell me over the phone you want to talk about Philip Smythe. You don't say Ray Sullivan, so I'm intrigued. I haven't heard that name in a lot of years. Not since I left my New York office in the nineties."

"Probably eleven years." I hope that stirs something.

Herbie looks surprised. "That's about right. Ray left the show — *World of Our Dreams* — and just seemed to disappear. I tried calling him after he got fired. Maybe I could have gotten him another job either as a writer or actor. I mean, he was still a sexy-looking old guy, but in this business old is dead. Look at me. But then again, he was behaving a bit nutzoid." He makes a whirling motion with his hand. "You meant it when you said this was a matter of life and death? If it was to get my attention, it did. You don't look like you're the police."

I hand him Morrie's card. "If you want to check, call this number. I am helping with a homicide case."

Herbie brushes the Danish crumbs off his pants onto the floor. "You're joshing me, right? You look like you should be living in a condo by the beach and playing mah-jongg every day."

"Close enough. But I am investigating a murder nonetheless. It's a long story; I can't fill you in completely. I'm sorry."

"And Ray is involved?"

"We think so. For the last eleven years he has been living under the name of Philip Smythe."

For a moment, it doesn't connect. "You're kidding." Herbie's face transforms as he puts things together in his mind. He gets up and removes a file from his old oak filing cabinet. "Here's something weird. For that same amount of years, I have been getting money orders from Ray. On almost the exact same dates. Ten percent of what used to be his salary. For a while I didn't cash them, trying to locate him. Figured maybe he was doing some kind of show in some local TV station. But those stations wouldn't pay this kind of money. Eventually I cashed them and kept the receipts in here. But what's that got to do with his using his character name from the show?"

"By any remote chance, did you save the

envelopes from where the money orders were sent?"

"No, sorry, I didn't think it would be important, but I remembered they were from various parts of Florida. So I figured he retired down here, too. Everybody does, eventually."

"The checks came each year at the end of March, July, and November. Yes?"

"Wow. Either you're a mind reader or he is in some deep —" He stops himself. "Trouble." He finds a less vulgar word to use in front of the little old lady from a condo.

"I need to talk to someone on his old show as soon as possible. The producer, Ms. Hill? Somehow I doubt my calling her will do any good. Could you arrange a meeting? I'd be willing to fly up to New York to see her."

His eyebrows lift at the sound of that name. "Like I said — everybody moves down here eventually. She lives in Boca. But I gotta tell you a couple of things. She left the show in New York; or rather they eased her out when she got to a certain age. But that woman could not just spend her money and live the good life. Showbiz was her life."

"What are you telling me, Mr. Feldkin?"

"You ever see a movie called *Sunset Bou-*

levard?"

"Yes, of course. With Gloria Swanson."

"Well, that's this Glory, too. She found some dumpy production company down here and she's producing a two-bit syndicated tape soap for them. But she still behaves like, like, Gloria Swanson. It's a weird scene. She's using her own money for the fancy offices and high salaries. Everybody's playing parts, playing up to Her Highness. But laughing at her behind her back. And taking as much advantage of her as they can. Still wanna see her?"

"Yes, please."

He picks up the phone. "It's a done deal."

I wait until Herbie speaks to what seems like one secretary after another until he is finally connected to Glory Hill herself. He talks to her as if she were royalty. She seems to be arguing. He uses his charm. "Glory, baby, for your old buddy, please? The woman is a fan. A big fan."

I wait eagerly.

He listens and then looks at me. "Noon, okay?"

"Perfect."

Herbie hangs up fast before she changes her mind. He writes the address on the back of an old envelope he pulls out of the trash and hands it to me. "I gotta warn you, she's crazy, but still a bitch on wheels."

Herbie pulls the photo of Ray Sullivan off the wall, blows the dust off it, and then hands it to me. He walks me to the door. "You were bluffing, weren't you? About this being a matter of life or death."

"No. I'm deadly serious." I can't stop staring at the photo of "Philip."

Herbie shakes my hand. "Listen, maybe you'll let me know how this goes down?"

"You might be reading it in the papers. Even *Variety*."

"Good luck, Mrs. Gold. You'll need it. She wasn't called the Black Widow of Daytime for nothing."

FORTY-NINE:
THE PRODUCER

The young, size-six, adorable blond assistant gives me a tour as we wind our way through many hallways, with walls totally covered with huge color portraits of the stars that've played on Glory Hill's very famous former long-running soap opera. I search for Philip Smythe/Ray Sullivan, but no luck. Another wall features the stars of the soap opera Glory is working on now. Of course Bree, as the assistant introduced herself, never calls it by that name. "Daytime serial" is the proper terminology, she instructs me. She walks quickly. I can barely keep up. But then I notice everyone I pass in the halls is moving at a fast pace.

Doors are open. I get glimpses of actors being made up, but I notice even their feet are tapping, or pacing as they practice lines in their dressing rooms. A woman pushing a hanging rod of costumes fairly runs past me.

I decide to ask Bree, "Doesn't anyone move slowly?" She looks horrified. "Not on this show! That's if you want to keep your job."

I peer at her, thinking she is kidding, but she is serious. We reach a door that says, in large gilt letters, GLORY HILL, EXECUTIVE PRODUCER.

Inside, I find three secretaries on different phones, earphones in ears and hands free to busily write down messages. The walls are filled with photos; I assume they must be of Glory Hill, shaking hands with many, many celebrities. There is also a huge glass china cabinet filled with awards.

At the far end of this large office, someone is sitting with a stack of what look like scripts. She is writing on each of the covers.

When I listen more carefully, I can tell the secretaries aren't on business calls but on personal calls, chatting and wasting time, and what they are scribbling on their pads is doodles.

My tour guide speaks to one of the women who just hung up.

"Cheryl, this is Mrs. Gold. She has a noon appointment."

"The queen is still on her throne." Mild smirking at that.

At that moment, a loudspeaker blares in

the room and a loud hoarse voice, with a pronounced British accent, is heard. "Get on the horn and get me eight tonight at La Funicular, table for two."

The voice stops. In the ensuing silence I just blurt it out: "Is your producer British?"

The room erupts in screaming laughter.

"Hoddley, m'dear." The one I was just told was Cheryl speaks in a falsetto British parody. "She was born in Flatbush."

The male tells me, "That's in Brooklyn. And don't ever mention you know that or heads will roll."

I wish I hadn't opened my mouth.

"You make the call, Jody," says Cheryl. "I'm not about to get screamed at by that maître d' again."

"Tim, it's your turn," says Jody, passing the buck to the young man at the third desk.

"Why bother. We know what they'll say." He puts on a snobbish accent. " 'Ms. Hill is no longer welcome at this establishment.' "

They laugh. Apparently they don't care that a total stranger is privy to their snide comments about the hand that feeds them. "Call La Finestre. She'll never remember which one of the 'La's she asked for. They haven't thrown her out. Yet." He makes an elbow/hand-to-mouth gesture that tells me he is referring to too much liquor and probably the behavior that went with it.

My tour guide giggles, but looks at me with embarrassment.

The voice of God blares again on the speaker. "Make the reservation for five more people. This whole frigging writing staff is having a working dinner meeting."

Now the laughter really erupts. "Poor SOBs," Tim comments. "Wait 'til you see the bar bill."

"It's the only way they'll survive it."

"And none of them will remember a note they take!" Tim sneers.

Bree touches my arm. "Would you like to see where the writers meet?" I think she wants to get me out of there.

In the hall, Bree feels she needs to apologize. "There's always a lot of tension on a show. I mean, we have so many deadlines. And sometimes the writers can be slow. I mean, they try hard, but Ms. Hill is so demanding. She comes from New York, you know, and she expects us to keep up the same standards. I mean, scripts have to be written over and over again. I mean . . ." She stops. She's run out of "I means". I'm getting the picture, though.

Apparently the writers' meeting has just ended. Five exhausted, angry-looking people drag themselves out of a conference room. Various ages, both sexes. They carry arms full of scripts and notebooks and look only at the floor. I hear the same hoarse voice coming from inside the room. "And I hope that by tonight one of you, just one of you, will have an idea. Any idea. Something that hasn't been rehashed a thousand times before."

And there she is, the famous Glory Hill. Tall, incredibly skinny, with very short bleached orange-red hair and — truthfully? Very ugly. I wonder how many face-lifts she's had, how many experts worked on attempting to change that mug, how much makeup was tried. But there was nothing that would fix that pointy jaw, the sagging eyelids, the ratty hair, the gray, sallow complexion, probably from years of smoking. Which would also explain the voice. All those experts at her command, all that beauty surrounding her, all that money — and there she is. Margaret Hamilton's twin, the wicked witch in *The Wizard of Oz*. Makes millions of bucks selling beauty she can't have. What irony.

"Who's she?" Glory Hill says, annoyed, pointing to me.

"Your noon appointment," Bree answers. I swear she's shaking.

She comes alongside me, dismisses Bree

with the back of her hand, keeps looking at her notes, and beckons me to follow. All without missing a step. Here we go again, fast walking. This would be a great place to work if one wanted to lose weight. Or have a heart attack.

"I don't have much time. Taping begins in fifteen. So state your business and be brief."

I don't work for her. I don't need to put up with her tyranny, but I could see how one could get caught up. I automatically get in step with her and state my case. "I need to know about Philip Smythe, the character, and Ray Sullivan, the actor-writer. Specifically I need to know as much as you can tell me about the seducer/serial killer character he created and acted out." Whew. See what pressure can do?

She turns and actually smiles at me, still not slowing up. "Very precise. Organized thoughts. Maybe you'd like a job writing this show. The losers I have to put up with are pathetic hacks."

I smile. "Thanks for the offer, but I'm a retired person. However, I'm working with the Florida police, who believe Ray Sullivan may be a serial killer who has been murdering elderly women for as long as eleven years, using his character's name."

Glory Hill actually stops in her tracks. Her

eyes light up. "Ray Sullivan. I fired that drunk from playing that part. And you're telling me he continued acting it out in the real world? Hot damn! I could redo this story as a sequel. Is Feldkin still his agent?"

"Slow down," I tell this whirlwind. "First things first. I want to know where he got the idea from. In fact, I want to know everything about this story line — and could we please sit down somewhere?"

She has incredible reflexes. Without missing a beat, she practically pulls me into a room that looks like a costume storeroom. There are two metal folding chairs. She points to one and takes the other. She kicks the door closed and lights up a cigarette. "Nobody but me can do this. Got it?" She takes out a portable, foldable mini-ashtray and looks at her watch.

"Got it." I guess I better talk fast.

Now I have to put up with her secondhand smoke. And the costumes will probably smell by the time we leave.

"Ray came up with the idea. He felt his character of Philip, the rich, lazy playboy, was getting stale. When we'd work late hours and he'd drink a lot, he ranted about his rich old aunt Dorothy, whom he hated and had to take care of all the years she was sick, and how he wished he could have

359

killed her and put her out of her misery. He was stuck with taking care of her until she died. I encouraged his rage. Turn your anger into a story, I told him. Good drama. I told him to write it up. He was around sixty at the time, and not only could he write it, it was perfect for Philip Smythe to evolve into this sexy older, sophisticated gent who went bonkers and started killing old ladies. But here's the funny thing. The next day when Ray was sober, I congratulated him on his story idea. He didn't remember it."

Glory Hill is a great storyteller herself. I'm sitting on the edge of my seat. "But, but —"

She shuts me up. Ms. Hill, I realize, does not like to be interrupted.

"When I told him, he gave me this funny look. He said he loved his aunt Dorothy and willingly took care of her. Ha-ha. That's booze for you. Some people cannot hold their liquor."

I smile, thinking of her secretaries' imitation of her drinking habit. "But being smart, Ray recognized a good plot when he heard it, and so began that story line. Even though, I must admit, he wasn't comfortable writing it. Audiences thought it was great. And scary. And, my dear, the ratings shot up to the sky."

"Do you remember the aunt's full name?"

"Yeah, she was some heiress, Dorothy Sullivan. Ray was the last in a line of a very rich family. It's in my files."

"The story line. What was in it?"

"So Ray, the writer, had Philip, the character, go from one retirement home to another. He'd pick a woman who had no living relatives. They must be real old and near death, or have an illness that would kill them soon. On a certain date, he helped them leave the world forever."

I can hardly sit still, I'm so excited. Everything fit. He was our man, all right. "What did he gain by killing them?"

"Ray didn't want to write the cliché of Philip Smythe being after their money. No, Philip was a mercy killer who dearly loved the old biddies and didn't want them to suffer. But he always took a souvenir."

I want to jump up and down for joy. Maybe this is the missing piece. "Such as?"

She laughs. "He was a killer with class. Whatever he took was in excellent taste. He took a painting or an Oriental rug or a rare piece of antique jewelry." She looks at her watch again and taps her long bright orange Cruella De Vil fingernails along the edge of the chair.

I spoke faster. "Why did you fire him?"

"Because we began to realize the audience was freaking out. Soaps are about love and sex, not about scaring the crap out of the viewers. We were getting terrified letters. Especially from old broads who were afraid to go to sleep at night. Now, get this, you'll love it: I told Ray to kill Smythe off or put him in jail, or have him find God and repent. Just stop the story. He agreed. It was even making him queasy. But Ray, the actor, wouldn't do it."

"What do you mean?"

"Ray, in his tuxedo, would get on the set and fling the script against a wall and say, 'Philip Smythe has to keep killing!'

"That was it, the booze had taken over. Maybe even drugs. Who knows? He was getting crazier and crazier. I like that in my writers, but he fell off the edge. He was drunk on and off the set. I had no choice. The network made me dump him. So goodbye, Ray."

Wow! I can hardly wait to call Morrie.

Glory snaps her little ashtray shut and she's on the move again.

I rush after her. "Did you ever hear about him or from him again?"

"Funny you should mention that. I get a note three times a year. Not signed, but I know it's from him."

"How do you know?"

"He includes a photo. A rug. A rare piece of jewelry. You know, like all the souvenirs he took on the show. I thought he was just teasing me. To tell me what I've missed by firing him."

I feel my heart popping out of my chest. "Please tell me you saved the photos."

"Of course I did. I never throw anything out. Everything goes in my memoirs. If I ever stop working and write them. A lot of people will be sorry when I do. You want them?"

"You bet!"

Looking at the watch again. She reaches the stage. "Time's up. We're through talking. Go back to my office, and tell Tim to go into my private files and get the photos for you. Videos of those shows, too, if you want them. Make sure he makes copies of the originals and you sign for them. I want first rights to the story of his trial. Hmm, I wonder if they'd let him out to play himself? Good-bye, Mrs. — uh, whoever you are."

And the whirlwind is gone.

I can't believe it. I have all the proof the police need!

And, while I was at it, I got a huge pack of autographed eight-by-tens of all the stars on both her old show and her new one to take home to Dora Dooley.

FIFTY:
ALL SYSTEMS ARE
GO

I call Morrie from home. "This is Gladdy. I have something very important to tell you."

I can hear Morrie getting angry. "What did I tell you? You didn't listen, did you?"

"Before you make a *tsimmis* out of it, I have positive proof. Positive proof that Ray Sullivan is a killer."

That stops him. "Then get it over to the station right away. I'll have the task force waiting for you." I guess he isn't mad at me anymore.

Ida picks up on my excitement. "So you got the goods on him."

"He's finished."

"When are they gonna rescue Evvie?" Sophie asks.

"It better be soon."

Bella is concerned. "But won't she be sore if they take Philip away from her?"

"Not when she realizes that he is a killer after all." I exchange glances with Ida. She knows how difficult that will be.

I hug them all. "See you later."

"Don't worry, we'll be waiting." Ida actually has tears in her eyes. "Good luck."

The huge conference room in the Fort Lauderdale police station is filled. The task force from all over the state and from Georgia, as well, listen to everything I report. The most chilling moments are watching actor Ray Sullivan, playing Philip Smythe, murdering one of the cast member "widows" on video.

Hearing him say, " 'Parting is such sweet sorrow,' " as he pushes the actress under the bubbles in the tub, horrifies me. I could imagine how it was for Esther Ferguson at the last moments of her life.

And now I am told what the task force has found. Widow after widow dying suddenly at the end of Philip/Ray's planned stays at each retirement home. They've already discovered seven so far. Unlucky women who had no families, so no one raised any questions. When Esther Ferguson's family showed up, Philip must have panicked. She'd hidden the fact of her family by changing her mailbox address, but when Alvin and Shirley came to visit unexpectedly, that sealed Esther's fate. That was his fatal mistake. He panicked. He should have left Esther alive. But he was too rigidly set in his patterns.

And none of these retirement complexes ever dug deep enough to see these coincidental deaths. I shudder. They are still searching. How many more will there be? Evvie, oh, Evvie, we've got to get you out of there.

Oz Washington comes over to congratulate me. He sees how nervous I am. "I'm worried about getting my sister out safely."

"It will be all right," he tells me. "I make fun of my bud, Morrie, but he's one hell of a good cop."

"Can I have that in writing?"

He pats me on the shoulder and joins the others.

They are all action now. Gathering up materials, conferring with one another, making phone calls.

Morrie walks over to me. "By the way, about his aunt Dorothy? He didn't kill her. He was away at boarding school."

"That's a surprise. I was so sure he did it. Morrie," I ask, looking at my watch, "it's already nearly three o'clock. When are we going up to Palm Beach?"

"Tonight. Late."

This upsets me. "Why?" I want to go now.

"Because we decided it was better to move

in fast, with everyone asleep; Ray Sullivan should be off guard and hopefully we can pull him out of his apartment without many people aware of it. Hope Watson and Donald Kincaid will let us in."

That is if Evvie doesn't start screaming and wake the entire place. The plan is sensible, but I am very nervous. I feel Evvie needs me. Now.

"Dearest, wake up. Please. It's almost four."
Evvie shakes Philip's shoulders gently.

He pushes her away. "Tired," he mumbles into his pillow.

She starts to pull the drapes.

"No," he shouts. "No light."

She knows how badly he slept last night. In fact, for the last few nights, it seemed like he was having more and more headaches. And more nightmares.

She is about to open the door and go downstairs, but she hesitates. The last thing she wants is to run into that cop, Donald. Something is very wrong in her room with Philip — and outside as well. Something is brewing. Part of her wants to confront this stranger, and another part doesn't want to believe her imaginings. Maybe Donald is just what he said — a guard at Wal-Mart.

Evvie picks up the phone and orders room

service.

The day drags on. I twiddle my thumbs while the cops continue to discuss their plans. They have maps of the facility and they are marking routes. When they need to know something about the layout of Wilmington House, they call me. Otherwise, I'm left on my own.

Evvie doesn't know what to do. He woke up for a while, took some pills, then went back to sleep again. The food she ordered for him was cold now. She thinks she might read, but the light would bother him, and she won't leave him.

She finds herself thinking of Gladdy. She wonders where she is. She needs to talk to her sister. Maybe she can call from the kitchen, but she's afraid Philip will wake up and catch her.

I go for a walk. My fingers itch to pick up the phone and call Evvie. I want to tell her to get out of there. Now! But if Philip is right there next to her . . . What if something goes wrong? What if she gets hurt?

When I get back, dinner is brought in. Everything tastes like cardboard to me. I can't eat.

■ ■ ■ ■

He finally wakes up.

"Are you all right?" Evvie asks.

"My migraine's really bad today. Nothing much to do but try to keep very quiet until it's over."

"What can I do for you?"

"Just sit here by my side."

"I will."

He closes his eyes again.

There is nothing for her to do but think, and her thoughts are troubling. Something is the matter with him. She can't keep pretending there isn't. She's been feeling this for some time now, but resisted its implications. It's as if Philip is at war with himself. And it's coming out in his dreams. It's important, but her mind won't reveal it to her. Maybe it's because she's afraid to know.

I come back to Morrie's office. It's empty. I have such a headache. I didn't really sleep much last night, so I lie down on his small couch for a few minutes.

The next thing I'm aware of is Oz gently shaking me. I leap up. It's actually dark out.

"I can't believe I slept."

"You needed the rest."

"Are we going?"

"Yes. Everyone's outside ready to roll."

Evvie convinces Philip to eat a little dinner.

"This is not fun for you." He pats her hand.

"I don't mind. Philip, dear, I know something is bothering you. Can't you share it with me? Maybe I can help."

He looks at her and she can't read his expression. His eyes grow dark and distant. Then he smiles. "Whatever are you talking about?"

Oh, Philip. Why are you lying to me?

Evvie is utterly exhausted. She lies down beside him and falls asleep

At last, we arrive at Wilmington House. The trip seemed endless to me. Everyone is taking positions.

"Stay in the car, Glad." The night air is cool. Morrie hands me his jacket to keep warm.

I take the jacket, but I jump out. "No way am I waiting here. I'm going with you." I grab on to his arm. "Don't even try to talk me out of this."

FIFTY-ONE:
PHILIP AND RAY

Philip is thrashing from one side of the bed to the other. It wakes Evvie, surprised to see she has fallen asleep in her clothes.

He leaps from the bed and crashes into the wall. Evvie gasps, fearing he hurt himself. She hurries to him as he starts banging his fists against the wall shouting over and over again. "Die, damn you, Ray, die!"

She tries to pull him away from the wall. "Philip, wake up. Phil, darling." His body writhes with some inner frenzy. She pulls her hands away. They're covered in his sweat. She doesn't know what to do. Finally she fills a glass of water from the bathroom sink and throws it in his face.

That stops him. He wakes up and looks at her, startled. It takes a few minutes for him to come to himself. He smiles crookedly. "Did I wake you from your beauty sleep?" He put his hands to his aching head and moans.

"Do you want your pills?"

He shakes his head and sits down on the edge of the bed.

"The migraines are getting worse. Darling, it's time to see a doctor."

"No! No doctor."

"Is it me? Am I causing you the nightmares?"

He reaches out to her and she comes and sits next to him. Philip puts his arm around her shoulder. "I actually think so."

"But why?"

"Because it's different. Because it's you that's different. You're not like any of the others."

"The other dying old ladies," she says ruefully.

"I didn't love the others. It was playacting. I pretended to love them so they would die in peace. I can't do that any longer. I'm not pretending anymore. I love you, Evelyn. I never expected that to happen."

His body shudders against hers. She holds him tightly.

"I'm not dying, Phil, dearest."

But he doesn't seem to hear her. "You're my only cure. You're the only one who can save me. The actor is dead. Long live . . . long live . . ." She can feel his tears running down both their faces.

Evvie takes a deep breath. "My darling. Long live who? Long live Ray? Who is Ray?"

His eyes blaze. Suddenly she sees the rage come over him. He throws her to the floor, and stands up. "Damn you! Damn you to hell!"

Evvie lies there petrified.

"Ray is dead!"

She crawls away from him slowly, never taking her eyes off him, as he paces the room. He reminds her of a tiger. About to pounce.

"Why did you have to mention his name? Now I have to kill you."

Evvie manages to slide up and sit down on the edge of the bed, next to the phone. She tries not to move. She's beginning to understand it now.

"Ray didn't want to kill them. Not him, not Mr. Goody Two-shoes. He wanted them alive and happy. I wanted them happily dead. Like her."

"You mean Aunt Dorothy?"

He looks at her sharply. His voice is rough, his breathing shallow. "I was so angry at her. The things she did to me. She tortured me. It gave her pleasure. Who could I tell? Who would believe me? When she got sick I thought I could get away. But I couldn't. I couldn't leave her. She demanded I wait on her constantly. But when things got very bad, her doctor insisted she send me away. So I never had my revenge. The crazy old bitch died while I was away. She burned down the house herself."

"So you took it out on all the poor old lady characters on *World of Our Dreams*?"

That stops his pacing; he turns to her, startled. "You knew? How long have you known?"

Evvie sighs. "Only a few minutes. I finally remembered where I'd seen you. I remembered a soap opera I used to watch."

"Daytime serial. Glory Hill would have a fit if she heard you call it a soap opera." He laughs madly at the memory.

She speaks softly, evenly. "Who's Ray?"

"Who's Ray?" She says it louder.

He lunges toward her. Evvie braces herself.

"Stop it! He doesn't exist anymore. I told you! I killed him, too."

"And Esther Ferguson. Real people like her? And more. Did you kill all the old ladies you pretended to love?"

Evvie's heart is pounding so hard, she's afraid she'll have a heart attack before he has a chance to murder her. She's thinking fast. Is Donald Kincaid outside again? She could try for the door. What about the phone? He said call 505. What were her chances of having time to dial?

As Philip reaches her, she kicks her legs out, slamming into his stomach. He's caught off guard for a minute. She makes it to the door, but he's too fast for her. He grabs her and throws her down once again.

Now she realizes that Donald tried to tell her he was here to help her, and that the police knew and were coming. Too late. They were going to be too late.

I'm going to die, she thinks.

He hovers over her, fists clenched. She tries to hide her terror. "I don't think you killed Ray. I think he doesn't want to stay hidden any-more. I think it's Ray who loves me. He doesn't want me to die."

He grabs her by the shoulders, hitting her head again and again against the floor "Liar. I'm the one who loves you."

She hears the sound of heavy knocking at the door.

"I don't want to kill you." Tears are stream-ing down his face. He picks up a pillow from the side of the bed and pushes it down over her face. She tries as hard as she can to push it off.

Through her muffled voice, she gasps. "Then let Ray go free."

"I can't."

She hears the key turning in the lock. Too late. With the last of her breath she cries, "You can. Philip, you must. Don't let me die."

With an anguished scream, he drops the pil-low and falls down on top of her. She wraps her arms around him as he sobs.

Evvie looks up startled to see Gladdy rushing into the room. With her, Morrie and four other policemen with drawn guns.

Though her throat feels raw, Evvie calls out, "Don't shoot. This isn't Philip. It's Ray. His name is Ray."

FIFTY-TWO:
LEAVING WILMINGTON HOUSE

We almost make it out of Wilmington House without anyone knowing, but a few light sleepers do get up and stare in shock as Philip Smythe is marched out wearing handcuffs. I'm sure they are equally astonished at our little parade — Morrie, Oz, and their men walk behind Smythe with guns drawn. The new "resident," Donald Kincaid, follows them. And Gladys Gold — what is she doing there? Hovering in the doorway is Hope Watson, wringing her hands.

When shivering Evvie is led out, with a blanket covering her, Hope Watson runs to her and hugs her. "You brave girl. You knew all along. You put yourself in harm's way to save one of our other guests from being murdered. Someone should give you a medal!"

Evvie is too numb to respond.

Hello? I'm standing here, too. Hope

ignores me. After all, what did I do? Nothing except listen to her harangues and take her verbal abuse.

All the way home, Evvie and I sit in the backseat of Morrie's police car, clutching each other and crying. Morrie and Oz sit up front, quietly talking.

"You were right about him," Evvie says through her sobs.

"You were right, too. Ray was a wonderful man. It was Philip who committed murder."

"I'll never see him again, will I?"

We both know the answer to that.

"Glad, forgive me. I'm so sorry for all the terrible things I said."

"I'll forgive you, if you forgive me."

Evvie manages to laugh. "Can you imagine the gossip at breakfast tomorrow? No Philip and now no Donald. The two best dancers in the bunch."

Her laughter turns into hysteria. I laugh and cry with her.

When we arrive at Lanai Gardens, it must be nearly three a.m. Out of the darkness I see a patch of color. As we get closer, there they are, under the lamplight, my girls, waiting up as they said they would. They're seated on a bench dressed in warm sweaters, with blankets over them, huddled together to keep them warm in the cool night air. Ida holds a flashlight and waves it toward us. There is no one else around in the quiet darkness.

Morrie pulls up. Oz gets out and opens the rear door for us. The girls look at me, worriedly. I nod and smile. Oz helps Evvie out of the car.

For a moment she looks at them, and they at her. Then, in a rush, the girls are on her, hugging and kissing and sobbing. They won't let go of her, nor she of them.

"We were so worried." Sophie pats her hair.

"We thought we'd never see you again." Bella touches her face.

"We love you." Ida kisses her cheek.

I join the group hug. "Welcome home." From all of us.

Evvie looks exhausted. Ida starts to move her. "She needs to rest."

"But we'll see you for breakfast?" Sophie needs to know.

"Of course," Evvie says, trying for enthusiasm. "Don't I have to hear all about what I missed?"

They help her to the elevator. Morrie holds me back for a moment.

"You are amazing, Gladdy Gold. Disobedient, but amazing."

"Not according to Hope Watson." I grimace.

"You're my hero, too," adds Oz.

They both hug me and I head for the elevator.

"I'm sorry about —" Morrie breaks off.

I turn. "Don't . . . But thanks for caring."

FIFTY-THREE:
THE MORNING AFTER

The girls eagerly peer through my screen door, and I tell them to let Evvie sleep some more and come for lunch instead. She slept at my place last night, not wanting to be alone

At nine a.m. their time, I phone Alvin and Shirley Ferguson in Seattle to tell them the case is over. Philip Smythe has been arrested.

"I knew it! He killed her, didn't he?" Alvin demands.

I hear Shirley in the background. "It can't be; he wouldn't kill her."

"You're both right," I say. "Does the term split personality mean anything to you? I'll send you a written report with all the details. The police will be in touch with you. They may want you to come back here to give your statement."

Shirley has grabbed the phone. "Can you sell those clothes back to the shop?"

"We'll see what we can do."

"If not, mail them to me. I'm sure they'll fit."

Sure. In your dreams, cheapskate. "Whatever."

Evvie wakes up right after my call. She comes into the kitchen wearing my bathrobe. She looks beyond weary. I hand her a cup of coffee. "Did you sleep?"

"Off and on. I had nightmares. It's beginning to really hit me now."

"Yes. And it will for quite a while."

We're both stiff with each other and we know it. The harsh words said — the hurts won't go away that quickly.

She sits down at the kitchen table warming her hands with the coffee cup. "A hundred things run through my mind. Some of them stupid, like how can I face anyone after the way I behaved?"

"Simple," I say. "Take a page from Hope Watson. We'll tell everyone you knew all along. The girls won't betray you. And you did figure it out yourself. That was so smart of you."

She grimaces. "Almost too late."

She starts to get up, but I bring the coffeepot back. I pour.

"Glad, what else did you find out about him? He killed other women, didn't he. I need to know."

"Not now. Later. We'll have lots to talk about."

She sees the troubled look in my eyes and lets it go.

Her eyes tear up. "How do I hide my broken heart? I loved him. If you could have seen how he was when he was Ray. Everything I could ever want in a man. He was wonderful."

I want to tell her someone else might come along. But it's not the right thing to say. Not now. Maybe never. Besides, I'm not sure I believe it.

She puts her head in her hands. "I can't bear it. How could I have been so easily fooled?"

"He fooled me. He fooled everyone. For years and years. Try not to be so hard on yourself."

I offer her some toast. She shakes her head. "My life is over."

"What are you talking about? Don't be ridiculous."

"All my life I've lived this fantasy, and my fantasy came true. But it was all smoke and mirrors. It was never real. I have nothing to live for anymore. Nothing but memories, turned sour."

For a moment, I remember Evvie in her

gorgeous red gown, dancing with Philip, looking beautiful and ecstatically happy. I want to cry for her.

I sit down in the chair next to her and pull her hands away. "Don't say that. You have me. And the girls. And your family."

And I think of a conversation when she said that to me when I first met Jack. It didn't work then and it won't work now.

"It's not enough. It never was. And it can't be ever again. I know what I've lost forever; nothing will be any good."

You'll have to grieve, Evvie, as if he died. You'll have to accept that torn piece in you forever. But I won't say it.

There is a pounding on the door and eager faces grin at us through the kitchen window.

"Evvie, I know how bad you feel, but if you just try to act like your normal self, maybe the old you will just kick in. Make an effort?"

"We brought lunch." Sophie waves a bag at us. I look at Evvie. She nods.

"Come on in," I call back at them.

I whisper to Evvie, "Will you be all right?"

"Sure," she says woefully. "You know what a good actress I am."

The girls plow in, emptying bags on the counter. Sandwiches from the deli. Dr.

Brown black cherry sodas. They are so happy to see her.

Evvie manages a smile. "Forgive me if I'm not too perky. Not enough rest." She digs around the choices. "Where's the pastrami?"

In a few minutes, everyone has chosen their lunch and we sit around the dining room table noshing away. The girls don't comment on the fact that Evvie is barely eating.

"Catch me up," Evvie says.

"Where do we begin?" Bella is all atwitter. "My favorite is when the Peeper finally got caught."

"He did? Who was it?"

Sophie laughs. "You'll never guess. Your old boyfriend."

I see Evvie wince at that word, but she pulls up, fast. "Not Sol?"

"Yes, Sol," Sophie adds. "He was peeping at one of the Canadians and they caught him and, boy, was he scared."

Ida says, looking righteous, "They were ready to string him up."

Evvie works hard at showing interest. "Sol, of all people."

I add, "He said he needed sex."

"And, yeah, is he gonna get a lot." Bella is laughing aloud. "Tessie saved him from being arrested. But only if he promised to marry her."

"You got back just in time. The wedding's next week."

"Sol and Tessie. Oh, my, what a combination." Evvie actually giggles. "That scheming woman — she's been after him all along."

Bella continues. "And you know what else — Sophie got high and she practically tore her whole apartment to pieces."

"I wasn't used to pot. But it was fun."

Evvie is really surprised now. "Pot? You smoked pot?"

Bella giggles. "You should have seen her in her underwear jumping up and down on her bed singing stupid songs."

Sophie and Bella break out into: " 'Oh, I danced with a dolly with a hole in her stockin' . . .' "

Ida adds, "And you should have seen the eating spree she went on."

Sophie giggles. "I must have gained ten pounds that night."

"How did that come about? Where would you get drugs? And why?" Evvie asks.

"From Dr. Friendly, who is no longer my doctor."

"Wow, that *is* news."

Sophie's face reveals her sadness. "He almost killed Millie with some drug he gave her. It was all my fault, because I recommended him."

"Now, now," I say. "We've been through this. You mustn't blame yourself." The girls agree.

"Is Millie all right?"

Ida answers. "She's still in the hospital. But she won't be coming home. Irving is looking for an Alzheimer's facility for her."

We're quiet for a few moments, thinking of our dear friend.

Evvie gets up. "Thanks so much for the lunch and the update. But I think I need more sleep now."

She walks out and we all look at one another worriedly. That's not Evvie. Not the Evvie we used to know.

I promise I'll help you, Ev. Someday you'll be all right again. I swear it.

The girls reach across the table and we all touch hands.

We'll all help.

FIFTY-FOUR: WEDDING BELLS

The wedding is a hoot. Phase Two is the official caterer for the marriage of Sol Spankowitz and Tessie Hoffman, but since all the Phases were invited, and it is an insult not to contribute food, there is enough chow to feed all of downtown Fort Lauderdale. Needless to say that makes Tessie very happy. Food and a husband — what more could she ask?

Not that Sol seems too happy. Since his engagement, he's been in a state of befuddlement. And today is no different. Irving helped him dress, so that his clothes would match. But Irving keeps shaking his head at the fate of his racetrack buddy. So far, Irving seems to be holding up, at least. He goes to the hospital every day to sit with Millie. It's when the realization hits that he can't take her home again — that's going to be a difficult time. Thank goodness for Yolie. And Mary, too. He'd be lost without them.

Dozens of chairs have been rented for the occasion. There is the *chupeh,* the traditional canopy under which the bride and groom stand during the ceremony. The rabbi is there waiting, chatting with members of his congregation.

So many people are here, all of them dressed in their finery, any excuse to get *fahputzed,* as Sophie would say. I can hardly count them as they are wandering and drinking and dancing all over the lawns of Phase Two. In fact, I can see Casey and Barbi, dressed in their unique way, doing a wild cha-cha together. At weddings it is not unusual for women to dance together, so their secret will still be safe for as long as they want to keep it.

They congratulated me earlier, and I thanked them again for their help. It was their information that broke the case.

Morrie and Oz are here, too. Women flock around them eagerly. I caught Sol looking at them almost wistfully. I bet he was thinking jail would be preferable.

Conchetta comes over to me. "I heard the news. My God, that was a close call." She looks toward Evvie. "Is she all right?"

I shrug. "Hopefully, in time."

Mother Nature is kind and the weather is balmy. Everybody loves a wedding and it's been a long time since we had one, so everyone is in a festive mood.

Yolie and Denny are maid of honor and best man. Denny has given her a sweet little ring. Maybe more wedding bells are about to ring. They also got to pick the music, so it's Latin salsa, blaring out over the happy conversation.

Evvie is putting a good face on it, but I know her heart is breaking. Ida is at her side to comfort her. Sophie and Bella still don't understand about Philip and Ray, but that's all right. Sophie comments, as she is wiggling in place to the music, "We got two killers for the price of one." So she's satisfied.

The announcement is made. The Spankowitz-Hoffman nuptials are about to begin, so we all start to gather on the big lawn.

I find my seat and wait for my girls to join me. Someone sits down next to me. "It's about time," I say, "they're starting." I look to my left and there's Jack. I actually gasp.

"I hope you don't mind. My sitting here." He smiles gently at me.

I wait for my throat to open so I can speak. "No, that's fine."

The girls don't show up. I assume they saw Jack and sat elsewhere so we could be alone.

Jack reaches over and holds my hand. We don't speak. I can't take my eyes off him, but he continues to watch the ceremony. I notice Evvie looking at us from across the crowd. She smiles bravely.

The ceremony is fun. Tessie is in high spirits. Sol can barely stand up, but not to worry — Tessie has a firm grip on him.

Afterward the happy bride throws the bouquet. Many eager hands are held high. Ironically, it lands in Evvie's crossed arms. She drops it as if it were the proverbial hot potato. Eighty-one-year-old Dora Dooley grabs it from the grass where it fell and cackles happily.

Evvie looks at me and I look at her. So many thoughts pass between us.

I look around for Jack, but he's disappeared as suddenly as he arrived.

I see Morrie walking over to me. Before I can say anything, he hands me an envelope. He shakes his head and walks away.

I open it and read the note inside. "Gladdy, I'm sorry. I have to leave. I don't know how long I'll be gone. Jack."

I don't know how to feel about this, so I hand the note to Evvie to read. Her voice rings with poignancy. "It's just you and me again, kid." She puts her arms around me and hugs me.

Who said getting old is criminal?

Sometimes it is sweet and lovely and many times filled with pain — but always full of surprises.

ACKNOWLEDGMENTS

As always, Howard, Leslie, Gavin, and James.

Caitlin Alexander, every single time. Lucky me.

Sharon Propson, PR maven.

My agent, Nancy Yost. Welcome to the club.

The amazing Margaret Sampson and the wild and wooly Women Who Walk on Water Book Club in Green Bay, Wisconsin. They better watch out or the next series might be about them.

Lynn Vannucci and Ginger Liebovitz, my loyal friends and first readers.

The always wonderfully helpful, talented

"kitchen klatch" mystery writers group for whom I travel (and never stop kvetching about) the dreaded 580. Camille Minichino, Margaret Lucke, and Jonnie Jacobs.

My sister, Judy, and adopted sister, Rose; my biggest fans.

Thanks to Guiamar Sandler Hiegert for Pago Pago and for my north coast "bookstore" at the Lost Whale Inn in Trinidad, California.

Dr. D. P. Lyle, physician to the authors. Thanks for your help.

And last but definitely not least. Thanks to Cheryl Jones, owner and "chef extraordinaire" of The Pleasure is Mine restaurant at Harbor Point. Most of the last half of this book was written in the San Rafael restaurant, with Cheryl keeping me strong by feeding me her wonderful food.

And to my faithful friends, my East Coast family and loyal fans who keep on writing. Thanks for your support.

ABOUT THE AUTHOR

Fate (a.k.a., marriage) took **Rita Lakin** from New York to Los Angeles, where she was seduced by palm trees and movie studios. Over the next twenty years she wrote for television and had every possible job from freelance writer to story editor to staff writer and, finally, producer. She worked on shows such as *Dr. Kildare, Peyton Place, The Mod Squad,* and *Dynasty,* and created her own shows, including *The Rookies, Flamingo Road,* and *Nightingales.* She wrote many movies-of-the-week and miniseries, such as *Death Takes a Holiday, Women in Chains, Strong Medicine,* and *Voices of the Heart.* She has also written the theatrical play *No Language but a Cry* and is the co-author of *Saturday Night at Grossinger's,* both of which are still being produced across the country. Rita has won awards from the Writers Guild of America, as well as the Mystery Writers of America's Edgar Allan Poe Award and the coveted Avery Hopwood Award from the University of Michigan. She lives in Marin County, California, where she is currently at work on her next mystery starring the indomitable Gladdy Gold. Visit her on the Web at www.ritalakin.com or e-mail her at ritalakin@aol.com.

The employees of Thorndike Press hope you have enjoyed this Large Print book. All our Thorndike and Wheeler Large Print titles are designed for easy reading, and all our books are made to last. Other Thorndike Press Large Print books are available at your library, through selected bookstores, or directly from us.

For information about titles, please call:
  (800) 223-1244

or visit our Web site at:
  www.gale.com/thorndike
  www.gale.com/wheeler

To share your comments, please write:
  Publisher
  Thorndike Press
  295 Kennedy Memorial Drive
  Waterville, ME 04901